Also by Ron Schwab

Sioux Sunrise

Paint the Hills Red

Ghosts Around the Campfire

The Lockes

Last Will

Medicine Wheel

The Law Wranglers

Deal with the Devil

Mouth of Hell

The Last Hunt

Summer's Child

The Coyote Saga

Night of the Coyote

Return of the Coyote

Twilight of the Coyote

Ron Schwab

Uplands Press
OMAHA, NEBRASKA

Uplands Press
P.O. Box 6105
Omaha, NE 68106
www.uplandspress.com

Ordering Information:
Quantity sales. Special discounts are available on quantity purchases by corporations, associations, and others. For details, contact the "Special Sales Department" at the address above.

Twilight of the Coyote/ Ron Schwab -- 1st ed.

ISBN 978-1943421312

In memory of my mother, Millie Schwab—gentle, patient and quiet, but strong as steel at her core

Twilight of the Coyote

Chapter 1

KATE

KATHLEEN ROSE CONNOLLY dismounted, plucked her binoculars from the saddlebags, and left her Appaloosa gelding in the shade of a solitary ponderosa pine that resided at the top of the granite bluff. She did not worry that War Paint would wander beyond the sound of her whistle. They had been together ten years now, since the gelding was a foal and she was ten years old. Kate had been sitting on a pile of straw in the corner of a stall at the foal's birth. She had named him for the three white streaks that extended like Sioux war paint from beneath the eyes down each side of his face, giving him a fierce look, she thought. Other than its namesake markings and some generous white splotches on its rump, the horse was coal-black.

She sat down on her favorite bench-rock and brushed back the silky strands of copper-colored hair from her green-tinted brown eyes and looked out over the lush valley as she had countless times over her young lifetime. She felt a cold, wet nose against her cheek and reflexively put her arm about the thick shoulders of Galahad, her black Labrador retriever and pulled him close. He had been her friend and companion for only a few years less than War Paint and was an early descendant of a breed finding its way to America from Newfoundland by way of England. His name had been inspired by her obsessive reading of Lord Tennyson's Idylls of the King, twelve narrative poems retelling the legend of King Arthur and his knights. Galahad was known for his gallantry and pure heart, and the traits had called to her as a young girl—and still did in her dream world.

As far as Kate was concerned, she was more than half way to heaven in this special place she had never shared with another human. It was her first trip to the top of the bluff since spring break. It was late June 1927, and the sun's warming rays more than offset the stiff, cool breeze that whipped the uplands this morning. She scanned the steep, craggy slopes of South Dakota's Black Hills National Forest across the valley to the west, but she was perched on Connolly Shamrock Ranch land—just barely.

As she looked out over the valley, she could not shake off the quarrel she had with her father, Owen Connolly, at breakfast. His Irish temper had flared when she announced she would not be returning to the South Dakota State College of Agriculture and Mechanical Arts in Brookings, where he believed she was enrolled in a home economics curriculum and diligently seeking a rancher husband. She had been an honor student at the college, but, unbeknownst to her father, she had enrolled in an agricultural program and was on track to graduate with the class of 1928 in another year. She would earn a Bachelor of Science degree in agriculture with an emphasis in beef production if she finished. She had not really lied to her father. He had just told her what to do and assumed she had done it and rarely showed any interest after that. She intended to ranch, with or without her father, and, while she had a healthy interest in the opposite sex, her destiny was not to be some man's brood cow. A husband would be nothing but a nuisance right now.

She already owned fifty Angus cows out of the Shamrock's five hundred cow herd, and she would cut hers out and lease her own place and start fresh and free of his pig-headed notions of where a woman's place was, if it came to that. She would find another job to subsidize her ranching until it could stand on its own. She was paying for her own education and could do what she darn well pleased. She would tell her father tonight what she had been up to and what she planned to do.

She pressed the binoculars to her eyes and, as they roamed the creek on the valley floor, she caught sight of a fisherman attired in hip-length waders and a fancy fishing vest, casting for trout in the fast-flowing stream that sliced through the Shamrock's ten thousand acres of pasture, hay and row-crop ground and half-naked hills. The fisherman's hat was perched evenly on his head, and, as serious fishermen tended to be, he appeared oblivious to anything but his quest. She pegged him as a dude, probably an Easterner. He was also a trespasser.

She would ride down and let him know he was on private property, and then she would give him permission to fish there. Visitors to the Hills frequently wandered innocently onto Shamrock range, the ranch being tucked between the Pine Ridge Sioux reservation lands to the east and Black Hills National Forest to the west and north.

She was curious. The fisherman didn't appear to have a horse. How did he get to the remote fishing spot? He was miles from any lodging or campground that she knew about. She turned her binoculars northward along the rocky park service road that snaked into the Hills and formed a rough boundary line between government and private lands. She paused when she saw the Model T Ford parked on the roadside midway up the steep hillside. The road was a path to nowhere carved from the granite slope and dead-ended a few miles further up. It was rarely traveled except by forest rangers and maintenance personnel, or the occasional hiker or lost tourist.

The nose of the automobile pointed downhill, so it had already been to the dead-end turnaround. What she found strange, however, was that there was a stocky man dressed in a white shirt and tie and suspenders leaning against the vehicle, his hat pulled down over his forehead in a losing effort to ward off the sun's glare. She swore she could make out a shoulder holster and pistol hitched on the left side of the man's torso, an outfit like she had viewed on screen at a Lon Chaney movie. Mobsters sometimes carried their guns that way in films. But, so did plainclothes lawmen. Was she watching a gangster of some kind? Or a good guy? Either way, he must be the source of the fisherman's transportation.

A swirl of dust moving up the service road caught her attention. Another Model T. Not surprising, since more than half the automobiles in the country were the economical Ford that sold for less than three hundred dollars.

The vehicle rolled to a stop, nudging the front bumper of the other Ford and pushing it back a foot or so. Mr. Suspenders had strolled toward the oncoming car with one hand raised in an apparent effort to halt its course, and now he was totally exposed when two men with pistols aimed leaped out of the car. The armed driver quickly joined them. In the middle of the road, three guns faced one. Mr. Suspenders dropped his weapon, and the driver walked over to the man and slammed the butt of his pistol into the side of Suspenders' head. He fell like a burlap bag of corn onto the road.

The newcomers engaged in animated conversation for several minutes, evidently plotting the next step of whatever they were doing. Finally, the driver and one of the men drug the felled man off the road and rolled him over the edge, where he slid twenty feet or so down the steep hillside until coming to a stop in a cluster of chokecherry and skunkbrush. She could not determine if he was alive or dead.

One of the men retrieved rifles from their car, and, with the driver remaining behind, the other two started down the deer trail that led to the valley below, and, ultimately, to the stream. They were obviously stalking the fisherman.

It would be a simple matter for her to take a back trail and reach the fisherman before the stalkers arrived. But what was the point? The fisherman was a stranger, and, for all she knew, they could be lawmen tracking a wanted criminal. It seemed unlikely, however, that such persons would have struck a man down and tossed him off the roadside. Would they have not taken him into custody and escorted him to the back seat of their Model T? Of course, the fisherman could still be a gangster. Maybe the Chicago mobsters were bringing their wars to the Black Hills.

She decided it wouldn't harm anything to take a closer look at the occupant of the trout stream. She could decide what to do about him after she had a chance to size him up. She whistled for War Paint, and, in a matter of moments, Kate and her companions were headed down the serpentine trail that took them back to the foothills. Less than a half hour later, she dismounted, pulled her Winchester from its saddle holster and abandoned the Appaloosa. Followed by Galahad, she inched her way through the aspen, birch and scrub oak that lined the stream. When she reached the clearing where she had sighted the fisherman, she found him standing in the knee-high water that broke swiftly around his legs as it followed its course downstream. His back was to her, but if he turned, he would certainly see her at the edge of the clearing.

He was a slender man, a few inches shy of six feet, she guessed. She saw no sign of a stringer full of trout, and she thought he seemed a bit inept at tossing the fly, almost as if he was not very serious about catching a trout.

"Good morning, young lady."

She started when she heard the man's voice. He turned toward her and began slogging toward the streambank, the rapid waters pulling at his feet. When he stepped upon the rocky bank, he tendered a closed-lip smile and cocked his head, obviously waiting for her to speak.

"I thought you should know, mister, that you're trespassing on private property."

He looked genuinely surprised. "Good heavens, I had no idea. I was informed this was park land. This is very embarrassing. I'll pick up my things and move out of here. My auto and driver are on the road up that way." He pointed northwest, where Kate had viewed the altercation.

"No, that's all right. Folks are welcome to fish here if they respect the property. That road separates the Black Hills National Forest from Shamrock Ranch land. I just thought you should know." She smiled. He seemed to be a soft-spoken man in his mid to late fifties, and she did not find him the least threatening.

"I do want to know," he said. "I have the utmost respect for private property. And, with your permission, of course, I would like to return to this little clearing. It's very peaceful here. I have a car and driver waiting for me on the road, however, and I really must be going. I am expected at the lodge for a late lunch." He peeled his rubber waders down his thighs and sat down to work them off his feet. When Kate saw him struggling clumsily to get free, she leaned her rifle against a tree stump and stepped over and knelt and helped tug the encumbrances from his feet. He stood and started a futile effort to brush the wrinkles from his trousers, which seemed a bit too nice for an outdoor expedition.

"You haven't done much trout fishing, have you?" Kate asked.

"First time. My wife said I should take a guide, but I wanted some time alone. I'm a pole and catfish man by heritage."

"Well, I'd be glad to teach you a few things about angling for trout, but time's wasting. Are you a crook or anything like that?"

"I've been called a crook and a lot worse. But, no, I don't think of myself as a crook."

"Well, forget about going back to your car." She told him about the run-in she had witnessed.

His face turned somber, but she saw no panic there. His brow furrowed, and then he said. "I hope Harvey isn't badly injured, or worse."

"I truly can't say. They didn't shoot him. I suppose they were afraid that would alert you."

"I guess I'd better be on my way. And you had better go, too. I thank you sincerely for the warning."

"And where do you think you're going?"

"I will stay with the stream. It will eventually take me to civilization of some kind."

"In a dozen miles, maybe. There's a cave in the rocks no more than a quarter mile from here. We'll go there. Even if they find us, I could hold them off for hours with my Winchester. If I don't get back home by lunchtime, Grandma will make Dad and Stretch come looking for me."

"I will be missed, also. I put my life in your hands, young lady."

"Kate. Call me Kate."

"You may call me Uncle Cal."

Chapter 2

KATE

UNCLE CAL SEEMED like an odd bird, but he was nothing if not a perfect gentleman. He didn't say much, but Kate could sense that a deep intelligence lay behind those translucent blue eyes. Wheels were turning in that head.

They had taken shelter in a deep cave with an entrance that made a tight squeeze for Uncle Cal to inch through. The opening would be difficult to see from the creek bed that lay some thirty feet below. She had never explored the depths of the cave. There were many in the Black Hills, and its tunnels might traverse for miles, connecting with countless openings in the region. She was a bit claustrophobic, and she was determined they would make their stand, if necessary, near the entrance.

Uncle Cal sat leaning against the wall on the opposite side of the cave just inside the opening. Galahad snuggled against him while his new friend stroked his head and scratched his ears. The dog slightly annoyed her with the instant rapport he had formed with the stranger. It meant nothing as far as the man's character was concerned. Galahad would make friends with an axe-murderer, so long as the axe was not directed at Kate.

"Kate," Uncle Cal said, "if you will allow me to take your rifle, I will keep an eye out for the men. I grew up on a farm in Vermont. I am a respectable marksman . . . or used to be."

She was not about to surrender her Winchester to a stranger. She still carried doubts about her judgment in interjecting herself into this situation. This man seemed pleasant enough, and, for that matter, he had a familiar look. But she might have seen his image on a wanted poster at the post office. "Sorry, I'm hanging on to the rifle. It's not a decoration for my saddle. I can use it."

She could make out enough of Uncle Cal's face in the beams of sunlight admitted by the cave's opening to see that it registered some surprise at her response. But he remained silent. She scooted closer to the entrance and peered out. They had arrived. The two men hurried along the stream banks, one on each side. She worried they would stumble onto War Paint. The gelding would be grazing a short distance downstream. Of course, the two men would never catch him, but they might scare the horse off, in which case it would probably head for the home place.

"They're here," she said, in a near whisper. "One's an Indian, probably Lakota. Braided hair, which you don't see so much these days. A chunky, older guy. The other looks like a dandy. Shirt and tie. Fancy shoes and a fedora hat. Kind of dressed up for an outing out here. A little on the skinny side, olive skin and sort of oily-looking. Dad would call him a 'wop.' Could these folks be friends of yours?"

"Your descriptions tell me nothing, but I don't suppose I would be acquainted with anyone who might be stalking me. An Indian and Italian seem a strange combination for such a task."

"You're not a gangster or anything, are you? The Italians are mixed up in the mobs, according to the newspapers."

"No, I'm not a gangster. I suppose I had better come clean, as they say. I'm the president."

"Of what?"

"The United States."

"And I'm Queen Victoria." She heard the pursuers' voices and cautiously looked out of the cave's entrance. "The scrawny guy has spotted the cave, and he's at the bottom of the slope." She positioned her Winchester against her shoulder and poked the barrel out of the cave opening, holding her fire until she was certain the man was going to approach the cave. She had him lined up in her rifle's sights, but she had never fired at a man before, and she did not know for certain he meant her or Uncle Cal harm. No, she could not shoot him down without warning.

She waited patiently. The Italian-looking man called to the Indian. "George, get your ass over here. I think there's a cave up this hill, and it looks like fresh scuff marks on the dirt."

The Indian splashed across the stream, stumbling, and falling to his knees when he clambered up the bank. He got back up and moved on like a clumsy bear, she thought. He bent over to catch his breath when he reached his companion.

The Italian said, "Up there." He pointed to where Uncle Cal and she were hiding.

"You need to climb up there and check it out."

"Why me?"

"You're the Indian. It's your job to sneak up on people."

"Go to hell. Do it yourself."

The stalkers did not seem to be over-endowed with courage. She questioned just how persistent they would be. She aimed carefully and squeezed the trigger. The rifle cracked, the echo in the cave stinging her ears, as her bullet tore through the Italian's fedora. She placed three more shots at their feet, kicking up rocks and gravel. The Indian was already backtracking as fast as his stubby legs would carry him. His partner raced after him ten paces back but gaining ground. The men displayed no inclination to regroup and continue their assault, but she decided they should wait a spell. She did not want to surrender the little fortress until she was certain they were in the clear. Besides, she needed to figure out what to do with her companion. She felt she had taken on responsibility for this man, even though she was not certain he knew his onions.

"They're gone?" Uncle Cal asked.

"It appears so. I don't think they'll be back, but we should wait a spell to be certain. Then I need to get home. I guess you'll have to ride with me." She looked at him dubiously. "Have you ever been on a horse?"

"Yes. Not often in recent years, but, as I said, I'm a farm boy. I used to ride bareback."

"That's good, because you'll have to ride behind me."

"Oh my."

"What?"

"I'm not sure that's very seemly."

This guy was trying her patience. "I guess if you can handle the reins, you can have the front seat."

"I think I would be more comfortable with that."

"Now, I think we'd better get better acquainted. I am Kate Connolly. My father is Owen Connolly. He's a rancher and owns this place. It's called the Shamrock Ranch. I'm a college student at South Dakota State, home for the summer and maybe for good, if I have my way."

"Very well. I was quite certain you were not Queen Victoria, since she is long deceased. I was born John Calvin Coolidge. My late father bore the same name, and he was a farmer, justice of the peace and jack-of-all-trades at Plymouth Notch, Vermont. I am currently employed as president and am spending my summer at the State Game Lodge in South Dakota. Alas, I will not have my way, and I will be returning to Washington at summer's conclusion."

It struck her then. The fisherman was not demented. He was the president. She had read that President

Coolidge would be spending the summer in the Black Hills and that he and his entourage would be taking over the State Game Lodge. Oh my God.

"I don't know what to say. I had no idea. I feel like such a fool. I'm sorry, Mr. President."

The president chuckled, "Please, Kate. Let me be Uncle Cal, at least in private. You likely saved my life today. My Secret Service protection was somehow taken out. The man you saw assaulted was Harvey Woods. Agent Styles was posted at the road entrance. I fear for his well-being. Edmund is going to be outraged over this breakdown, if he does not first suffer a heart attack when he learns I am missing."

"Edmund?"

"Edmund Starling. He's head of the Secret Service detail that came with me to South Dakota. A serious man, who does his job very proficiently. But he does not take it well when life does not follow his script, as it rarely does for any of us."

"Well, I think our best bet is still to ride to the Shamrock home place. There is a telephone there, and we can contact the State Game Lodge and let somebody know where you're at. I'll warn you, though, we're on a party line and half the county will know where you're at before the day's out. I know Grandma Beth will be thrilled to have you at the house. She voted for you, I'm sure. I'm worried about Dad, though."

"What do you mean?"

"I don't know what he'll think about me dragging home a Republican." She smiled at the thought.

"Your father's a Democrat, I take it."

"Yes. He says every good Irishman has a 'D' stamped on his butt at birth. Pardon my French."

"Well, when I was elected Governor of Massachusetts, I ran very well in Boston's Irish precincts. I daresay there were a few good Irishman who did not get stamped. I look forward to meeting your father and promise not to talk politics."

Chapter 3

TREY

THE FIRST LADY entered the room in the State Game Lodge that had been set aside for budget work. When she appeared, I was hunched over the table with my tin crank adding machine, trying to make sense of the budget for the Department of Agriculture. I stood immediately. This was not my job, but I was sort of a guest of President and Mrs. Coolidge during my assignment in South Dakota and could not refuse the president's request to help with budget matters during time I was not otherwise occupied.

Grace Coolidge was a ritzy lady in her late forties and looked a decade younger. I had something of a crush on her, and I could not understand what enamored her so with her husband. She was cheerful and vivacious. The press called him "Silent Cal," a moniker well-earned, and I had never heard him cut loose with a good old belly laugh. It was a challenge to draw out a smile. That's not to say he was without a sense of humor. In fact, he had the quickest, driest wit I had ever encountered, and he often had a twinkle in his eye. But he had a knack for confounding both friend and detractor.

"The president is late. We were to have lunch at one o'clock."

"Perhaps the fishing is good."

"But one of the agents should have reported in. Edmund is not pleased."

I would never say it aloud, but Edmund Starling, the Secret Service agent-in-charge was never pleased. I think his undershorts were too snug and pinched his privates. "Well, I'm certain Edmund has everything under control, and the president will be here shortly."

Mrs. Coolidge pushed aside a chair across the table from me and sat down without giving me time to assist. "Sit down, Trey. I would like to chat."

I complied. "Yes, ma'am."

"I invited your grandparents to join us for the Independence Day celebrations. July 4 is also the president's fifty-fifth birthday, you know."

"I imagine he is really looking forward to the occasion."

"You know better, Trey. He'd rather go fishing or read . . . or work on the budget. But he will not. I have planned several days of Black Hills experiences."

"I suspect my grandparents will have to decline the invitation. Gramps is getting up in years. He's a few years short of eighty and looks it. Gram Skye's six or seven years younger, but you'd never guess she is past seventy."

"I have good news. They've already accepted. You forget, they visited the White House in March. They both were fit as a pair of fiddles. You are just seeing your grandfather from a young man's perspective."

This could not be happening to me.

"You don't seem excited about the news."

"Well, I do have an assignment here, and I don't know that I can take off to spend much time with them. And Gramps and I have something of a testy relationship these days."

"I cannot imagine why. You are such an easy-going young man. Calvin loves to spend time with the senator, and I adore Skye. You must make time to patch up any differences with your grandfather." She stood. "We'll talk again. Perhaps, you can tell me what kinds of activities your grandparents might enjoy."

She flew out of the room like a lovely butterfly, carrying my heart with her. I was grateful for her exit, however. I did not wish to be the one to tell her Gramps would rather spend his time fishing with the president. Everybody might be happier if the first lady and Gram Skye took on the social schedule together and left their spouses at the State Game Lodge. The unwary husbands, of course, had no choice but to surrender.

I ended up with the presidential party on this journey indirectly because of political connections. My full name is Ethan James Ramsey III, hence "Trey." My father was "Deuce" Ramsey. Gramps must have still had a sense of humor when he tagged Dad with that nickname. Major Ethan James Ramsey II was an infantry officer killed in action by the Krauts. He's buried in France. Gramps and Gram, accompanied by my mother, Zoe, crossed the Atlantic and visited his grave five years back. I declined to make the trip. I don't know why. Maybe I'll go someday, but it seems rather pointless to self-inflict additional wounds.

My father, Deuce, was a West Pointer and a career soldier. With the likelihood the politicians would stir up another war or two, he was destined for at least a star or two. He was thirty-seven when his life ended in 1917, a dozen years older than I am now. I worshipped my father. I wonder sometimes if that would have changed if I had not lost him and learned more of his humanness as the years passed. It doesn't matter; those years won't pass for him.

Gramps, of course, is the first Ethan—Senior, if you will. I love and respect him. And I don't know how to deal with him. There is a stiffness in our relationship. He's a lawyer-rancher near Lockwood, Wyoming, but Gram Skye has always run the ranching operation. Skye de-Paul Ramsey is half-blood Brule Sioux. Her father was a French trader. Gramps was a scout for the cavalry out of Fort Laramie during the Indian wars, and Gram says the Sioux called him the Puma for his skill in stalking his quarry, usually Indians, I guess. He still moves silently and with considerable grace. He is far from decrepit, as I may have intimated to Mrs. Coolidge. When a United States Senator from Wyoming died six or seven years ago, Gramps, who was a political supporter of the governor, was appointed to fill the interim vacancy, serving only six months before a successor was elected. He had no interest in seeking election to the unexpired term.

It was during his Senate service that Gramps became a fast friend of then Vice-President Coolidge, who resided with Mrs. Coolidge and their sons in a Washington hotel. Mrs. Coolidge and Gram hit it off instantly, and despite a generation's age difference, formed their own enduring friendship. The relationship seemed to tighten after the Coolidges lost their own son three years ago. Calvin Junior died at age fifteen as the result of a bacterial infection invading a blister incurred in a tennis game on the White House lawn.

Mrs. Coolidge returned to the budget room fifteen minutes after she departed. Her face was pale, and her eyes glistened with tears. I was not accustomed to seeing her in a distressed state. Calm, composed and cheerful constituted her usual demeanor. I stood and stepped toward her. "What is it?"

"Someone tried to assassinate the president," she replied, before falling into my arms.

I said nothing, and I must confess I savored those few seconds. The waft of her perfume. The closeness of her body. I can be a despicable rogue when it comes to women, and the first lady is a bona fide Sheba. She is even more attractive because she seems unaware of her effect on men, especially me. At the same time, I was uneasy. What does one do with his hands with the first lady in his arms? I certainly couldn't pat her shapely fanny.

"But the president is all right?" I asked. Sorry, I am rarely articulate with a lovely woman in my arms.

She pulled back and seemed to pull herself together. "He is apparently fine. His Secret Service agents were injured, but not fatally. Mr. Starling is outraged. He has already arranged to send the men back to Washington and called for additional agent support. He is fuming, of course."

"Do you know what happened?"

"Only that he was rescued by a cowgirl, of all things. He's with her family at a place called the Shamrock Ranch about ten miles from here. Edmund wants to send two cars for him in case extra protection is needed. Edmund will take Agent Quinton with him. He would like to have you ride with Mr. Caputo."

I was not Secret Service, but I could not deny this woman. Besides, I was an agent with the Bureau of Investigation—the BOI or BI. Pick your acronym. My boss, J. Edgar Hoover, who was appointed by the president a few years ago to head the agency, would be pissed if I didn't nose in to whatever was going on here. He would probably figure out a way to wrest control over any investigation from the Secret Service anyway. He was one hell of a political strategist. Also, I was not unmindful that he made a job for me when Gramps sent an inquiry his way.

I was grateful to be riding with Frank Caputo to retrieve the missing president. Frank, who might have reached five and a half feet on his tiptoes, was a stocky, swarthy Italian, with a smile that melted the ladies' hearts. In his late thirties, he appeared to be a confirmed bachelor, but I am certain he slept alone only when on assignment. He looked and spoke like a guy from the Chicago mob. I suspected he could kill with the same ease. A good man to cover your backside.

I was equally thankful not to be accompanying Quinton Q. Quinton. I never asked what the middle initial stood for. He was a prude with zero sense of humor. Some called him a bluenose. I called him an asshole, but not to his face. Grudgingly, I admitted he was a more than competent agent.

Regardless, I hoped we could make this a quick trip. I was scheduled to meet with a fellow BI agent in Rapid City tonight to tend to the real business that had brought me to the Black Hills.

Chapter 4

TREY

THE ROCK AND gravel road that led to the Shamrock Ranch twisted deep into the foothills that framed the higher, more mountainous reaches of what folks knew as the Black Hills. The present-day park lands were sacred to the Sioux, and my ancestors owned this part of South Dakota several generations back, first by right of occupancy and, later, by treaty when the politicians and bureaucrats in Washington decided it was all a big chunk of worthless rock. Then, prospectors discovered gold and the hills were ultimately opened to white settlement. As a consolation prize, the Sioux, particularly the Lakota, ended up with the Pine Ridge Reservation spanning miles of untillable wastelands across southern South Dakota and northern Nebraska. My Brule ancestors, along with the Lakota, Hunkpapa and several other sub-tribes are Lakota. I don't know if my twelve and one-half percent Sioux blood entitled me to set up a shack on the reservation or not. These productive grasslands are, of course, outside the reservation.

I didn't know what the acres to cow-calf grazing ratio is in this part of country, but I soaked in some sense of pasturing rates when we lived on the Ramsey Lazy R spread after my father's death. A rancher could run a lot of cows on this range. I surmised we were threading our ways through Shamrock land right now, and it seemed these folks had settled on Black Angus. Gram Skye was firmly committed to Herefords.

When we arrived at the Shamrock Ranch headquarters, it was almost like coming onto a village that had been swallowed up by the surrounding shortgrass foothills. Clustered in a bowl-like setting were three houses, including a large ranch house, a bunkhouse, a huge barn, an apparent separate stable, a chicken coop and a collection of assorted outbuildings. Twenty or so people were gathered near the ranch house, so Starling led our duo of Model T Fords toward the activity. Nobody seemed much interested in our arrival.

As we got out of our vehicles, I caught sight of the president sitting back in a lawn chair and munching on a pastry. He gave me a small wave, and I was surprised to see traces of a pleased smile on his lips. He seemed unfazed by the aborted assassination attempt.

There were some small children playing tag in the dusty ranch yard. Adults of varying ages, the men wearing scuffed cowboy boots and battered hats, sat at a nearby picnic table or in the weathered chairs and benches scattered around the president. From the vehicles parked in the yard, I assumed some of these folks were neighbors invited over to see a genuine live president.

As usual, the president appeared to be doing more listening than talking. As I drew nearer, I noticed a barrel-chested man with curly white hair and a matching brushy moustache good-naturedly scolding the president for vetoing the McNary-Haugen farm bill earlier in the year. The bill had been supported by his fellow Republicans, but Calvin Coolidge said it cost too much and interfered with the free market. The president responded by asking if he might have another glass of lemonade.

Starling's face had turned crimson, no doubt horrified by this breach of security, with the president seated in the middle of a horde of unvetted strangers. I was not Secret Service, so I determined to let the agent figure out how to gracefully extricate the president from this situation. Then the president got out of his chair, accepted a fresh glass of lemonade, and strolled toward me.

"Trey," he said. "There are a few folks you should meet." He waved at the white-haired man. "Owen, come over here. I would like for you to meet my budget assistant."

The man joined us under a ponderosa pine, the largest of a dozen scattered about the ranch house. "Trey," Coolidge said, "this is Owen Connolly. He owns this ranch and has been the gracious host for my visit here. We have a bit of disagreement over the farm bill, but we've discussed it without rancor. Owen, meet Trey Ramsey."

Connolly seemed to flinch at the mention of my name. I shook the rancher's hand. It was like sticking my hand in a vise, but I persevered until he released me, and I did not cry. He was a big man with beefy shoulders and a thick torso, but no beer gut. He stood a good six feet. I was taller by two or three inches, but, somehow, I felt smaller. He was the kind of man who had what Gramps called a 'dominating presence.' The ruddy-faced rancher studied me with pale blue eyes that said he disapproved. "You're sure as hell no Irishman," he said.

"No sir. Pure American mongrel." I smiled, but he frowned, evidently finding no humor in my response.

"Where you from?"

"Wyoming, I guess would be where my roots are." He just stared at me.

The president interrupted. "Here she comes. The young lady who saved my life."

I turned my head and saw a copper-haired girl strolling my way. The hair was shoulder-length and pulled back in a ponytail. She was dressed like a man. Boots. Denim britches that were indecently snug but hinted at nice gams. The green cotton shirt didn't stretch much at the chest, so her bubs were modest at best. I know I shouldn't have been undressing her in my mind, but I couldn't help it. I swear she was the most stunning creature I had ever seen. My infatuation with Grace Coolidge died at that moment. I think the president was taken with her, too. I'm certain I saw a smile when she approached. Poor Grace. Her stock was sinking by the minute.

When she reached us, I saw she had a sprinkling of freckles on the flesh below her green eyes and across the bridge of her nose. Without her boots, she was probably a foot shorter than I am. She stared at me inquisitively, no doubt wondering what this stranger dressed in suit and tie was doing here.

The president introduced us. Her grip was firm, but we did not engage in a squeezing match. "My pleasure,"

I said. I was much more verbal with the floozies I tended to run with.

Coolidge said, "Why don't the two of you get acquainted while Owen introduces me to the folks I haven't met yet? I suspect Agent Starling wants us to be on our way to the lodge."

Owen Connolly tossed me a suspicious glance and joined the president.

I suppose it was only seconds, but it felt like the two of us stood there tongue-tied and looking each other for an hour. Thank God, she broke the silence.

"So, you help President Coolidge with his budget?"

"Uh, yes. I'm good with numbers." That no doubt impressed her.

"Why does a budget assistant carry a gun?"

Shit. She must have noticed the bulge beneath my shoulder where my .45 Colt Government Model was cradled in its holster. "Well, in light of the attempt on the president's life, it was thought we should all be prepared."

"That makes no sense. You don't just put a weapon in the hands of a numbers cruncher on a whim. I think you're Secret Service."

"I'm not Secret Service."

"I guess it doesn't matter."

"You seem hostile toward me for some reason."

"I'm sorry. This has not been a happy day. I had to fire my rifle at some men."

"Let's walk. Tell me about it."

We strolled slowly away from the gathering, and she told me the story of her encounter with the President of the United States. "I feel so foolish I didn't know who he was," she said. "I was quite brusque with him. And I'm angry he didn't tell me. Well, I guess he tried to tell me, but I thought he was crazy."

"He's not upset, I assure you. I'd guess he enjoyed the entire adventure."

"Before I came to meet you, I spoke with a Mr. Starling. He seems very upset. He said I am not to speak with the press, and I am not to tell anyone else what happened this morning."

"He's embarrassed. He's the agent-in-charge. But he's also right. They need to track these men. Publicity probably would not be helpful."

"That suits me. I don't want any publicity."

"Think about anything you may not have mentioned about those men. I would like to speak with you again about this." I was grasping for an excuse to see this woman again.

"Why would a numbers cruncher want to ask me questions about what happened? Mr. Starling said I should talk to nobody but him. That's what I'll do."

I may have to kill Starling. "We don't have to resolve this right now."

"Who are you?"

"Trey Ramsey. Just like President Coolidge said."

"But who is Trey Ramsey?"

"Perhaps you would find out if we met again."

"I don't have time for games."

She veered away and headed toward the president, presumably to render her good-bye. I didn't think she liked me.

Chapter 5

TREY

RAPID CITY, WITH a population approaching ten thousand inhabitants in 1927, sits in the southeastern corner of South Dakota as the gateway city to the Black Hills from the east. I was told it was the third or fourth largest city in the state. I had visited the city, about a half hour's auto trek from the State Game Lodge, immediately before the president's arrival and almost daily since. The president's executive offices had been set up in the Rapid City High School building, and that was where most of his official business was done. The annoying budget project was an after-hours endeavor. Calvin Coolidge was probably the only president since the founding of the Republic to review and edit every line of the federal budget. His penchant for a balanced and frugal budget bordered on obsession.

Tonight, I was enjoying a late supper at Dog's Restaurant, an off-main street hash house specializing in hamburgers, which were gaining ground on hot dogs for claiming the title as the All-American sandwich. Strange, when you thought about it, since the Krauts concocted both. The hamburger was a little on the bloody side for my taste, but the apple pie looked promising. I sucked without enthusiasm on a bottle of Coca-Cola. Elsewhere I might have sought out a speakeasy. Because of my unilateral break-up with the first lady, I was in the mood for something stronger. Panther piss from a home whiskey still would have suited me just fine. Since the Bureau of Investigation was leading the war on hooch, it would have been unseemly, though, for a couple of BI agents to get caught in the net of one of J. Edgar's raids.

A lanky Negro man slipped into the opposite side of the booth. He was attired in work boots and bib overalls with the straps pulled over a faded red shirt. I had dressed in my well-worn blue jeans and scuffed-up cowboy boots, so we should have looked like a couple of working stiffs. From the curious looks directed our way by the other patrons, it appeared we were not blending well into the general population, however. I wondered if that might have something to do with Gabriel Riley being the only black man in the entire city, possibly even in the whole state.

"What the hell are you supposed to be?" I asked.

"I'm a farmer, and you're a cowboy."

"I think we're both clowns." I could talk with Gabe like this. He was my best friend in the Bureau. He also kept me on the straight and narrow. He was the senior agent on this mission, where the BI had assigned a massive force of two. He had served as a sergeant with the Buffalo Soldiers, Ninety-second Infantry Division during my father's war. He was married with three children, morally upright and responsible. In short, he was everything I was not.

Gabe ignored my remark. "Tell me about your day and an attack on the president that I heard about first in a call from Washington."

I gave him a short version of the aborted assassination attempt and the rescue by the cowgirl.

When I finished, Gabe observed, "About the only thing I got out of this is that you met this dame who has a nice butt, small bubs and terrific gams, none of which you have viewed in raw flesh."

"Well, no. But it's not for lack of willingness."

"What about the president? How is he handling the scare?"

"Stoically, of course. But I'm keeping an eye on him. I think he's my main competition."

Gabe shook his head in disbelief. "I'll tell you about my day. I drove out to the reservation."

"You would have made a better impression if you had ridden a horse."

"I don't ride horses."

"I do. I'll go next time."

"Twenty miles?"

"Maybe I'll drive."

"Anyway, I spoke with several chiefs. They claimed they were chiefs anyway, but it seems like everyone out there is a chief."

"You know what they say: 'Too many chiefs and not enough Indians.'" I could see my attempts at humor were starting to grate, so I shifted gears. "Did they know anything about the killings?"

"One of the chiefs had some insight and useful information. His name was John Buffalo Horn. He said one of the girls was his niece. He was the contact who had written to the Bureau of Indian Affairs last January. It only took three months to deliver the letter to the BI, a few blocks down the street."

"And only another two months for the BI to assign the murders for investigation."

Gabe and I are in the Black Hills to investigate the rapes and murders of two Lakota girls, ages fifteen and sixteen. The case was cold as Alaska, the bodies having been found partially uncovered in a dry creek bed the previous November. Lucy Eagle Feather and Nelda Two Horses had evidently been buried there and later dug up by predators and partially devoured before discovery. Freezing temperatures had preserved enough of their remains for autopsy and medical evaluation in Rapid City. Local law enforcement had no jurisdiction, since the bodies were found on the reservation, which was legally a separate nation, and the reservation police had neither the personnel nor equipment to do much more than to pick up drunks or dispose of the suicides.

Gabe said, "I also received word from my superior that J. Edgar wants us to discreetly inquire into the assassination attempt. He doesn't want a pissing contest with the Secret Service until he knows he can win it."

"Are they sending out more agents?"

"Nope. Everybody's either in Chicago or down South investigating the Klan. I'll give Coolidge his due; he's put the heat on Hoover about taking on the KKK."

"So where do we start?"

"I'll work on leads involving the Lakota girls. You focus on the failed assassins. And keep your ears tuned in when the Service guys are around. We'll make a move if you pick up a clue."

"I think I need to talk to Kate Connolly . . . on an official basis."

"I think you need to keep your nozzle some distance from the fire. Now, I learned something new today. Chief Buffalo Horn says there are as many as twenty-five Sioux girls between the ages of fourteen and nineteen missing from the reservation. The Pine Ridge stretches across most of the southern part of the state, and the occupants are scattered, so an accurate count is impossible. The chief says some are probably runaways, but not that many. And there could be others missing who haven't been reported."

"We're on to something a lot bigger than two murders, aren't we?"

"I asked the chief to compile a list of any missing girls who lived on the reservation with the names of possible family member contacts. We will split up those names, which will include family members of the known deceased, interview them on or near the reservation and try to find a common connection."

"That's going to take a few weeks."

"At least. I'll find you on July 4 and give you your list and what background information I can put together. In the meantime, I'm hoping to identify a few locals, white or Sioux, who can help us with the lay of the land and give us a better idea of where we might look or furnish names of other people to talk to. We're grasping at straws. But we're going to solve this."

"Maybe Kate Connolly would help."

"Jeez, Trey. Talk to the woman, if you want. But I'm telling you now, stay out of her pants. Promise me that."

I don't lie unless it's expedient, so I did not promise.

Chapter 6

THE RAPID CITY OUTFIT

BOSS BULLOCK WAS outraged. The boobs had totally screwed up the job, Now the feds would be looking for them, and they didn't have a damn thing to show for it. They could have gotten a hundred grand for a president, maybe more. Bullock, whose proper name was Claud, had spent two years with the South Side Gang, also known as the Chicago Outfit. He had worked for Scarface Al Capone, now in prison for a tax evasion conviction, and Hymie Weis, dead since last October because of his failure to recognize it was time to get out. When the North Siders or some Judas rubbed out Hymie, Boss had the good sense to beat it out of Chicago. He was tired of being somebody else's muscle and hit man anyway, and he decided not to wait for somebody to give him his own "retirement party," as the mob called an inside hit. He was nearly thirty-five years old, and it was time to set up his own operation.

Boss went back home to Rapid City and began putting his own gang together. His enterprises were small-scale compared to Chicago, but there was no serious competition, thereby increasing his life expectancy. He had already made deals with local moonshiners and booze-runners to service Rapid City's two preeminent speakeasies, as well as the dumpsites he had set up on the reservation for marketing the cheap hooch to the Indians. He still had his Chicago connections, and that was where he sent the reservation girls for stocking the whorehouses in the Windy City. Some signed on voluntarily for a future in the "entertainment industry." Others were just captured like wild animals and hauled like so many cattle across the plains. He had marketed at least thirty now at two grand each, and he couldn't keep up with the demand. The Sioux girls had evidently become novelties in the Chicago bordellos. He would have to up his price.

Boss leaned back in the swivel chair and swung his feet up on the desk. That's what bosses did. He didn't do much of his own killing anymore, and he only occasionally raped the female captives. He missed that. A man of his stature did not pay for pussy. He liked the idea of having a special moll to service him, but two had run out on him already, evidently rebelling against the rough stuff. He had found one and strangled her. The other was still in hiding, but the boys had their eyes out for her. He feared she knew too much for him to just shrug off her disappearance.

He gazed out the window of the unpretentious house he had acquired on the outskirts of Rapid City for a headquarters. It was a clapboard, two-story structure that would not attract undue attention, but the interior was elegantly finished and decorated. His office was the former parlor, and his expansive oak desk was placed so his back would be to the wall, allowing him to keep guests sitting in any of the cluster of upholstered chairs in front of the desk within his sight. He trusted no one, not even his older brother, Bull Bullock, who was as huge as his namesake and half as smart.

Bullock tensed at a rap on the door, and he lifted his feet off the desk and opened the top drawer to reassure himself his .35 Smith & Wesson was there. He did not close the drawer. "Who is it?" he asked.

"George."

"You alone?"

"Yep."

"Come on in." Bullock slipped his hand in the desk drawer, and his fingers closed on the butt of the pistol. He was there when Hymie Weiss was taken out, and the scene at that bloodbath was burned in his memory.

He relaxed when George Many Knives entered the room alone. He nodded for George to take a chair in front of the desk. "What do you hear from the State Game Lodge?"

"My snitch says they don't have any suspects. Their only interest is in protecting the president. We will not have another opportunity. Good news is they don't have enough people with the Secret Service to look for us and stay close to the president, too."

Many Knives thought Bullock did not know the identity of the snitch, but Bullock knew the spy was Willy Hobson, a handyman at the lodge. His job would make him invisible throughout the facilities. Willy was half-blood Lakota and a nephew of George's, and always open to picking up an extra sawbuck or two. So far, his intelligence had been reliable. He had called George the morning of the president's fishing sojourn. He had also informed George later about the young woman who had intervened to remove the president from harm's way.

"I can't believe you and Solly were chased off by a young babe."

"We weren't expecting anybody else, and young babe or not, she could shoot. I told you we should have stayed away from the president. Too risky. It was a dumb idea."

Only George could talk to him this way. He was the outfit's connection to the reservation. He also had more brains than the other three of the outfit's core combined. Unfortunately, George Many Knives was a serious capitalist and would sometime try to squeeze Bullock out and take over the reservation business for himself. Of course, he would have to kill George before that happened, and he would take care of that personally. But, first, he needed to find another connection to the Sioux. Bull had told him about a younger Pine Ridge Indian who could take over the reservation business. Bullock was going to talk to the young man within a few days to check out his potential. He was skeptical because Bull usually had zero ability when it came to judging people. But he might get lucky.

Bullock asked, "Did you find out who the babe was?"

"Yeah. Kathleen Connolly. Her old man owns the ranchland where Coolidge was fishing. The Shamrock Ranch. My snitch says she just happened to be there."

"She and Coolidge weren't up to funny business?"

"Doesn't seem likely. No reason to think he ever knew of her before."

Bullock had a thought. "What if we nabbed her?"

"What do you mean? What would we do with her?"

"Hold her for ransom. She saved the president. Government would pay some serious money to get her back. They're trying to keep the whole thing quiet it seems. Her family would yell if Uncle Sam didn't foot the bill. Also, her old man could probably scrape up a few bucks."

"I don't know why you think you got to kidnap somebody. This is another dumb idea."

"We wouldn't give her back. But we'd get rid of a witness, if nothing else. We'd take her and sell her in Chicago or bump her off. After we take our turns with her, of course."

"Well, I heard she's looker. But it's still risky business. It's not like taking some reservation kid nobody will miss."

"But she needs to pay for what she did to us."

"I'll ask Max to check her out. Keep an eye on her. We need to wait till the president thing cools." Max Waters was half-blood Lakota. He rarely spoke to Boss, but he was Many Knives's trusted ally and key reservation contact. Boss knew where the squatty man's loyalties lay, and he did not like it.

"And cut off your pigtails."

George glared. "They ain't pigtails. Why?"

"In case the cow-babe saw you. Change your look. Get a suit."

"I suppose that makes sense."

"Figure out a way for Solly to change his look, too. She wouldn't have seen Max. He stayed with the Ford. Right?"

"Yeah. But the agents saw all three of us."

"I hadn't thought about that. Tell him he needs to do something. Shave his moustache and chin whiskers, for sure. Dump those Chicago-style duds he likes to wear and turn Indian till this blows over."

"Nobody's seen Bull. He doesn't have to lay low."

"That's a blessing. There'd be no way to disguise the big ox."

Chapter 7

KATE

KATE WALKED INTO the kitchen, carrying the day's mail, and dropped envelopes and a Montgomery Ward's catalog on the table. "Grandma. I don't know what to do. I've been invited to the State Game Lodge to celebrate Independence Day and President Coolidge's birthday. I am to stay over and join the president and first lady and attend the Tri-State Roundup rodeo at Belle Fourche the next day. They would like me to stay at the lodge three nights." She handed Beth Ridgeway the invitation which had been handwritten and signed by Grace Coolidge and delivered by a Secret Service agent a few minutes earlier.

Her grandmother examined the invitation. "Impressive. What a nice gesture . . . and opportunity for you."

"What am I going to do?"

"Go, of course. There is a phone number here for you to call with your acceptance."

"But it's just three days away. And I won't know what to wear or how to act."

"You just be yourself. And I'll help with the clothes." She plucked another tiny slip of paper from the invitation envelope. "You missed something. Who's Trey Ramsey?"

She remembered Trey Ramsey. The numbers cruncher. "He works for the president. Says he's a budget assistant, but I think he really does something else. He's arrogant and kind of standoffish."

"I remember him. That handsome young man who came with the agents to pick up President Coolidge that day. What do you call men like that these days? A sheik? He almost made me swoon. That thick black hair and light Mediterranean complexion. Those dark, bedroom eyes."

"Grandma, you're disgusting. You are reading too many of those magazines. I've seen the stacks of Ranch Romances and Parisienne in your cottage. I'm surprised Stretch doesn't take them out to the burn pile."

"Stretch reads them, too, but he'd never admit it. And I know who else has been helping herself to my old issues of Parisienne," her grandmother responded. "Don't pretend you're a bluenose with me."

Kate blushed guiltily. The Parisienne, edited by H.L. Mencken and George Jean Nathan, was a scandalous magazine in the view of self-appointed guardians of the nation's morals. It published sex-advice columns and risqué articles and stories, as well as advertisements for lingerie and sex merchandise such as performance-enhancing tablets and breast-augmentation products. The crème she had ordered while away at school had been ineffective.

Her grandmother continued. "Anyway, Mr. Ramsey will be arriving about five o'clock on July 3 to escort you to the State Game Lodge and dinner."

"Oh God. I am not going."

"You would insult President Coolidge?"

"Well, no."

"Of course not, and all Mr. Ramsey is doing is driving you to the lodge. If you like, I'll tell him how to take the long way."

"No thanks. I will show him the short cut."

Beth Ridgeway shrugged and gave Kate what her granddaughter called "the eye."

Kate took the invitation from her grandmother and went out onto the porch that stretched the length of the large log house that had been constructed in 1916, just a bit more than two years before her mother's death. She sat down on the porch swing that was suspended from one of the thick beams that support the roof. She began swinging slowly, letting the rhythmic motion lull her just to the edge of sleep. A gentle breeze drifted down from the Black Hills, nullifying the warming efforts of the mid-afternoon sun. She gazed at the small cottage about seventy-five feet to the west, where her grandmother, Elizabeth Ridgeway, now resided with Jim Ridgeway, her husband of two years, and lover for nearly ten.

Beth was a slender, supple woman just shy of seventy years now. Her face was lined and bronzed by an outdoor life, but she was still a striking woman, Kate thought. Stretch Ridgeway was the Shamrock's foreman, tall and lean, as his name suggested. He was an easy-going, hard-working man, who was evidently content with his lot, and had been with the ranching operation since before Kate's birth. He was like the indulgent grandfather to her before he became the real thing. She guessed Stretch was ten years younger than Grandma Beth.

A widowed Beth came to take over running the Connolly household a year before the death of Kate's mother, Coleen. She had been Chief of Nursing Staff in a Columbus, Ohio hospital for some years prior to that time and had been granted a year's leave of absence to attend to family matters. The year expired, and she never returned. Shortly after Kate's tenth birthday, Grandma Beth became Kate's stand-in mother.

Recalling Grandma Beth's naughty remarks a few minutes earlier made Kate smile and carried her back to that night when she was barely past eleven and she had opened the door to Grandma's bedroom in the big house to see if Grandma was still awake for some girl-talk. Thankfully, she had opened the door quietly, because she discovered Stretch and Grandma entwined naked on the bed. Grandma was moaning, and, for a moment, Kate feared Stretch was harming her. But then Grandma giggled, and Kate softly pulled the door shut and returned to her own room. She had grown up on a ranch and seen stallions and bulls doing their business on the females, so she roughly understood what Grandma and Stretch were up to that night. But it had not occurred to her that grandmas did such things. She never said a word to Grandma. But she had never erased the image from her mind.

Kate wondered if lustiness could be inherited. She knew that righteous and moral young ladies saved themselves for marriage, but last summer, home from college, she had attended a petting party with Liam Karlsson, a ranger and firefighter with the forest service. Petting parties were the rage on college campuses and even some high schools these days. The concept was simple enough. Young men and women went to gatherings, indoors or outdoors, where there would be refreshments, and sometimes music and dancing. But the objective was for males and females to pair off and kiss and touch and, perhaps, fondle to the point the partner would permit, short of doing "it." She had never discovered a boy's stopping place, and none of her friends had either.

There was boot-legged beer at the Rapid City party, however, and she had been giddy and lightheaded just enough that she had slipped into the woods with Liam, a blond muscular Swede, hailing from Minnesota, and returned without her virginity. She was tormented by her sin, but that did not stop her. She went out with Liam a dozen times, and she never returned home without slipping into sin again. Because she liked doing it and didn't want give up doing it, and Liam was darn good at doing it.

And she did not even love him. She liked him, but she could not see herself married to Liam, and she doubted he had marriage in mind. She had reason to suspect she might not be the only girl he was servicing that summer. It was Grandma Beth that brought her to her senses.

Grandma knew, of course, and she had sat Kate down for a serious talk about pregnancy and condoms and other devices and, most embarrassing of all, how she might satisfy herself. Grandma was a registered nurse, and she was very clinical and matter-of-fact about it all, but, nonetheless, Kate had wanted to crawl under the kitchen table.

Kate had declined to go out with Liam the remainder of the summer, and she successfully stopped short of surrendering her tattered virtue at the few campus petting parties she attended during the school year. She held out hope she had not turned into a common chippie or slut. She was determined to avoid seeing Liam this summer, but the thought of him was suddenly unsettling. Well, she had the upcoming visit to the State Game Lodge to distract her for now, and Mr. Ramsey wouldn't be so hard on the eyes, even if he was a boring numbers cruncher.

Chapter 8

TREY

WHEN I PULLED the Model T up in front of the Shamrock Ranch house, I was surprised to see an elderly couple holding hands, of all things, and standing in front of the porch swing on the veranda. I hoped I wasn't taking grandma and grandpa with me, too. I had not seen their names on the guest list. I was not surprised to see Owen Connolly at the top of the steps with his arms folded across his chest and a scowl on his mug. I was not a suitor picking up his daughter. I was on a mission for the President of the United States. It wasn't my fault Coolidge is a Republican. I am somewhat open-minded about politics. I've never taken the political wars too seriously. I confess, however, that a bit of Coolidge had rubbed off on me. I would not mention it to Gramps, though, and risk setting him up for future disappointment.

I got out of the car and started walking up the stone pathway that led to the porch. I waved a greeting and got waves and smiles from grandpa and grandma, who was quite a tomato. She reminded me of Gram Skye in her bearing. The man I assumed was her husband appeared a bit weather-beaten, but vigorous enough. I received a glare from the Irishman. I was starting to take this personally.

I was rescued from an awkward conversation with Mr. Happy when the front door opened, and Cinderella stepped out. I was stunned. This girl cleaned up good. I swear I had never seen such a beautiful creature. The ponytail had galloped off, and a mane of silky, red hair swirled around her neck and swept over her shoulders like an ocean wave. She wore a jade-colored dress with a soft, clingy fabric, tastefully dropping just below her knees. And standing where I was in front of the porch looking up, I confirmed my earlier judgment. She had perfect, endless gams. Then I caught her father's eye and realized I might have been staring inappropriately at his daughter's legs, so I worked my eyes up to her lovely face. "Good afternoon, Miss Connolly," I said. "President and Mrs. Coolidge are looking forward to you joining them."

"It should be an interesting holiday," she replied. Then she turned to her father. "I know you have met Dad." I stepped up onto the porch and offered my hand, which he promptly crunched and crippled. Fortunately, Stretch Ridgeway and Grandma Beth inflicted no further damage and were very friendly and welcoming. I had the feeling Grandma liked me, since she gave me a tight, lingering hug. In fact, it almost felt like she was flirting with me, which, of course, she was not.

After exchanging inane pleasantries for a respectable time, Stretch helped me load the luggage in the back of the Model T. The bags all belonged to Cinderella, who explained she did not know what wardrobe items might be needed, but she had brought her boots and riding outfit for possible rodeo attire. I thought naked in my room would be sufficient, but, gentleman that I am, I did not say this aloud. This woman had taken me to the brink of obsession. I was struggling now to remember Mrs. Coolidge's first name.

I opened the passenger door, and Kate Connelly climbed in. After that, I went to the front of the car and got it started with a single go at the crank. When I slid behind the steering wheel, she commented, "I expected you might arrive in a Packard or a Cadillac, being the president's numbers cruncher and all."

"Model T Fords make up President Coolidge's four-car fleet. Henry Ford's a campaign contributor, and his vehicles are cheap. Budget concerns," I replied.

"Your life does not sound very exciting. Are you serious about this budget stuff?"

"The president is, so I am. And I like working with numbers, and I like and respect the president. Did you know that six years ago the federal budget was over five billion dollars?"

"That's exciting."

I ignored her sarcasm. "The president's next budget will be about three billion dollars. He's run surpluses every year of his administration, and that's making serious income tax reductions possible."

"Dad says we don't pay income taxes. He loses money every year."

"That's not a recipe for long-term financial success."

"Our conversation is going to take a nasty turn if we keep talking about money."

I concluded I was a long way from getting this lady naked in my room. "Okay, let's talk about family. I really liked your grandmother and grandfather."

"Grandma obviously liked you back. You didn't say you liked my father."

"He seems to be a fine gentleman." Maybe I should have been a lawyer like Gramps wanted. Those weren't bad weasel words.

"You don't like him."

"He doesn't like me."

"He only approves of prospective young ranchers who will provide him with a grandson."

I thought I could meet half of the expectations. "He wants you to marry a rancher?"

"Yes. And I might, but I don't like him pushing it."

"And your mother?"

"She died when I was ten. Grandma Beth raised me since I was nine."

"I'm sorry. She had a long illness?"

"She died in 1918 in France during Wilson's war. That's what Grandma calls it. Dad would never speak ill of Woodrow Wilson."

This was spooky. A chill raced down my spine.

"What was she doing in France?"

"She served in the Army Nurse Corps. She was a registered nurse, like Grandma Beth. She was discharged from active duty a dozen years earlier, just before she married dad. But she volunteered for the Reserve Corps and got called up after war was declared. Because she was married and had a child, she could have applied for an exemption. Dad says she would have received it automatically, but she refused to request an exemption. So, they sent her to France. I don't think Dad's ever forgiven her. I'm not sure how I feel about it. We don't know how she died. Nurses supposedly weren't sent to the front, and the Army claims no nurses died in combat. She was in Paris the last we heard. We received word she died 'doing her duty for her country.' She's buried in a military cemetery in France. That's all we know. God, I don't know why I've jabbered on like this."

I turned the Ford onto the main road. I didn't know what to say, and I remained silent for several minutes, reaching for the right words. Finally, I blurted, "My father died in 1918. In France. Infantry officer. He's buried in a military cemetery there."

Neither of us spoke for the next ten minutes, but as we neared the lodge I broke the silence. "My grandparents will be joining us for dinner tonight. They're friends of the Coolidges. They came from Lockwood, Wyoming by train. Arrived in Rapid City this noon and were just getting settled in when I left for your place. They're my father's parents. You'll like Gram Skye. Your Grandma made me think of her, for some reason."

"I won't like your grandfather?"

"Oh, yes, you will. He and I just have an uneasy relationship."

"Your grandparents are friends of the president and first lady? Is that how you got your job?"

"I guess you could say that. Indirectly." It stung to admit it to this woman.

"But you're more than a numbers cruncher, aren't you? That's a bunch of bushwa. You're packing again today, and I don't think I'm considered dangerous."

Of course, she would have noticed the bulge caused by the gun under my jacket. I had a feeling she never missed much. "I'm an agent with the Bureau of Investigation, and sometime during the next few days we'll talk business."

Chapter 9

KATE

DINNER WITH THE first couple had been a surprisingly informal and intimate experience. Kate had anticipated a formal occasion and a dining room filled with dignitaries and public officials. But the only diners had been President and Mrs. Coolidge, Ethan and Skye Ramsey, Trey Ramsey, and herself. The fare had been simple: baked trout, beef sirloin strips, roasted potatoes and an assortment of vegetable dishes. Dessert had featured a multi-layered German chocolate cake. Mrs. Coolidge said it was a birthday cake, but the president would have scolded her if she arranged for just one candle. He did not like fusses, Kate learned, and he would have declined to blow out a single, lighted candle.

The first lady was warm and cheery, her expert orchestration of the dinner conversation reflecting her experience and natural charm. She teased her husband when he became too serious, and she enjoyed the man's dry wit that tended to pop up at the most unexpected times. Kate had been seated between Trey and his Grandma Skye with the first lady sitting across the table between the president and Ethan Ramsey. There was not a chair at either end of the table. She thought it strange that the president did not sit at the head of the table. Skye Ramsey and Grace Coolidge had carried the conversation, the men speaking only when specifically addressed or nudged into the dialogue by the first lady. The three men had retreated now to a sitting room off the dining area for cigars and coffee or whatever it was men did after such meals. Given these were prohibition times, she assumed there was no alcohol. Trey had looked like he was a reluctant participant.

Mrs. Coolidge excused herself to speak with staff about Independence Day and birthday arrangements that would take place at the lodge the next day, evidently starting by mid-morning. She had suggested Kate and Skye enjoy a walk or relax on the veranda. She would join them when her tasks were finished.

Kate and Skye strolled leisurely down a crushed-rock pathway that edged the gardens surrounding the lodge, chatting amiably about Kate's family and the Shamrock Ranch. Kate noted that Skye Ramsey was not only knowledgeable about the cattle business but had unusual skill at turning the conversation to her companions; Kate had found herself rambling on at length about her father and grandparents. For the second time that day she told her mother's story. It was also the second time in nearly ten years. The realization startled her.

"Mrs. Ramsey, until today I had never spoken to anyone other than my grandmother about the circumstances of my mother's death. The subject is verboten with my father, and I always just told friends my mother had died and left it at that."

"Please, call me Skye. I think we're going to be great friends. I don't think your experience is unusual. Some people try to pretend a tragedy did not happen by not talking about it, I think. Of course, that doesn't work. Ethan will not mention Deuce's name for the longest times. I get comfort from talking about his life. He is still with me, in my heart. You did know we lost a son in the war?"

"Trey told me. I didn't know his name."

"Ethan Junior . . . Deuce."

"I get it. And Trey is the third. That's different."

"The nicknames weren't planned. They just happened, like they usually do."

"I didn't ask Trey. Do you have other children?"

"One. And he's been a godsend to us. He runs the ranch operation now . . . but tolerates my unsolicited advice. His name is Jacob Fox Ramsey. He is our adopted son. He's full-blood Brule Sioux. That's another story. He's fifty-seven years old, married to a lovely Sioux woman, and they have given us three special grandchildren . . . two girls and a boy. Jake's son, Clay, finished his degree at the University of Wyoming this spring and has started reading the law in Ethan's office. Ethan is delighted. He had hoped that Deuce and Trey might find their ways to the law, but it didn't happen. Trey tried, but he and his grandfather always seem to lock antlers, like a young buck fighting an old buck. I hope to see them make a comfortable peace before I die."

"They seemed civil at dinner."

"Yes, that's the word. They are civil. But friendship and warmth would be better."

Kate thought of her father. She could relate to the situation.

"Things will ease in few months. Late spring, Ethan becomes increasingly tense and more easily aggravated.

He's ordinarily an almost irritatingly calm and relaxed man. I cannot upset him if I try, but as we draw nearer the anniversary of Deuce's death, Ethan grows agitated and terribly moody. It will pass after that day passes, and he will do well until the cycle commences again."

"When is the anniversary date?"

"August 5."

Kate's heart hammered in her chest, and she suddenly felt short of breath. She caught sight of an axe-hewn bench beside the trail and stumbled to it and clumsily plopped down.

Skye sat down beside her and wrapped her arm around Kate's shoulder. "Kate, what is it, dear?"

Kate took a deep breath. "My mother, Coleen, died August 5, 1918."

They sat silently for some minutes, as Kate regained her composure. In the hills above the lodge, a coyote howled. Another responded. And then a pack began barking in the distance.

Kate said, "Dad hates coyotes. Shoots them whenever he gets the chance. I never could. I love to listen to them at nights. They give me peace somehow. I miss my coyotes when I'm away at school."

Skye said, "The coyote is my spirit animal."

"Really. Is that like a good luck charm?"

"I suppose you could say so. It comes from a vision my uncle, Lame Buffalo, had. It was during the period I met Ethan and had the spill from a horse that cost me my hand."

Kate would never have inquired about the infirmity, but it would have been impossible not to notice the pinned-up sleeve on Skye's blouse. It appeared she had lost her left arm a few inches below the elbow. "Can you tell me about the vision?"

"It is a long story. It involved a tragic lynching of two Indian boys near Lockwood. My uncle Lame Buffalo's son rode with the boys but escaped to the village. I taught at a Quaker school near Lockwood and employed Ethan as a lawyer for my cousin. We went into the mountains to convince my uncle to send my cousin back to stand trial. He was obviously reluctant, and at night Lame Buffalo went off into the hills alone, seeking a sign from the Great Spirit. When he returned the next morning, he ordered my cousin to return to Lockwood with us. He explained that while waiting for a sign, he heard a male coyote calling for his mate from the far-end of the valley. The female answered from somewhere above the cave where Lame Buffalo sat. He closed his eyes, and the vision came."

"You're giving me chills."

Skye continued. "In his dream, my uncle saw a river, the flat water . . . the Platte, it is called today. On one side stood warriors painted for war and armed for battle. On the other were soldiers of the U.S. Cavalry, who were also prepared for war. My uncle raised his arm to signal attack, but suddenly Ethan, known among the Sioux as the Puma, appeared from the mass of soldiers. He waded into the shallow flat water and crossed it to where the Sioux warriors waited. Standing before my uncle, he held out his arm and cut his own wrist with his knife. My uncle said blood flowed like milk from the teats of a nursing mare. And then, seemingly from the river's mist, I appeared next to Ethan. I was known as Sky-in-the-Morning among my Brule family, and I was dressed in the doeskins of a Sioux woman."

Spellbound, Kate asked. "Go on. Please."

"I took Ethan's knife and cut my own arm and pressed my flesh to his until our blood mixed. And when my uncle looked across the river, the soldiers were turning their horses away from this place they had chosen for battle. Then, the Puma took my hand, and we walked away, crossing the river to follow his people. Lame Buffalo turned to the Brule warriors and said, 'Return to your lodges; we shall fight the white man no more.'"

"Were you and Ethan in love already at the time of the vision?"

"No, he was my lawyer. And, I must say I found him rather annoying at times. Some days later, even after he saved my life and was going to ask me to marry him, I cut him short and returned to my people. It was months later, and after much bloodshed that we reunited and were married."

"And the vision. Somehow I think there is more to your story."

"Ethan does not believe in visions or prophecies, but I am open to such possibilities. Many people in my village were later massacred by raiders seeking ill-gotten gold bullion that had come into the hands of my trader father. He had hidden the treasure near his abandoned trading post in Wyoming's Powder River country. I, and several other young women, had been taken captive by the renegades. Ethan and several of his friends tracked the raiders and obtained our release, although he was seriously wounded and nearly died. We found the gold and established an organization called the Lame Buffalo Foundation. All the money was used to purchase ranch and farm land, which would be sold first to survivors of our Brule village and then to other Indians who chose to establish lives outside the reservation. The foundation carries the mortgage. After operation of the ranches or farms for at least five years, the mortgage debt is cancelled, and the operator owns the land free and clear. It pleases me that many of my people became very successful and productive over the years and that most of the land remains in the hands of their families. They have prospered and become a part of the fabric of America far beyond those of my people who have remained on the reservation."

"And you see this as the prophecy from the night of the coyote fulfilled."

"Yes, and I think it is a harmless enough thought, don't you?"

"I'm sorry to be so late, ladies. The arrangements for tomorrow are starting to overwhelm."

Kate looked up and saw Mrs. Coolidge stepping carefully down the path, which was shadowed by darkness now. She also caught a glimpse of a Secret Service agent a few steps back and off the pathway. It must be awful to have someone trailing you all the time, Kate thought. Rarely a private moment to be yourself. Perhaps, she should have her own agent to keep her away from the likes of Liam Karlsson.

Skye said, "We've had a nice time getting acquainted. The coyotes are howling and barking this evening and gave me a wonderful opening for my storytelling. And you didn't have to listen to the tale again."

"Oh, but I would love to hear it again. You and Ethan had quite harrowing adventures in your early years. Have you ever considered writing about them? It would be such a gift to new generations."

"I would have to tell our stories as fiction. No one would believe the truth."

"Regardless," Grace Coolidge said, "You should think about it."

The women moved along the path back to the lodge, Kate trailing along behind a few paces, the Secret Service agent behind her. In the soft moonlight glow, she caught a glimpse of a man stooped over next to a bucket in the garden. He appeared to be pulling weeds. What a strange time to be engaged in such a task. She supposed, though, with guests arriving tomorrow, the staff was working overtime to spruce-up the grounds.

Chapter 10

TREY

PRESIDENT COOLIDGE HAD excused himself for the evening. He was a creature of undeviating habit, and an early bedtime was deeply ingrained in his routine. Unfortunately, for me, he would be awake with the sunrise, and he told me he would like to work a few hours on budget details before preparing for the day's festivities.

Gramps, on the other hand tended to be a night owl, like he was looking for reasons to avoid bedtime. I wondered if it had to do with ghosts who visited when his eyes closed and he surrendered to sleep. Gram had mentioned she worried because Gramps often moaned and tossed and turned in their bed and occasionally cried out and awoke in a cold sweat. Peace increasingly eluded him as the years slipped away.

Gramps and I remained in the room, seated in cushioned leather-covered chairs and overseen by walls of elk, deer and buffalo heads. A stuffed black bear stood on its back legs in one corner, and a bobcat crouched on the mantel above the fireplace. This room had not previously been opened to presidential guests, but I assumed it was a private meeting room of sorts. When the president left the room, I thought of getting up and following, but I didn't see any way I could do that without making it obvious I was avoiding Gramps, which, of course, was precisely what I had in mind. I would have given my last nickel for a bottle of corn bourbon right now.

"A drink of something stronger than coffee would be nice, wouldn't it?"

"Well, if we're law abiding, we can't. Besides, I'm BI." I thought these were careful statements. Gramps was known for his aversion to liquor, although he had opposed prohibition. I remember him saying, "A free man has an inalienable right to be a fool. Just leave folks alone."

"Well, Mr. BI man, I have a shot or two of giggle juice every evening these days, and the feds are toothless to do anything about it. Prohibition has tripled crime of all kinds in this country. Legalize booze and half the Chicago mobs will collapse."

Gramps shocked me with his words. Straight-laced Gramps, drinking illegal hooch every night. At the same time, it strangely concerned me.

"I concede that too many BI resources are committed to the unenforceable."

"Tell me, how are you liking your work with the BI?"

"It's interesting enough." I said noncommittally.

"I was wrong to push you to take the job with Hoover. I realize now, it's dangerous work. I thought they'd put you in an office working numbers. I understand you are on an assignment here that involves murderers . . . and now there is the matter of the attempted assassination."

I bristled. "You don't think I can handle a dangerous assignment?"

"I know you can. And I'm certain you will do so more than competently. I'm selfish. I don't want to see your life at risk. Losing Deuce was something I will never come to terms with. It troubles me that I placed you in harm's way. My God, you lost your father, and all you've ever got from me was platitudes. I've felt so sorry for myself, I haven't had your back the way I should."

I didn't like this conversation a bit, and it was making it tougher for me to blame my problems on Gramps. It's tougher to go through life without scapegoats, isn't it? "I haven't always used good judgment," I said.

"Well, that's true enough. After you got your business degree from WU, I was wrong to have pushed you into law clerking to prepare for the bar. That's not to say you wouldn't make a fine lawyer. But we all must choose our own paths. I say this as a man who has made a wagon-load of mistakes a six-horse team couldn't pull. I blame myself for your father's death because I always thought he applied for an appointment to West Point to get away from me and do things his own way. No father was ever prouder when Deuce graduated and got that officer's commission. But I never told him that. I never told him I loved him, but no man ever loved his son more. These are just a few of the mistakes in my wagon. Thank God, I did one thing right when I convinced your grandmother to marry me."

Tears trickled down Gramps' cheeks. He had left me struggling for the right words, but I could not come up with them. "I'm sure Dad knew those things."

"Well, it's too late to change it. But I vowed before we left Lockwood, I wouldn't make that mistake with you. Trey, I'm proud of your graduation from WU with highest honors and that unbelievable numbers brain of yours. I wanted you to read law in my office because I thought you'd be a great lawyer. But I also hoped that it would give me a chance to get closer to you and know you better. Rectify past mistakes. I just want you to know I love you, Trey. I always have. And I always will, whatever course you take in your life. I do understand you've got to blaze your own trail. And I will have your back if you need me, so long as I can take a breath."

Frankly, I had had enough of this, and I just mumbled, "I love you too, Gramps."

"How's Zoe?"

Gramps was prone to shifting topics in an instant, but I figured he had spat out the words he had probably rehearsed in his head many times and was pressed to make a quick escape. This was fine with me.

"Mom's doing very well. She and Ted love San Antonio." Three years after Dad's death, Mom remarried. After seven years, she remained deeply in love with the Texas wildcatter she married, as near as I could tell. It was a rags-to-riches and back again sort of life, but she didn't seem to mind.

"She's a fine woman. I'll always be grateful she brought you with her to Wyoming after we lost Deuce. She and your Grandma Skye became close during that time and I know they still write."

"Yes, Mom's a writer. I'm a little slow getting back to her and have to answer three or four letters sometimes."

He shifted again. "Can I ask you something about the assassination attempt?"

"Yes. I may not know the answer to your question."

"How did assassins know the president was going on a fishing outing?"

"I suppose they had someone watching the lodge from a safe distance. But that's conjecture. I can't answer your question, and the Secret Service isn't keeping me in the loop on their thinking. It's a good bet they resent a BI agent being anywhere near the case. Gramps, these agencies are as territorial as mountain cats."

"They wouldn't have a crew of three killers watching just on the chance the president would leave the lodge. And from what the president told me, they seemed to know exactly where he and his agents were headed. He said the destination is always reported to the agent-in-charge whenever he or the first lady depart for any purpose."

"I see what you're getting at. You think there is a leak from the staff." I had to give Gramps his due. He never missed much. He saw things that others did not with some consistency, a carry-over, perhaps, from his days as an Army scout.

"Who's that young man I see scurrying about the property? He's always sweeping or painting or tinkering with some damned thing. And he's always working where there's a gathering of people, usually not far from the president or first lady. Before dinner, he was hammering on the floor just outside the dining room, but I noticed he didn't have any nails."

"That would be Willy. I don't remember his last name. Now that you mention it, he does seem to be everyplace. I guess we're so accustomed to him being around, he's become invisible."

"Exactly. Somehow this man doesn't feel right to me. I assume he's not a part of the presidential contingent?"

"No, he's an employee of the State Game Lodge. But I'm sure all of the staff members were checked out by the Secret Service."

"But there isn't much they do but verify statements with a few references and ask a few questions at the county sheriff's office. I'd say the young man is at least half-blood Indian, no doubt Sioux. If he comes from the reservation, any background report is probably a blank page."

"I'm sure you're right."

"He's sure watching that young lady friend of yours, too. Of course, that's hard not to do. She's a looker. I'll probably get scolded by your grandma tonight for roaming eyes."

Gramps smiled, and somehow that warmed me. I remember him smiling a lot before Dad's death. After that, it seemed like he suddenly turned old and grumpy. "I appreciate your thoughts, Gramps. Willy's not going to be invisible anymore."

Chapter 11

SKYE

SKYE HAD CAUGHT a glimpse of Ethan and Trey in the private lodge room, but she chose not to join them. Ethan carried many secrets but few were kept from her. She hoped tonight he would tell Trey the things he so badly needed to say. If he did, he would start to build the bridge between them. But Trey would need to work on the bridge from his side of the gulf that separated them, also. Ethan, at his core, was a kind and giving man. It was time for Trey to grow up.

Skye lay in bed with pillows propped up behind her, engrossed with Elmer Gantry, the recent best-selling novel by Sinclair Lewis. The book was a page-turner and a bit titillating in spots. She had read most of Lewis's works, including Main Street and Babbitt, and she loved his characterizations and plots. But she also found him pompous and, sometimes, uninformed and economically naïve in his thinly-veiled attacks on small town and rural culture and what he evidently saw as excessive American materialism. She suspected he was not entirely forego-ing the luxuries of life when he spent his royalty checks. But he told a good story and provoked thought. For pure escapism, she preferred Edna Ferber, or Zane Grey, who seemed to have every western novel he wrote adapted to the silver screen in its seemingly insatiable appetite for westerns. Of course, she and Ethan had lived those times, and the stories were greatly sanitized versions of real life in the old west.

The bedroom door opened, and Ethan entered. He lay his dinner jacket over the back of the chair and sat down, his gaze fixed on her with eyes that showed more spark than they had for a spell. She liked it that there was no liquor available here, and she longed for his teetotal-ing days. He was not an obnoxious or mean drunk, but Ethan, with a few drinks down his gullet, became a silent and moody man. It was past time for a talk. When they returned to Lockwood, she would bring up the subject.

"Hello, beautiful lady," Ethan said.

"Hi, handsome man. I sense you had a nice evening."

"I did. I may have started mending the fence. Time will tell."

"Fence fixing's an endless job on the ranch. We're never done."

"I get your point. How was your evening?"

"Fun. Grace was busy with arrangements for tomorrow, so I spent most of my time with Kate. You remember Kate? The young woman you were ogling at dinner?"

"Ogling? I don't ogle anyone but you, my love."

"Liar. That's okay, as long you don't sleep with anyone but me. If you do, you're a dead man."

"Good Lord, Skye, I'm seventy-eight years old."

"Remind your friend." Should she tell him what she had learned and risk spoiling his good mood? She considered the question only a few seconds. They didn't keep information like this from each other.

Skye said, "I learned something tonight."

"From Sinclair Lewis? Not from that socialist bastard."

"Don't get worked up. No. From Kate Connolly."

"And what did you learn from Miss Connolly?"

"Brace yourself. Her mother served with the Army Nurse Corps in France during the war." She could see Ethan's jaw muscles tense and tighten.

"Connolly. I think I know where you're headed with this. I suppose her first name was Coleen?"

"Yes. And she died August 5, 1918."

Ethan shook his head in disbelief. "This has to be the most bizarre coincidence I've ever encountered. Did you say anything to her?"

"Only the date of Deuce's death. I told her the date, and then she responded with the date of her mother's death. She was stunned by what she apparently saw as a coincidence."

"Do you think we should tell her anything?"

"No. I don't see any point. I can't imagine what I would say."

"I agree. Leave it alone."

"The coyotes started howling immediately after she gave me the date."

Ethan gave her a look of mild exasperation. "We've heard a lot of coyotes over the years, dear."

"I think these were telling us something. I just haven't figured out what."

"I need to get to bed. Do you and Sinclair have room for me?"

"Definitely. And I'm going to shuck my nightgown. I want you to hold me."

"Is that all?"

"That's up to you and your friend."

Ethan shed his clothes and stretched out naked beside her on the bed. She snuggled up to him, and he wrapped his arms gently about her shoulders, as she rested her head upon his chest. She never tired of lying with this good man she had loved so passionately for so many years. They would never share enough nights together.

Ethan said, "My friend is willing."

Chapter 12

TREY

MRS. COOLIDGE HAD asked me not to stray too far from Kate Connolly during the birthday and Independence Day activities. I gathered that meant I was not an official host for the young lady, but I was to be available upon command. Sort of a loyal dog, if you will.

Hundreds of South Dakotans were swarming on the State Game Lodge grounds by mid-morning, and the main road and driveway were clogged with cars and horse-drawn buggies and wagons. The torrid sun would have everybody stinking with sweat before the day was out, and I would be among the worst, wearing a jacket to cover my .45 pistol. I thought I looked rather sheik, though, with my head topped with a flat-brimmed straw hat. Then I saw Kate step out of the house, and I felt like a hobo. She wore a navy-blue skirt, thankfully showing as much of the exquisite gams as western decency would allow. Her red blouse was high-necked and unrevealing. And patriot that she was, she had a little white, beret-type hat cocked at an angle atop her head.

She caught a glimpse of me, holding a prime spot under a ponderosa not far from the veranda, and, to my surprise, she hurried down the steps and walked straight toward me. As she came near, she showed traces of a smile. This shored me up some and gave me a shot of optimism for a civil conversation.

"Good morning, Kate," I said. "You look lovely this morning." Was that pouring the sugar on a bit thickly? I had no idea. My female relationships heretofore had pretty much been confined to floozies, and I felt awkward in polite society.

"Flattery will get you nowhere. But it's nice of you to say so. You clean up quite nicely yourself. You'll roast today in the coat, however."

"You do understand why I'm wearing a jacket?"

"So you can pretend you're hiding the gun?"

"Perhaps not everyone is as observant as you."

"There were hundreds of sidearms and a scattering of rifles checked in by your Secret Service at the gate before

I came downstairs. I was watching from my bedroom window. By my count, almost every agent is at the gate. No more than one Service agent and somebody who claims to be a Bureau of Investigation agent here on the grounds. That's terribly thin protection, if you ask me."

She was right, of course. "I don't think they anticipated this many people."

"Anybody could slip a gun in here. There is something I've been thinking about. If somebody wanted to kill the president, this would be the place to do it. All these people and the vehicles and horses blocking the roadways. Position a marksman in a high spot around here, and he could do his job and make it to a getaway car before a search could even be organized."

She was making me uneasy, and I found my eyes roaming the outbuildings and hillsides for likely sniper posts. "So, what are you suggesting?"

"I'm wondering if the so-called assassins were actually planning to kidnap the president?"

I thought about her remark. I was not certain their intent mattered since they did not carry it out. But, in casting for suspects, the character and backgrounds of abductors might be different than those of assassins. A presidential killer, for instance, would likely have a political grudge. An abductor's motive would more likely be money. "I think what you suggest is certainly a possibility. I should be screening the grounds before the president comes out. Would you care to join me for a stroll?"

She took my arm, and we strolled leisurely about the grounds, sometimes having to squeeze between the clusters of people. A cowboy band added to the festive atmosphere with its guitars and fiddles and an accordion or two. Traditional songs filled the air, but the band included several new songs in its repertoire, including a current hit by a new hillbilly star, Jimmie Rodgers, called Blue Yodel or T for Texas and a tune recently released by the Carter Family titled Wabash Cannonball, which didn't appear to have much of a future.

There were countless unofficial food and drink vendors lining the edges of the rolling lawns, much like the county fairs I attended with Gramps and Gram as a child. I bought us lemonades and promised lunch later, if she would join me. To my surprise, she quickly agreed. Strangely, I was no longer thinking of her as a potential conquest—well, not too much anyway. I was just enjoying her company, a new and rather scary experience for me.

"Let's go down by Squaw Creek," Kate suggested, taking the lead down a sloping path that led to the clear, fast-flowing mountain stream that descended from the hills and raced over a rocky bed past the lodge grounds.

"The president's been fishing here almost every morning—with great success, I might add." I decided not to mention staff rumors that Starling and South Dakota Governor William Bulow had colluded to have the stream stocked with ancient trout from a state fish hatchery and wire netting stretched across the creek downstream to hinder their escape. Also, there had been a few local complaints that the state legislature was on the verge of passing a bill to rename the stream Grace Coolidge Creek.

When we reached the stream, Kate claimed a large boulder for her perch and sat down and positioned herself with her legs discreetly crossed, leaving me standing awkwardly beside her. A hint of perfumed fragrance wafted upward, and, for fear of my nose starting to twitch like a bird dog picking up a scent, I staked out my own smaller flat-headed stone some six feet distant that forced me to look up at her. I felt like an accused looking up at a judge in a courtroom, but the nice-gam view compensated some.

"I had breakfast with your grandparents this morning," she said. "They are such an interesting couple, so obviously crazy about each other after all these years. Your grandfather seemed especially spry today. More talkative. He still cuts quite a figure, and your grandmother is so poised and beautiful."

The old fart. He was more politician than Coolidge. Gramps could turn on the charm when he wanted. But he could also turn it off in an instant. "I had intended to meet up with them, but I got caught up in something."

"You overslept is my guess," she said, displaying a mischievous smile and a twinkle in those gorgeous greenish-brown eyes.

I shrugged. "I hadn't committed."

"But you would have pleased them if you had been there."

I think I was being scolded. And it worked. She had pressed the tip of a spear in my conscience. Guilt had been an infrequent visitor in recent years, but the past day it had been making itself decidedly unwelcome. "You're right. I should have joined them."

"I had a wonderful conversation with your grandmother last night."

I sensed this was leading to something, but I was not too concerned. Gram Skye had always been my defender, although she probably had not helped my spoiled state. "That's nice. I'm glad you enjoyed some time with her."

"She told me the date of your father's death. August 5, 1918."

"Yes, that sounds right." Actually, the date was engraved in my mind.

"That's the same date my mother died."

She sent my head spinning with that remark. This was beyond weird. What were the odds? "That is a really strange coincidence."

"Yes, it kept me awake last night thinking about it. Skye also told me about Lame Buffalo's vision on the night of the coyote."

"I've heard that story until I could repeat it word for word. Gram told me the story once, but the Brule around Lockwood told me the tale until I was sick of it."

"I think it's romantic and kind of spooky at the same time."

"I'm certain old Lame Buffalo believed in his vision, but we all have strange dreams sometimes. Then some things in a dream happen, and we can choose to call it either prophecy or coincidence. I lean toward coincidence."

"You don't believe in the vision?"

"No. I don't believe in things that can't be proven with hard facts."

"That's why you're a numbers cruncher?"

"I'm not an accountant. I'm a BI agent, who has some ability to work with numbers."

"Skye said you were a mathematical prodigy as a child, that they had to find books for you to read because you were advanced beyond the abilities of your teachers. I can't imagine. I've always struggled with numbers. But she said you see your ability as a curse, because you don't even enjoy working with numbers. You tested out of every mathematics class in college and obtained a degree in business because you promised your mother you would graduate."

"Gram talks too much."

"She worries about you. She's afraid you find no fun in life."

"I find fun." But do I truly?

"What is 1,166,676 divided by fourteen?"

"Eighty-three thousand three hundred thirty-four." Damn, I never responded to these little games.

"Impressive, I guess. But, of course, I can't do that in my head, so I really don't know if you're right."

"I'm right. And please, don't do that again," I snapped.

"I didn't mean to make you angry."

"Not angry. Annoyed."

"Well, I wasn't trying to annoy you. I was enjoying your company until now."

I could see the concern on her face, but I sensed that I had a situation that needed defusing. Perhaps, I was starting to pick up some emotional awareness. I had been told by my mother I needed that. What would Gramps say here? "I'm sorry. I've been having a wonderful time. I'm just a bit too sensitive about my numbers curse. I'll do better. Second chance?" Her eyes studied my face, and I thought I saw a tad of empathy there.

"Second chance."

"Will you be offended if I talk business?"

"BI business?"

"Yes."

"I'm listening."

"I asked you to think about anything you might not have mentioned to the Secret Service about the day you helped the president. Have you thought about this?"

"I have. I thought I heard one of the name's called out—the Sioux's. And I don't remember mentioning the name. I thought the president would have said something, but then it occurred to me he was in a corner of the cave and probably didn't hear the voice."

"What was his name?"

"George."

"This could be important."

"There could be a hundred Lakota named George on the reservation."

"But, as compared to Indian No-Name, this greatly narrows possibilities."

"Of course, he might not be Lakota. He might not be from the Pine Ridge Reservation or Rapid City. He might be in Kansas City by now."

"At least it's something."

"You were already here when those men were stalking President Coolidge. You're not in the Black Hills to chase assassins."

My mission was not top secret. Gabe had probably already shown his credentials a dozen times. "Another agent and I are investigating the rape and murder of two Lakota girls. There is also the possibility there are other killings or abductions. A number of young women appear to have turned up missing."

Her brow furrowed. "I've heard about the murders. The Shamrock borders the reservation, and I have several good friends about my age who live not far from the ranch. Sage Rainmaker teaches at one of the reservation schools. She knows everybody in the western part of the Pine Ridge. She's very bright. She could go anyplace, but she's chosen to stay here and help her people."

"Do you think she would talk freely with me?"

"If I went with you. She's my best friend. I haven't seen her so much, since I went away to college. She attended the Haskell Institute in Lawrence, Kansas for a year after she finished high school, got teaching certification and came back home. But I've been planning on riding over to see her anyway."

"Ride? Like on a horse?"

"It would be much shorter from my place, and we could find her without attracting so much attention. You can ride, can't you?"

I gave her an exasperated look. "When I wasn't living on army posts, I lived on Gram and Gramps's Lazy R. I'm rusty, but I can ride. I suppose I could rent a horse from the lodge for a day, but we'd have to figure out how to meet up."

"Belle Fourche rodeo's tomorrow. Day after, you drive over to the Shamrock. I'll ride my War Paint and pick you a gentle mount from the remuda. I'll show you some of God's country on the way to the reservation, which belongs to the devil. And don't worry about Dad. He'll be on a cow-buying trip down at Chadron, Nebraska for three days starting tomorrow."

I passed on her gentle mount remark, and I wasn't looking for trouble with Owen Connolly. "I don't want to cause any conflict between you and your father."

"Dad and I have had trouble ever since Mom died. I don't lie to him if silence doesn't count." She pointed up the slope toward the lodge. "There was a man looking down the hill at us, longer than casual. Maybe he was just curious."

I turned. "Was it the handyman?"

"No. I can't say for sure, but I thought he looked like a darkie. Dressed in bib overalls and a straw hat. Like a farmer."

Chapter 13

TREY

AS WE WALKED back toward the festivities at the lodge, I explained to Kate that Gabriel Riley was the senior agent for the BI investigation and that I doubted he would take kindly to be referred to as a "darkie." She assured me she would never want to offend anyone because of his race. She had seen few Negroes during her lifetime, and folks she knew, who did not use the derogatory "N word," tended to refer to black people as "darkies."

Gabe had disappeared by the time we returned to the chaos on the grounds. I started to escort Kate to a flatbed wagon where some ladies appeared to be making sandwiches and selling pie when the celebrants nearest the lodge veranda began clapping and cheering.

Kate and I veered off in the direction of the racket but were eventually blocked by the hordes who were pressing forward. We backed away, then, for a clearer view, and I was shocked to see the president standing on the top porch step wearing a huge ten-gallon hat, a red silk cowboy shirt, a purple kerchief and a pair of white chaps with "Cal" emblazoned on them. The usually staid president was smiling like a kid at Christmas. I learned later that a Boy Scout troop from Custer had given him a bay mare with saddle and other tack. The chaps had been a gift from the cowboy band.

"Isn't he cute?" Kate said.

Insane, I thought. "Well, everybody seems to be loving it."

"It's nice to see him having fun on his birthday. He seems to carry a great sadness on his shoulders."

"Let's go eat while everyone's preoccupied with the president."

"Okay. I'm starving."

We made our way to the flatbed trailer, where we each selected ham sandwiches, baked beans and potato salad for lunch. We also were given a complimentary slice of chocolate birthday cake, one of hundreds on tables scattered about the grounds. As we walked away to search for a place to sit down, I caught sight of Gabe waving for us to join him at a small folding table where he sat alone with his own lunch. He stood and doffed his straw hat, as we approached.

"Kate," I said, "this is Mr. Gabriel Riley, the other BI agent I mentioned. Gabe, this is Kate Connolly. I may have mentioned her name when we met." I shot him a warning look.

"Why, yes you did. You spoke very highly of her. I would be honored to have you join me, Miss Connolly. And you can sit with us, too, Trey."

"Please, call me Kate."

"If you will call me Gabe."

Kate chatted amicably with Gabe about his family and military service, quickly eliciting more information about his life than I had garnered in the months I had known him. Since I was cut out of the conversation, I focused on my lunch, which was superb country fare, my kind of food. The church lady at the concession had informed us that the cake was sour cream chocolate, from a recipe for a cake presented to President Coolidge by a Rapid City resident. I had never eaten better. Finally, I was included in the conversation.

"Trey," Gabe said, "here is your list of families with missing daughters. There are ten for you to contact." He handed me a folded sheet of paper.

"Kate is going to go with me to meet a friend or two of hers who might be helpful. I'll have her look at this list and see if she knows any of the families. I've informed President Coolidge that I have to give this case priority now and won't be available so much to go over budget numbers. He understands, but if I come in before his bedtime, I'll probably be conscripted."

"I have a list of a dozen families I'll be interviewing. I don't think we'll have much time to devote to the attack on the president."

"Kate has a name for the Indian who was involved. George. She heard that name called. Not much, but it's a start. I'll inform the Service. There is also an employee here at the lodge who might bear watching. Willy Hobson. He's apparently part Lakota. If nothing else, we might look for openings to find out more about him."

Gabe asked, "And you have a reason for singling out this man?"

"First, it seems highly likely to me that these assassins, if that's what they were, had to know where the president was going that morning. That suggests a leak from the State Game Lodge. Willy is a handyman here who always seems to be working near the president or Secret Service agents, or wherever there is serious conversation taking place. It could be anyone, but I think we should find out more about this man." I did not attribute the uncovering of a suspect to Gramps, rationalizing he would not want to claim credit for his observations, but I felt a bit of guilt at taking credit. There it was again. Conscience. This stranger could become a problem.

"Is that Willy?" Kate asked, speaking in a near whisper and nodding toward a black-haired young man with a gunny sack in his hand, stooping and picking up litter not more than twenty feet behind Gabe.

"Don't turn, Gabe," I said. I glared at the young man, and when he turned his head and looked our way, our eyes met for an instant. He quickly started working his way toward the lodge. "Now, Gabe."

Gabe turned his head and watched Hobson walk away. "How long was he there?"

Kate said, "I don't know. I said something as soon as I saw him."

Gabe said, "We need to find out about this guy. Trey, you alert the Service. We should all be asking some questions. He's probably okay, but we'd better be certain."

Chapter 14

KATE

KATE HAD WAR Paint and Nipper, a big-boned sorrel gelding with a white mane and tail saddled and hitched to the rail in front of the house. She sat on the top porch step, dressed in boots and well-worn riding garments, her hair tied back in a ponytail that fell from beneath her wide-brimmed hat. The sun was not always a redhead's friend. She had gotten out of bed early this morning in anticipation of Trey's arrival. They had spent most of two days together at the State Game Lodge, and, after getting past the early tension between them, they had fallen into a comfortable friendship. At least that's the way she saw it. But it didn't hurt any that he was pleasant to the eye with his dark, rugged features and slender, rangy body. Liam Karlsson was physically more muscular and thickly-built and had a flawless, pretty face. But there was something about Trey's brooding, coffee-brown eyes that pulled her into dangerous territory. She would have to be on guard.

Yesterday, Trey had accompanied her to the rodeo and they sat in the grandstand with his grandparents and President and Mrs. Coolidge. The first couple had been alternately thrilled and shocked as the events unfolded. In one instance they had been horrified, when a steer broke its neck during a bulldogging contest and had to be shot and drug off in front of the silent crowd. Kate had been delighted to see the president roar with laughter during an event where range cows were turned loose in the arena, and cowboys competed to see who could rope and milk a jarful from a cow the fastest. Mostly, the cows won the event. Kate smiled now, just remembering those moments when this stoic, serious man let down his guard. She sensed he was enjoying his visit to the Black Hills enormously, and the residents of his host state were excited to have him there, and welcoming, except for the few who had attempted to turn the occasion into tragedy.

Trey's Model T pulled into the yard, and she waved at him before hurrying back into the house to grab the two paper bags she had packed for their lunches. She had included several extra oatmeal-raisin cookies to go with the apple and ham sandwich in Trey's sack. The bread and cookies she had fresh-baked this morning to the surprise of Grandma Beth, who usually had to drag Kate into the kitchen for domestic chores.

She was surprised that her grandmother was not here to see them off, but she, for some reason, had become uncharacteristically quiet and subdued when Kate told her about the coincidental dates of deaths of Deuce Ramsey and Coleen Connolly upon her return from the State Game Lodge yesterday morning. Kate supposed it had set Grandma Beth to thinking about the loss of her daughter.

She rushed out the door with their lunches. She had looped a water-filled canteen over the saddle horn of each mount, and there would be several icy springs to stop at for refills along the route she had planned. Trey was leaning against his car as she approached, his eyes fixed in her direction. It had annoyed her slightly, when they first met, that he seemed to be appraising her like a cattle judge looking at a heifer in the show ring. She hoped she wasn't as obvious when she studied him. This morning, he looked like a working cowboy, attired in scuffed cowboy boots and a dusty, black low-crowned hat pulled down on his forehead. He wore faded denims and a short-sleeved cotton shirt that revealed, sinewy, muscular arms, inconsistent with her image of him as a sedentary numbers cruncher. She guessed his naturally-tan skin immunized him against the mountain sun's searing rays.

He pushed his hat up and smiled as she approached. "Howdy, ma'am. Appears you've got the critters saddled and ready to ride."

"I do. I wasn't sure you knew how."

"I assure you I can saddle a horse, but I don't mind having it done for me."

She thrust the lunch bag toward him, and he took it and peeked inside. "I'm hungry," he said.

"Too bad. Picnic spot is about two hours from here, just about a half hour from the reservation school. You can put your lunch in the saddlebags."

He opened the Ford's passenger door and reached in and plucked out his pistol and shoulder holster. "Along with these. Hopefully, it won't be needed."

"I've got my Winchester. Do you want me to get another?"

"No. We should be adequately armed. I can't imagine we will need a gun for this little trip."

"Very well. Let's ride."

Trey followed her to the horses. She patted War Paint on the rump. "This is War Paint. He's mine. You're riding Nipper."

"Why am I suspicious about that name?"

"You'll be fine. Just don't turn your back to him. Or jerk too hard on the reins."

Trey stepped into the stirrup and swung gracefully into the saddle. They rode, side by side, across the valley in the direction of the low mountain range that overlooked the reservation that spread into the southern portion of the Badlands. Kate noted that Trey was far from the tenderfoot she had suspected him of being. He was certainly a more than competent horseman, and Nipper had evidently sensed this, for he had been on his best behavior

When they climbed into the foothills, Kate pulled ahead and took the lead. "The trail to the top is not especially treacherous, but it's too narrow for two abreast."

Trey fell in behind her. Kate looked back from time to time as they picked their ways up the shale-covered trail. Her eyes never met his because he appeared to be searching the slopes above and the floor of the canyon below. She suspected this was an instinctive thing for him, and he was probably not even aware of it. Perhaps, his Army scout grandfather had passed on more habits than Trey would admit.

When they reached the summit, they dismounted and staked out the horses to graze on sparse grass that creeped through fissures in the granite surface of the narrow mesa. The area was treeless and offered no shade beyond the shadows cast by two enormous boulders, perched side by side like two sentinels overlooking their domain. They each chose one and sat down, with legs crossed Indian-style, facing each other as they opened their lunches.

"That was a steep climb," Trey commented. "Are you sure that's the fastest route to the reservation?"

"It's not. We can cut more than a half hour off the return trip by taking the trail on the canyon floor. But I wanted you to see the contrasts of this country from here. Look to the west, and it's all mountains and valleys. To the east, it's all barren wasteland that even cactuses reject. Enough grass to support a few sheep and goats in wet years."

"That's the reservation, I gather."

"The Pine Ridge Indian Reservation. Miles and miles along both sides of the South Dakota and Nebraska borders, more on our side of the line than Nebraska's. If you travel a short distance you will find the commencement of the Badlands, which are essentially many, many square miles of deep gullies and canyons carved by erosion, where only the toughest creatures can survive. The Sioux claim ownership of the Black Hills, including the Shamrock Ranch. They were granted the land by the Laramie Treaty of 1868, but five or six years later, gold was discovered in the Black Hills, and the government opened the land for settlement."

"I had read there is a lawsuit by the Sioux to reclaim the land or to recover damages."

"Yes, but it's likely to go on for years. Dad's always been a little bit nervous about where the Shamrock fits in to any settlement. Coolidge seems openminded when it comes to settlement. He has some personal support among the Sioux for supporting and signing the Indian Citizenship Act three years ago."

"Interesting that the Indians inhabited the country for centuries before the Europeans and Spanish settled, but it took an act of Congress to make them citizens."

"Of course, there were ways to acquire citizenship before. Marriage. Military service. Owning property and residing off the reservation for a specified time. But it was all very complicated."

"You seem to be a student of history."

"I do like history, but I'm not all that good with dates. I suppose you would be."

"Maybe. If I studied it. Frankly, I spent most of my college years focusing on good times."

"Good times?"

"Parties and drinking, for instance."

"Petting parties, too, I suppose?

"Not so much."

Trey appeared reluctant to talk about his past, so she decided to shift the subject. "Are you uncomfortable talking about your father's death?"

"Not really. It's been so long ago, I don't dwell on it now. I used to, though. I was angry at him for leaving me like that. Stupid, isn't it?"

"I don't think it's unusual. I felt the same way about my mom. She was in the Army Nurse Corps reserve, but she could have claimed exemption. She was not career Army like your father. She wasn't subject to the draft. She had a choice. The war or her family. I resented that for a long time . . . I suppose until I got out of high school and started to see the world a little differently. We all make choices every day that change the directions of our lives. But we often cannot even imagine the consequences of those choices. Mom didn't go off to war planning to be killed. She had valuable training that was needed there, and Grandma said she was always a free spirit, looking for the next adventure. I'm not certain, but I can remember her and Dad quarreling a lot when I was a child. I just lately started to recollect those times, and I've wondered if she was running from him. Yet, that meant leaving me, too." It occurred to her she had never spoken to anyone of these thoughts, not even Grandma Beth. It made her uncomfortable now, to think she had spoken the words to a young man, who was still a near-stranger.

Trey spoke softly, "Before the war, we moved a lot from post to post, but Lockwood, Wyoming, near Gram Skye and Gramps, was always home base. We had a cottage on the ranch property where Mom and I stayed when Dad was away on short assignments, and that's where leave time was spent. I worshipped Dad, and we played baseball together and enjoyed each other's company when he was around. But he was gone a lot and always a little distant . . . just his nature, I guess. I was closer to Gramps before Dad's death. He was easy-going and fun and always made time for me. Until Dad was killed. Then he changed and turned sad and withdrawn, when I needed him most. I was angry at him, too, until recently. I've just started to re-think things. Gram always says not to judge a man until you've walked a mile in his moccasins. When a man loses a child, I guess he's got some ghosts of his own to deal with."

"Forgiveness. Grandma Beth says it's a powerful force. It lets you put stuff behind you and start fresh. Why waste away our lives fretting about some wrong, perhaps, even imagined, that we think somebody's done to us? It gets in the way of enjoying the now and anticipating the future with enthusiasm."

"Sounds like we both have wise grandmothers."

"Maybe they've just learned from years of living." She hesitated. "Speaking of grandmothers, Grandma Beth seemed upset when I told her about your father dying on the same date as my mom. I thought it was kind of strange."

"Probably just reminded her of her own loss. Like I said, we both know about losing a parent before their times, but we can't relate to the death of a child."

"I think there's something else."

Trey looked at her expectantly. When she said nothing, he finished the cookies in his paper sack. "These are scrumptious. So was the fresh bread. Did your grandmother bake them?"

She feigned insult. "No. I baked the bread and cookies. Why would you assume Grandma did?"

He raised his hands defensively. "I apologize. I just thought it would take many years' experience to make something this perfect. My thanks for an excellent lunch."

He was overdoing it now, but she didn't mind the fuss. "We'd better be on our way."

Chapter 15

TREY

AS WE RODE onto the reservation lands, headed in the direction of what I assumed was the faint outline of the school building in the distance, I was struck by the dismal scene that unfolded. Scattered helter-skelter over the parched, brown prairie were indistinguishable bleached-out, unpainted shacks, many with spaces between warped boards that would not bar snow, let alone wind drafts. Most of the occupants owned at least several half-starved dogs, it appeared, and an occasional cow or a few head of sheep or goats occupied the yards of some residences.

This was a sharp contrast to the thriving, prosperous farms and ranches owned individually by the Sioux in the valleys lying east of the Powder River and outside

Lockwood in Wyoming. I realized at that moment how important Gram Skye's tireless work with the Lame Buffalo Foundation during her lifetime had been. Gramps, too, had been her silent anchor and supporter all those years. These were people who made a difference in their little corner of the world. How could I have been so blind?

From time to time I sighted a wizened and ancient man or woman, sitting on a rocking chair or bench in front of a shack, watching the visitors, seemingly only with mild curiosity, as they passed by. Strangely, I often saw school-age children playing in the yards, but rarely young or middle-aged adults. I sidled Nipper up closer to Kate.

"Why aren't the kids in school?"

"They go when they feel like it, which may be not at all, if their parents don't make them."

"But why don't they make them?"

"Many on the reservation don't understand the importance of education. Some don't want their children to leave the reservation. If they don't go to school, they're pretty much stuck here. There are Sioux parents who demand that their children attend school and encourage their studies at home. They cling to hope for a better future. But too many here are resigned to their situation and are not motivated to improve lt. The government allotment lets them subsist, and that seems to be enough."

"And where are the adults?"

"Some are working at the few jobs on the reservation. Others work for local ranchers or have jobs in town. Unfortunately, many gather at the crude speakeasies that are set up in dilapidated barns or old-time tipis for sale of boot-leg liquor. Their kids are likely the ones that aren't in school."

When we rode up to the schoolhouse, we dismounted and led our horses to a metal trough that sat under a pump in the schoolyard. I worked the pump handle and filled the nearly empty receptacle while our horses drank and Kate filled the canteens. Then we hitched our mounts at one of the rails in front of the building. A half dozen horses and ponies were hitched at the several rails adjacent to the school, so I figured there must be a few pupils inside.

Kate said, "Why don't you wait out here? I'll slip in and call you in after I explain to Sage why we're here, or I'll bring her out. It's a two-room school, and another teacher usually has the second room."

While I waited, I strolled the perimeter of the school. The framed, rectangular building and two privies out back were freshly white-washed, as was another structure that looked like a ranch bunkhouse set off some fifty feet from the school. The grounds were immaculate. Someone even had a sizable flower box set up along the bunkhouse building, and it was overflowing with purple and yellow flowers of some kind. I knew roses and tulips, but flower identification was something I had never worried much about.

I observed that neither telephone nor electric wires had made it this far yet, but that was not unusual in most rural areas. Gram and Gramps's Lazy R had a telephone, but electricity had not yet arrived. Gramps's Lockwood law office, though, was thoroughly electrified and even included one of the new Frigidaire refrigerators. Gram had to settle for an ice box on the ranch, but I had never heard her complain about that, or much of anything for that matter.

I heard voices at the front of the building, so I hurried back, and, when I turned the corner, I found Kate engaged in animated conversation with a woman, whose back was toward me. I could only tell that she had short-cropped black hair and wore a gray professional-looking outfit and black shoes with short heels. Oh, she had quite a nice behind as well. When she turned toward me, her initial promise was fulfilled. She was decidedly more buxom than Kate, taller and more curvaceous, too—a bit more meat on her bones, one might say. She had flawless, bronzed skin, and her dark eyes said I'd better stop my appraisal of her forthwith.

"Sage," Kate said, "this is Trey Ramsey, the Bureau of Investigation agent I was telling you about."

"Pleased to meet you, ma'am," I said.

She seemed to consider it a moment before extending her hand. She gripped mine firmly but did not try to do harm like a certain Irishman I had recently encountered.

"Mr. Ramsey," she said.

"Please, call me Trey."

"Mr. Ramsey," she said pointedly, "I have an eighth-grader supervising study time while I am absent from the classroom. I will try to answer your questions, but I do not have time to waste with pleasantries. How may I help you?"

She was not quite hostile, but she was not going to be charmed. I must have left my charm with that floozie in Washington the night before I departed with President and Mrs. Coolidge on their Black Hills journey.

"Miss Rainmaker, an associate and I have been sent by Washington to investigate the murders of two Sioux girls."

"Yes. Ruth Gray Horse and Lark Pipe Maker. They were killed, and one can assume they were raped and beaten. What has taken you so long to get here?"

"I can't account for that, ma'am."

"Government bureaucrats, I suppose."

"Did you know the girls?"

"Not Ruth, but I was acquainted with Lark. Her ten-year old sister, Frannie, attends my school, off and on. She's not here today."

"Do you know anything about Lark's social life ? Friends? Anyone she was spending time with?"

"I didn't know her that well. I think she stayed home and cared for the children her mother produced. She had six siblings. She was the eldest and seemed to be quite responsible. Her father, Reuben Pipe Maker, was married to her mother, but I'm told he disappeared after Lark was born. This did not stop her mother, Lucy, from reproducing. The children would have increased her allotment, and I do think the children got fed. But I gathered from Frannie that Lucy is absent from home several days at a time, occasionally a week or more. I'm worried about who is looking after the children now that Lark is gone. I plan to drop by next weekend and see what I can find out. If there is a serious problem I will report it to the Tribal Police, and they will do nothing."

"They don't care?"

"They're overwhelmed. They try. But this would not be high priority. I could take two of them here. I have three in the dormitory now, and it holds five."

I nodded toward the bunkhouse. "That's the dormitory?"

"Yes. The other teacher, Alice Potter, and I share a room at one end. We have two rooms . . . one for girls and the other for boys at the other end, and a small kitchen and eating area in between the sleeping quarters."

"Would this Alice Potter be helpful?"

"I think not. She just joined me two months ago. She's here for the summer, and then she returns to a Quaker school in Missouri in the fall. I operate this school over the summer months and close three months in the winter because we can't cope with the wind and snow in these facilities. Most of the time I don't have a second teacher, so I'm grateful to have Alice here now. The Quakers will send other relief when they can."

"Have you heard that other girls have gone missing?"

"Yes. Young people, especially girls, frequently disappear from the reservation from time to time, some for better and others for worse. But the numbers are concerning. I do not think they are all voluntary runaways. They could be dead like Ruth and Lark. It would be easy to dump a body in the Badlands, and it would never be found. Somebody didn't have time to do that with those girls."

"I have a feeling you have a theory."

"White slavery. I have heard that Sioux girls are either being lured away or outright kidnapped and delivered to Chicago for sale to houses of prostitution. I have been told of a girl who escaped and found her way back home. Perhaps, Ruth and Lark resisted and paid with their lives."

"That's certainly a possibility. Do you know the name of the girl who escaped? Can you tell me where I can find this young woman?"

"I can, but I will not. She fears her life is in danger if the abductors learn she is on the reservation."

"I can see that she is protected or help her leave the reservation and start a new life elsewhere. Also, if we apprehend the kidnappers, she can live here without fear again."

"The Sioux have endured too many broken promises for me to leap at that bait."

"I can understand the distrust, but she might have information that could save the lives of many others. Would you at least get in touch with her and tell her what I have said? This could be very important."

"I will do that much. I will contact Kate. If the girl is willing to speak with you, I will inform Kate of the conditions."

Sage held the cards. "I am agreeable to that. I have another question. Do you know a young man named Willy Hobson who works at the State Game Lodge?"

She rubbed her chin thoughtfully before responding. "I do not know him personally, but I am acquainted with some of his family. His cousin, John Black Feather, is in my classroom now. He is twelve-years old. A bright and diligent student who has prospects of a good future if demon rum doesn't catch him."

I said, "I don't think Willy is full-blood. From his name, I assume his father is white."

"Yes, the relationship with John would be through the mother's blood. There would be many cousins because there were nine children in his mother's family. John's and Willy's mothers are sisters. I appreciate that you did not refer to Willy as a 'breed,' like so many whites do."

Her eyes seemed to soften a bit. I had almost forgotten a card I could play that might help me here. "Well, I'm mixed-blood myself, but my Sioux is diluted some. My grandmother is half Brule. She's president of the Lame Buffalo Foundation. You may have heard of it." Her hostility evaporated noticeably at that remark. Perhaps I was wrong and I am devious enough to make it as a lawyer.

"Yes, I have read a great deal about the foundation and its founder. I never connected you with Skye de-Paul Ramsey. I have always wanted to visit Lockwood, Wyoming and see firsthand the work that has been done there. I am Oglala, and the Brule, of course, are part of our Lakota family and speak the same dialect."

"I would be honored to arrange a visit so you could meet with Gram Skye. She and my grandfather were just in the Black Hills visiting President and Mrs. Coolidge. Unfortunately, they left for Lockwood on the morning train. I will make her aware of your interest. I know she would love to have you visit." This elicited a smile, a quite engaging one, and I decided I should not overdose with the sugar.

"I would love that. And I will talk to the girl who says she was kidnapped."

"I mentioned Willy Hobson. Do you know anything else about him?"

"No, not really. Just his family. It is probably a recommendation of sorts that I don't know much. I tend to hear about the troublemakers and the tormented. I think he pretty much grew up in Custer. His father, Luke, is a skilled mechanic and contracts vehicle maintenance work with both the state and federal governments."

"Just one more question. We're looking for a Sioux man with the first name of George."

"I could quickly come up with a dozen Sioux males with that first name."

"It would be helpful if you could make a list of any you can think of."

"I could do that, I suppose. I will give my list to Kate when I report back about my contact with the girl." She paused. "You asked about Willy Hobson. He has an uncle named George."

"He does?"

"Yes. George Many Knives. A man of less than stellar reputation."

"Could you explain?"

"He is said to be the source of most boot-legging on the reservation. Those who want to sell alcohol must go through Many Knives to buy their stock. His competition has a way of turning up dead or disappearing."

"If you know about this, why doesn't the law?"

"Most find it safer not to get involved. Many do not want to jeopardize their supply. And if it does get to the tribal police, money talks."

"I can't thank you enough, Miss Rainmaker. You've been very helpful and given me much to ponder."

"You may call me Sage, and, if you like, I will call you Trey."

"I would like that, Sage."

She gave me a quick smile and turned to the door. "And now I must return to the classroom."

When I looked at Kate, her eyes were shooting little daggers at me. "Nice lady," I said.

"You have no shame when it comes to sweet-talking someone, do you? She was actually starting to flirt with you before she went back in the school."

"Oh, I don't think so. She'd just decided I wasn't such a bad guy after all."

"And you were undressing her with your eyes when you met. That's a bad habit that could get you in lots of trouble."

I couldn't deny it, so I said, "I'll work on that." I thought that was noncommittal enough.

Chapter 16

GABE

GABRIEL RILEY SAT at a corner table in the new White Castle restaurant, one of over a hundred springing up across the Midwest over the decade since opening of the first in Wichita, Kansas in 1921. The structure was boxlike and cramped with stools in front of a long counter, and no more than ten small dining tables were squeezed into the building. The exterior design attempted to present the image of a miniature medieval castle. Its specialty was a hamburger smothered with cooked onions for a nickel. Gabe had ordered two.

Tonight, Gabe was dressed in a blue suit and matching striped tie. He was comfortable in this attire and was glad he had abandoned his farmer charade of the past week. He had flashed his badge enough times that he was certain he was fooling no one.

A frosty mug of root beer and a plate nearly covered by two hamburgers with steaming onions drooping over the edges were placed on his table by a young, blonde waitress with a cardboard crown perched precariously on her head. "Anything else for you now, sir?" she asked.

"No ma'am. This should be fine. Thank you."

She seemed like a nice young lady. Reminded him of Clara the first time they met. Of course, Clara was just as black as this girl was white. But where it counted, underneath the skin, this young lady came across as chipper-dispositioned and kind. He missed Clara and his two little girls, Chloe and Jessie, and baby Gabe. His family was everything to him, and he wouldn't mind a desk job if it would keep him closer to home. He just wanted to get this case solved. But he would chase clues for as long as it took, and he would not give up for the sake of a quick trip home. Fellow agents had nicknamed him Bulldog for his tenacity and persistence.

As he ate, his mind turned to Trey Ramsey. He hoped his meeting with the Indian teacher turned up something helpful today. Trey was smart as hell, and what made him so likable was that he didn't even know it. It annoyed Gabe sometimes that Trey didn't appear to take his job as seriously as Gabe did. But he suspected much of Trey's seemingly flippant attitude was a façade, covering up a hurt inside. Perhaps, the loss of his father had something to do with it. But Trey must get a handle on his drinking and partying. It wasn't just a matter of sowing wild oats; a stage Trey should have passed by now. Prohibition was the law. And Trey was a law enforcement officer. Beyond Gabe's notion that Trey had a responsibility to carry on his life as a model for others, his career would be over if the young man was caught up in the net of a speakeasy raid.

As he ate, Gabe chided himself for eating too many hamburgers since his arrival in South Dakota. But they were cheap, besides being darn good-tasting. He'd go off the wagon when he got home. Clara would see to it. He looked up when the door opened, and two rough-looking types, with guns holstered at their hips, walked into the restaurant and sat down at a table at the opposite end of the room. They might have been twins the way they dressed, with cowboy boots and leather vests and crumpled hats, which they did not bother to remove. But they were Mutt and Jeff, one tall and string-bean thin, and the other short and on the stocky side. He pegged the shorter man as Sioux. They both glared at him like movie outlaws. Perhaps, they had watched too many of the old silent westerns, which were starting to be quickly displaced by the new talkies.

The men ordered from the blonde waitress, evidently giving her a rough time over something. This was not a time or place for a solitary Negro to butt in, but he could pull his badge if forced to. Fortunately, she got the order and left to place it with the cook. These guys spelled trouble, and he had a hunch they had more than a casual interest in Gabriel Riley.

Gabe finished his hamburgers, pretending he did not see the glares directed his way by the two men. When they were served, he decided it was a good time to high-tail it out of the place. He didn't want a distracting incident to flare up, and he sensed the pair across the room were primed for trouble. He dropped a generous tip on the table and got up and made his way to the door, watching the men warily out of the corner of his eye as he passed their table. They seemed to be absorbed in their meals when he stepped out the door.

He decided to return to his hotel and place a call to the State Game Lodge, hoping to get a preliminary report from Trey on his visit to the reservation school. As he strolled down the new sidewalk, he heard a woman's voice scream, "Mister, behind you."

He reached beneath his jacket for his .45 Colt, as he spun around, but he heard the cracks of gunshots and crumpled to his knees from the force of slugs that drove into his body before he could place his fingers on his weapon. Fumbling, he finally grasped the butt of his pistol and pulled it out. The forms were hazy in the dusk, but he could make out the attackers. The weight of the pistol was almost more than he could lift with his fading strength, but he got off two shots before he collapsed on the concrete. Clara and the kids. What is going to become of them? That was his last thought as blackness descended and shrouded him in its blanket.

Chapter 17

TREY

FORTUNATELY, THE VALLEY was lit by a brilliant full moon, as Kate and I rode through the thick grass in the meadow near the ranch house. Something stirred off to one side and leaped from the grass and made a beeline for Kate and War Paint. I started to reach for my gun before I realized it was Galahad, the black Labrador retriever. He barked a greeting, and Kate praised him for being a good dog, although I could see nothing he had done to deserve the commendation. In fact, the friendly canine had spooked Nipper for a few moments. I like dogs, but I must confess, I was always more of a cat aficionado. A special orange tabby cat owned me when I was a boy, and I still mourn his death. If I ever plant my roots someplace, I'll find a cat again, although I suppose some would see such a pet as not very useful or manly.

"Is your grandmother going to be worried?" I asked Kate. I checked my Ingersoll pocket watch. "It's half past seven."

"If you hadn't noticed, I am an adult. Why should she worry?"

I had noticed, and I could not stop noticing. But I was seeing her with less predatory eyes now. "I don't think parents and grandparents ever stop worrying, and, in their eyes, you may never be a full-fledged adult."

In confirmation of my worldly wisdom, Kate's Grandma Beth was waiting under the porch light when we rode in. I hadn't thought about it before, but I assume the benefits of telephone and electrical service in ranch and farm country had come with tourist development in the Black Hills.

"I'd better check with Grandma before I put the horses up," Kate said, as we dismounted.

As we walked toward the porch, Beth stepped off the porch and hurried toward us.

"Trey, Mister Starling called about fifteen minutes ago. He wants you to call him."

"Okay, I'll help Kate with the horses, and then I'll give him a call."

"He said it was very urgent. You make your call. He said you have his special number at the lodge. I'll help Kate. Go on in the house. The phone is on the parlor wall, just next to the kitchen doorway. Remember, it's a party line, so you'll have be careful what you say. Agent Starling knows this, too."

Everything was urgent with Starling, so I was not especially concerned. Not until I spoke with him, that is. After he explained the reason for his call, I told Starling I would leave for Rapid City immediately.

I trotted out to the stable which was attached to an enormous hay barn. The horses had been unsaddled and put in their stalls, and the women were fetching water and graining the geldings when I walked through the wide door opening. "I have to leave for Rapid City. My partner's been shot. At least three times. Starling thinks he's dying."

Both women froze and looked at me with horror-stricken eyes. Kate spoke first. "He's at the hospital?"

"Yes. Can you tell me where it's at?"

"I'll do better than that. I'll take you there. Let me drive. I know these roads blindfolded."

"That's not necessary."

"Get your butt in the car. I'll run to the house and grab some more cookies, if Stretch hasn't eaten them all."

"He hasn't," Beth said. "I've got some hot coffee on the stove. I'll pour some in fruit jars for the two of you. I'll come back and finish with the horses."

"Really, that's not necessary." My words were wasted. They had already brushed past me and headed for the house.

I waited for no more than a few minutes by the Model T before Kate emerged from the house and hurried toward the car with a bulging cloth bag. She climbed in on the driver's side, I worked the crank, and the Model T roared to life. As soon as I climbed in, she plopped the bag in my lap. I quickly grasped the drawstring and lifted it and lowered it to the floorboard between my feet because it was hot as blazes and threatened vital parts. She put the car in gear and hit the gas, and we tore out of the yard. It occurred to me that I had never been a passenger with a female driver before.

Kate was good. And she was fast, racing along those mountain roads, with occasional hairpin curves, like the proverbial bat out of hell. She didn't say a word, focusing her attention on the road, and I was not about to say anything to distract her. I had lost my appetite and decided I would drink my coffee cold if we made it to our destination. Finally, I just closed my eyes.

Chapter 18

TREY

WHEN WE ARRIVED at the hospital, after making a forty-five-minute drive in thirty, we were greeted at a night nurse's desk inside the entryway, given a room number on the second floor and directed to a stairway. The nurse warned us that Gabe was unconscious and might be in surgery for a considerable time. When we arrived at a waiting area on the second floor we were met by a lean, towheaded deputy sheriff who could have passed for a sixteen-year old. He identified himself as Bing Compton. I showed him my credentials, and he confirmed that Gabe was in surgery and that it might be a long wait.

The waiting room included a small, sagging leather couch and two stuffed matching arm chairs, one of which was occupied by a young, blonde woman who, at first glance, would have triggered more thorough inspection under different circumstances.

The deputy spoke to the young woman. "Carrie, you can leave now if you want. This is Mr. Ramsey, he's Mr. Riley's partner, and he'll stay now." He looked at Kate. "I should know you."

"I'm Kate Connolly."

"Oh, yeah. You're Liam Karlsson's girl."

Kate flushed a bit, and replied, "You may have seen me with Liam last summer."

The deputy continued. "This here's Carrie Swanson. She saw what happened and tried to warn Riley about the shooters. Riley killed one of them, but the other got away."

"That's what the Secret Service officer told me."

"Carrie had somebody from the White Castle call the sheriff's office and the ambulance from the hospital. She stayed with Riley and stanched the bleeding of a major vessel below the neck. His prospects don't look too good, but he wouldn't have made it here if not for Carrie being there."

"There wasn't anybody else," Carrie said. "And I came with the ambulance because I didn't want him alone with strangers in case he died."

"You knew him?"

"He was a customer at the White Castle. He seemed like such a kind, gentle man. I'd never have guessed he was a BI agent."

"He was in the restaurant before he was shot?"

"Yes. And then those men came in. They were rude, and I could tell Mr. Riley was close to stopping them."

"So, you could identify the man who got away?"

"Absolutely."

"I'd like to sit down and ask you some questions and have you tell me about what you saw. Is that all right?"

"Yes, of course. If I can help in any way, I'm glad to."

I took a seat on the couch next to Carrie's chair, and Kate sat down beside me. The deputy stood nearby, keeping an eye on the entrances. I decided he might be more experienced than his appearance indicated. I liked this guy.

Carrie told me about what had happened earlier in the evening, down to Gabe's two onion-smothered hamburgers and root beer, which was a bit much for my starving, queasy stomach. I hate onions. She said that the two men had moved from their chairs instantly, leaving their unfinished meals behind, as soon as Gabe went out the door of the restaurant. It had not occurred to her that they planned to shoot Gabe. She thought they were going to give him a beating or hassle him some way. She had pegged them as Negro-haters. She added there were some folks in Rapid City like that, many of whom had never met a Negro in their lives. She hastened to say that most people there had mixed with Indians regularly over the years and dealt with a few Negroes who worked for the railroad, and the large majority of folks had little interest in racial matters at all.

I said, "The dead shooter was described as short and stocky. He's not going anywhere, so he can be identified, hopefully. What did the other man look like?"

"Well, he was built about like Bing. About his height, too, I'd guess."

I called down the hall to Bing. "How tall are you, deputy?"

"A tad over six feet."

"The similarity stops there," she said. "He's a darker-complexioned man . . . but not like an Indian or Negro. Black hair, neatly trimmed along the edges. The top of his head was covered with a hat. They were dressed like cattle tramps, but I think this man was more of a dandy. He had smooth hands and clean, trimmed fingernails, not the calloused hands of a cow puncher. His face was smudged with dirt, but underneath was a clean-shaven face and pencil-thin moustache. Given some time, I could sketch his face."

"You're an artist?"

She shrugged and gave a sad smile. "Wanna-be artist. I've been told I can draw a passable likeness of a person. I do some water colors. I'd like to learn oils. Couldn't afford to go off to art school, but I'm saving up."

"That's why you noticed all the details, isn't it?"

"Well, I suppose, but I play a private game when strangers come in. I try to guess what their lives are like. What kind of work do they do? Where do they come from? Do they lead miserable lives? I make up stories about them in my head. I observe things about them, and the most interesting ones, I go home and sketch on my pad. I have hundreds of drawings."

"So, can I ask you to go home and sketch this man?"

"Of course."

"Ma'am. I can't thank you enough for what you did for Gabe Riley. He's not just my partner. He's my good friend, and he is worthy of the help you gave."

"I just hope he makes it. He will be in my prayers."

"He will need help wherever he can get it." The deputy had edged back our way, and I turned to him. "Bing, can you arrange to have someone take this young lady home?"

"I have a relief officer coming in a few minutes, so I can take her home myself."

"I'd like to see a twenty-four-hour watch on Carrie and her house. The other shooter knows she can identify him. It's not likely he would try anything, but we don't want her to be in danger just for being a good Samaritan."

"I'll get hold of the sheriff and volunteer for first watch." He nodded toward Carrie. "Where do you live Carrie?"

"I live with my folks. Pa has a pig farm on eighty acres east of town."

A short time later, Bing escorted Carrie out of the hospital. I promised to keep her updated on Gabe's condition, and she said she would have a sketch by noon tomorrow. Bing was obviously taken with the young woman and welcomed the opportunity to look after her. I had no concern that he would do anything improper. There were some bad people out here right now, but I had sure been running in to some darn solid folks in this corner of the country. I turned to Kate, who still shared the couch with me, and sat within a few inches because of the sagging cushion that put us in sort of a trough. I was not inclined to fight gravity this night, and she did not seem to be resisting the incline that pushed us closer.

"Trey," Kate said. "I've been thinking. The man Carrie described. His description, other than his clothing, could fit one of the men who came after the president. You don't suppose—?"

"It would be quite a coincidence, but it's not impossible. That would mean our two cases are one. Interesting possibility. Did you get a good look at the man's face?"

"Well, there was some distance between us, but I always thought I would recognize him if I saw him."

"You've got to look at the sketch when Carrie finishes it." I changed the subject and reached for the sack of cookies and coffee jars I had set on the floor by the couch. "I'm starving. How about some cookies and cold coffee?"

"No, thanks. Go ahead. I'm sleepy."

She leaned her head against my shoulder and fell dead asleep before I bit into the first cookie. There was something more intimate about her leaning against me like that than I'd ever experienced with a woman. I guess it was the idea she felt comfortable with me and trusted me. It drew me to her in a curious way and made me determined to never hurt her. This Ethan James Ramsey III was a stranger, and I wondered for a moment what was happening.

Chapter 19

KATE

WHEN SHE AWOKE, she found herself with legs folded up in a fetal position on the couch and her head resting in Trey's lap. His arm was draped over her shoulder, and she could hear soft snoring closer to a cat's purr above her. She looked up and saw Trey, his head drooping with chin on chest. She thought he looked like an innocent boy, even with the morning stubble that cast a shadow on his face and failed to mar that handsome face. He would be pleasant to wake up next to mornings, she thought, before chiding herself for being such a hopeless slut.

It was a bit of a struggle, but she raised herself up and swung her legs off the couch without waking Trey. She saw that the deputy was awake, sitting in a straight-back wooden chair, thirty feet down the hallway, not far from the entryway to the second floor. Then, from the other direction, she heard a commotion caused by rattling doors and squeaking wheels and the flurry of footsteps. This alerted Trey and his eyes fluttered open, and he lifted his head, looking at her with confusion, as if he did not recall where they were.

Momentarily, an orderly and a nurse came around the corner pushing a gurney with a sheet-shrouded patient on it. A dark face, contrasting to the white sheets assured Kate that Gabe survived. She and Trey stood while the orderly maneuvered the gurney into Gabe's room. They started to follow but were intercepted by a stocky, gray-haired man in a surgical gown who had trailed the procession.

He turned toward Trey and Kate and, with a reassuring smile, extended his hand, gently clasping Kate's first and then shaking Trey's. "You must be the patient's friends," he said. "I'm Dave Harrington, Mr. Riley's surgeon."

Trey said, "I'm Trey Ramsey, Gabe's BI partner. This is my friend, Kate Connolly."

"Owen and Coleen's daughter. My God, you're the spitting-image of your mother. You were my third baby. You turned out fine despite my inexperience."

Kate remembered now that her father had said she had been delivered by a Dr. Harrington, who specialized in surgery and obstetrical work and women's problems, whatever that meant. "Yes, I remember your name. Dad has mentioned it."

Dr. Harrington turned businesslike. "Well, you don't want my chit-chat. You want to know about your friend. First, his status is in limbo at this stage. We'll know more by tonight. If he's going to make it, I would expect him to regain consciousness by tomorrow sometime. The longer he's in a coma, the worse his chances of survival. Of course, he then must survive any infection that may set in. We still have no drug that accomplishes miracles when that happens. It will be a week before we can make a prognosis with any confidence."

"Where was he hit?" Trey asked.

"Three places. He's got a shattered knee. I patched it. My guess is it will end up stiff, but, if he lives, there are surgeons in the big cities who may be able to help. He had a wound that passed through the flesh between his neck and shoulder and nicked an artery. If it hadn't been for the intervention of a young woman, he would have died from that before he got here."

"So, it's the third wound you're most concerned about?"

"Yes. Lung-shot. The bullet tore things up seriously. I entered beneath his right shoulder blade and recovered the slug. There was a lot of internal bleeding, and, besides infection, there is risk of pneumonia. I think I've done all anyone can do about this wound, though. From this point, we just treat symptoms."

"So, it's just wait and see?"

"Yes. But it's a miracle he made it this far. Let's hope he's a miracle man. I have seen such people often—those who defy odds."

"I'm betting Gabe's one of those," Trey said.

"Now, Trey and Kate, I must take another look at my patient before I call it a night. Leave word at the front desk how you can be contacted. No news will be good news. If you don't hear from us, check back late in the afternoon. I make rounds about five o'clock."

After the physician entered Gabe's room, Trey turned to Kate. "Breakfast?"

"Do you like hotcakes and sausage?"

"My favorite, as long as we can get some good coffee with it."

"If you like mud, The Griddle, has great coffee. But the hotcakes offset any deficiencies in the coffee."

"I'm sold. Let's go."

With the sun barely peeking over the eastern horizon, the usual breakfast crowd had not taken over yet, and Kate and Trey had privacy at a small table in the back of the dining room. They had both ordered the hotcakes and sausage, and after drenching her pancakes in hot maple syrup, Kate had torn into her breakfast like a ravenous bear. The coffee had not improved since her last visit. It occurred to her they had not spoken a word since the waitress delivered their plates, and she suddenly realized she had nearly cleared her plate. Trey, on the other hand, was plodding through his breakfast. Oh well, she wasn't going to abandon a soggy crumb. She would finish and dawdle with her coffee.

She looked up and saw that Trey's dark eyes were fixed on her. He had a small, amused smile on his lips. "What?" she said.

"You have been up most of the night. You're still wearing what you started off with on horseback yesterday morning. Yet, you don't smell bad from here, and you look darn good. Very impressive." He raised his hands in defense. "Please, don't be offended. I'm not coming on to you."

She didn't mind the remark. It was about as close to romance as the guy had come. And it wasn't much. "You've worn adversity well yourself." She thought that was noncommittal enough, especially since slut that she was, she likely would have let him lure her to bed with only token resistance. Thankfully, he didn't seem to be one of those men who was fixated on bedding every woman he came across.

Trey said, "Do you mind staying in town this morning? I would like to have you look at Carrie's sketch. Then I can take you home."

"I'll be glad to stay the rest of the day, if you don't mind my tagging along. I'd like to stay in touch with Gabe's condition. I do know people around here. I might be helpful if you want to talk to folks."

"I'm sure I can use your help. If you want to call your grandmother, you can tell her you will be home before dark."

"I'll call Grandma Beth." Of course, the gentleman would have her home before dark. Maybe he would give her a goodnight handshake.

Chapter 20

TREY

KATE AND I stopped at the sheriff's office, and I asked a deputy if the dead gunman had been identified or if they had learned anything that might connect the man to anyone else. The deputy, a big man, carrying about a hundred excess pounds of blubber, most of which lopped over his belt, struck me as something of a sloth and did not seem particularly interested in my inquiries. He knew nothing and suggested I check back later, when I was confident he would still know nothing.

When we stepped outside the sheriff's office, I nearly bumped into someone, and, when I realized who it was, I wished I had. Liam Karlsson. I had taken an instant dislike to the man when he and Kate had exchanged pleasantries at the Belle Fourche Roundup. He had seemed a pleasant-enough man, and I suspect women found him charming and quite dashing. But I was annoyed by the way his eyes roamed Kate's body with too much familiarity. And she didn't seem to mind at all.

Kate spoke first. "Liam. I'm surprised to see you in Rapid City. I thought you were working in Custer. And you're out of uniform. Did you leave the rangers?"

"No, I've got the day off. I was hoping to spend it with you. I called your house last night, but your grandmother said you were staying over in Rapid City, and I thought I might find you here. Did you stay at Alice's?"

I gathered Alice was a friend, and the muscle-bound lout cast me the evil eye when he asked the question. I wished he would move on, but he didn't seem to be in a rush.

"No," Kate said. "Trey and I have a friend in the hospital . . . you do remember Trey? We stayed at the hospital last night." She hastily added, "In the waiting area."

"I see."

But, of course, the oaf did not like what he was seeing. I supposed he thought we had secured a private hospital room for the night. Kate was looking a bit flustered now, evidently sensing the man's displeasure. Gallant knight that I am, I came to her rescue.

I pulled out my pocket watch and feigned worry. "Kate, I'm sorry to interrupt, but we are running late. We should be moving on."

"Oh, you're right. We are late. I'm sorry, Liam. I'll have to talk to you another time."

"I'll call next time I have a day off," Liam said, as we hurried to the car.

"Yes, that would be nice," Kate called back.

When we were seated in the Model T, I said. "I don't think Mr. Karlsson likes me."

"You weren't very friendly yourself."

"So, he's your boyfriend?"

"No. We saw each other some last summer. We haven't been out since I got back from school."

"But you led him to believe you would go out."

"That's because I don't foreclose possibilities. He's really very nice and can be fun."

That was not what I wanted to hear. "You have the directions to Carrie's place, don't you?"

She pulled out a slip of paper. "Yes, but it's not even ten o'clock. She thought it might be noon before she would have the sketch."

"We can check now and go back later if she doesn't have anything."

When we rattled up in front of the box-shaped, clapboard farmhouse not far from the city, I was pleased to see that a sheriff's office vehicle was parked there and that local law enforcement was looking after Carrie Swanson. I was surprised, however, when Deputy Bing Compton emerged from the house and walked down the brick path to greet us.

"Bing," I said. "Are you still on duty?"

"Not on paid time. The department's short-handed, so I volunteered to stay over a shift. Someone else will be out here by noon."

It's amazing how a pretty lady can bring out the volunteer spirit in us. "How is she doing on the sketch?"

"She finished that an hour ago. I was going to track you down, but Carrie's mom forced me to try her Swedish sweet rolls first."

"And your priority was your stomach."

He smiled sheepishly. "Wouldn't have been polite to turn her down. Anyways, Carrie said to tell you to come on in." He waved for us to follow him into the house, where Carrie was sitting at the kitchen table surrounded by the mouth-watering aroma of baking breads. No wonder Bing was hanging around the place. He was a goner if Carrie's mom was setting a trap for a husband for her daughter.

We went over to the table, and Carrie lifted the sketchpad, so we could see. Instantly, Kate said, "It's the same man."

"You know him?" Bing asked.

Kate looked at me, and I gave a barely perceptible negative nod.

"No, but I've seen him someplace."

"Carrie," I said, "I'd like to take your sketch back to the sheriff's office and have someone take some photographs of it. They can distribute it to all the officers, and, perhaps, put something in the newspaper. You will be safer then, too. Once the public has viewed the likeness, the killer wouldn't have much incentive to come after you. I can't thank you enough for all you've done. The surgeon told me Gabe wouldn't have made it to the hospital alive without your help."

Carrie tore off the page and handed me the sketch, "I just hope Mr. Riley pulls through. I didn't do anything anybody else wouldn't have done under the circumstances."

She was wrong, of course, but I decided we needed some unrealistically optimistic people in the world to balance out the cynics, like myself.

After we left the house, Kate and I delivered Carrie's sketch to the sheriff's office. Sheriff Matthew Johnson was in, and during this visit, I received some cooperation. A bear-like man with snow-white hair and a brushy moustache, the sheriff seemed an easy-going, good-natured sort, but his translucent blue eyes suggested this man was nobody's fool. I strongly suspected he was one of those men who gained an edge by having others underestimate him. The sheriff instructed the sloth I met earlier—his name was Orville—-to get some photographs of the sketch and to get something to the local newspaper. Before my eyes, the man turned into an efficient machine.

"Do you suppose somebody could get a photo of the dead man?" I asked. "He looked like an Indian, I understand. If he's Oglala, somebody might know who he was."

"We can do that. Body's over at the undertaker's. I'll get Orville on it, and we can get this picture out there, too."

Sheriff Johnson invited us into his private office, and Kate and I took chairs in front of his cluttered desk. He sat down in his hardwood swivel-chair and leaned back, slinging one booted foot over his knee. He looked at Kate with a twinkle in his eyes. "So, how's the old Irishman doing these days, Katie?"

"Oh, he's fine," Kate said, "Cranky, as usual. He's on a heifer-buying trip in Nebraska right now."

"I saw him a few weeks ago. He said he was recruiting a good Democrat to run against me next election. I told him that finding a Democrat was tough in this county, and a good one, tougher yet. He said he might run his self to get me out of here. Now, that would give me cause for concern. He might give me a run for the money."

"He wouldn't run. It would take too much time away from his cows."

The sheriff looked at me. "So, Mr. Ramsey, is the BI taking over this murder case?"

"Please, call me Trey."

"Matt."

"No, Matt, I don't work that way. I'm not taking over anything . . . besides, the BI doesn't have any arrest powers. We need you folks on the case. Gabe Riley and I were sent here to investigate some reservation murders. It's kind of a jurisdiction entanglement, with the BI, your office, the city and the reservation police. I suppose the state could intervene separately, also. The assault on Gabe took place in your domain, and I'm not going to interfere with how you approach the case."

I could tell he was sizing me up, as he studied me in silence for several moments, before responding.

"The state won't come in unless I ask. The town cops back off felonies, and there's no overlap with reservation authorities. That's not to say this isn't related to your investigation on the reservation. I think we ought to team up. How can I help you out?"

"We didn't have enough people before Gabe got taken down, and the Secret Service can't spare anybody. I could use a man to work with me and be liaison with your office. That way, you can be certain you are in the loop, and I'll have an extra officer with arrest powers to rely upon."

"I could take care of that."

"Could you spare Bing?"

The sheriff grinned. "Herbert Compton? He's not dry behind the ears, but he's smart as a whip and works like a plow mule. Sure, you can have Bing. I'll get word to him that he's working for you for a spell. Get ahold of this office when you have something you want him to do."

Herbert? I could see why he adopted Bing. The latter sounded much more like a western deputy's moniker.

After departing the sheriff's office, Kate and I located the White Castle and decided to try the hamburgers for lunch. I thought, perhaps, a visit to the crime scene would inspire me. I ordered my burger sans onions, and the waitress's look of disbelief made me feel like a namby-pamby. Kate took the works. So much for stealing a kiss. It occurred to me she might be ingesting male repellant. I also wondered if she would have ordered onions if Liam the Ox had been dining with her.

While we waited for the hamburgers, I asked, "No doubt that the guy in Carrie's sketch is the same guy who was stalking the president?"

"None. He didn't wear a battered cowboy hat or boots that day, or an open-collared shirt, but I would swear under oath it's the same man."

"Most of Gabe's inquiries were about the murdered and missing girls. We certainly should consider the possibility we're looking at the same perpetrators for all the crimes. If the Sioux girl will talk to me, that's my best chance for a lead, so I'll still concentrate on that. I'm also going to have a conversation with Willy Hobson first thing tomorrow morning. I'll have the Secret Service detain him as soon as he shows up for work at the lodge."

When we left the White Castle, I decided to swing by the hospital and try to get a report on Gabe's status. Doctor Harrington would not likely be there yet, but, perhaps, we could learn something. As I pulled out of the parking stall, Kate said, "You're a man to watch out for. You really are one sweet-talking fool."

"What do you mean?"

"You sweet-talked Matt Johnson into going along with you slick as a whistle."

"I didn't sweet-talk him. I just told him I wanted to work with him."

"With more syrup than I put on my hotcakes this morning."

"I haven't been with the BI long, but I've seen a few cases stalled just because a federal officer steps on local toes. That's not going to be my style."

When we entered the hallway outside of Gabe's room, I was pleased to see that one of Matt Johnson's deputies was posted outside the door. I showed him my credentials and vouched for Kate, but she was already exchanging small talk with the middle-aged man, and they obviously knew each other. It seemed that everybody knew Kate.

"Is there any news about my partner?" I asked.

"He woke up. Doc just got here and is checking on him now. He ought to be out in a few minutes."

"That's good news," I said. "We'll wait."

Kate sat down in one of the chairs in the waiting area, where we had spent the previous night. She seemed to be watching me curiously as I paced the hall like an expectant father. I was anxious for a status report on Gabe. I had been informed that Starling had notified Gabe's wife, Clara, of the shooting, but she was a thousand miles away in Washington. It must have been driving her crazy, waiting for word of her husband's condition. I promised myself I would call her personally as soon as I could confirm his status. I prayed that I would be able to deliver good news.

The door to Gabe's room opened, and Doctor Harrington emerged. He saw me and walked in my direction. I felt Kate's fingers clutch my arm. Somehow, like a silent, slinky cat, she had eased beside me when the surgeon appeared.

"He's conscious," the surgeon said, "and surprisingly lucid. This is very positive. My biggest concern is infection. That could set in anytime, especially with the lung wound. If he pulls through, he's going to be down for a long spell. He will need to be hospitalized for several weeks. It will be considerable time before I can make a serious prognosis on outcome, but this is the best news we could hope for right now."

"Can we see him?" I asked.

"For a few minutes, I suppose. But you're not helping him if you don't hold it to that."

Dr. Harrington hurried down the hall, evidently planning to check on another patient while he was at the hospital. Kate and I entered Gabe's room and found a nurse holding a thermometer in his mouth. Gabe was awake, but his eyes were glazed over, and his head was motionless as he watched us approach his bedside. The nurse removed the thermometer and noted something on a chart and left the room after tossing us what I took as a warning look. Kate broke away and moved next to Gabe, placing her hand on his cheek and planting a soft kiss on his forehead. That won a faint smile. She would be a tough act to follow, as they say.

I stepped closer. "I guess I won't ask you how you feel."

He answered anyway in a near whisper. "Like shit."

Those words gave me hope. Same old Gabe. "Can we do something for you?"

"Tell Clara I'm fine. Not to come. Stay with the kids."

"I'll call her, as soon as we leave here."

"Tell her I'm going for a desk job." With those words, he closed his eyes and drifted away.

Chapter 21

THE RAPID CITY OUTFIT

BOSS BULLOCK WAS outraged. His clumsy thugs had messed up again. Max Waters was dead. Not a great loss to the outfit, but he was another dot for somebody to connect. And some woman could identify Solly. He should kill Solly and have his body dumped out in the Badlands someplace. He decided he would do this. But not yet. He needed him out at the chick coop until they shipped out another load. As soon as the shipment headed for Chicago, Solly was dead meat.

His brother, Bull, Solly Cleaver and George Many Knives sat silently in the chairs across from Boss's desk. "Listen up. I got some plans here. First, George, I want you to contact Chicago. Tell your contact we want a delivery truck at the pick-up point north of the chick coop one week from tomorrow, an hour before sundown."

"But we only got eight chicks. We're two short," Many Knives protested.

"Then get off your ass and fill the coop. And one better be that bitch, Connolly."

"Boss, the Connolly woman is trouble. Leave her alone."

Bullock slipped the pistol from his desk and pointed it at the Sioux. "Are you planning to call the shots now?"

Many Knives didn't flinch and returned an icy glare. "No. I gave you my opinion. But we'll pick up the Connolly girl and find one or two others. The woman will die in Chicago in a week, though, after they've used her up. They can't hold somebody like that. Sooner or later, she'd escape. And she would know what to do. The reservation girls have never been anyplace. They're afraid to try to get away. And some have been sold for wives or mistresses after a bit. Bettered themselves. The Connolly woman's a different animal."

"Get her to the coop before the truck comes. And I might want to try her before she's shipped out, so let me know when you've got her. I'm thinking we might hold her for ransom, and then we'd have to kill her and forget about her Chicago vacation. Do you have enough help?"

"I've got two Oglala, who are in too deep to get out now, and Charlie. I might pull my nephew, Willy Hobson, in on this one. He needs work. He's been my snitch at the lodge, but I told him to disappear. It's too risky for him to go out there now. If somebody makes a connection and they squeeze him, I don't know what he'd say. I told him he's in big trouble if they find him out . . . from them and us. I'm going to teach him the business. I'll put Charlie and the two Oglala on rounding up the girls. I'll take Willy with me to corral the Connolly girl. And I'd like Bull, too. We'll camp on the back side of an overhang that gives a good view of the Shamrock building site. We can hide the truck up there, too. We'll take my spyglass and watch in shifts. The girl moves about by herself a lot, as near as I can tell. It won't take but a few days to catch her alone."

Bullock didn't like it, but he agreed the breed had already served his purpose at the lodge. He turned to Cleaver. "There's a picture out on you, Solly. You're poison. I want you out at the chick coop. George will run you up to the drop-off. Grab your stuff and get out of Rapid City. When the delivery truck comes for the merchandise, you'll ride with the driver to Chicago. You've done it before. Only this time, don't come back . . . ever. I'll give you all you've earned before you pull out." He did not add that the moron had earned a bullet in the brain.

Grim-faced Solly Cleaver nodded assent.

"Bull, as soon as you trap the girl, I want you back here in case I need something in a rush. Nobody can connect you to anything that's happened, so you can go downtown, if necessary."

"I want to go with Solly. Get me some poon tang up at the coop. I saw one of the Indian chicks I took a liking to."

"You will stay close by till I say otherwise. Move your brain from your pecker to your head for a while."

Bull Bullock scowled, but he didn't challenge his brother.

Chapter 22

TREY

I HAD LEFT KATE off at the Shamrock Ranch well before supper the night before. Thankfully, her father had not returned yet, so I did not have to deal with his foul temper. I had walked Kate to the porch of the ranch house, but somehow it seemed awkward when we said our good-byes. I told her I would talk to her soon, and she said she would let me know if she heard from Sage Rainmaker, and then turned and scurried into the house.

We had spent a lot of time together since my arrival in the Black Hills with the presidential party, and, after a rocky start, we had formed a comfortable friendship, or, at least an alliance, I thought. I liked Kate a lot, too much to chance hurting her. But I missed her company when we were not together, which was an alien feeling for me where women were concerned.

I had hoped to speak with Willy Hobson this morning, but he had not shown up for work. He had not called in, so I did not take this as a positive sign. I checked with the hospital and received a report that Gabe's condition was stable, which I was told was the most we could hope for at this stage. The nurse said Clara had already called. I had spoken to Clara after my own visit with Gabe at the hospital the previous afternoon and was informed she was already arranging for a train trip to Rapid City. She indicated the connections were terrible, but the Bureau of Investigation was helping with logistical details, and she expected to arrive within three days. The kids were coming with her. I decided not to forewarn Gabe.

I had spoken briefly with the president after breakfast. He planned to spend the afternoon at the Rapid City high school building, where the official presidential offices had been set up. He understood that I would not be available for budget work any time soon, if ever. He seemed worried and preoccupied, not quite his usual calm, focused self. I had decided to go to Rapid City myself and recruit Bing Compton to go with me to Gabe's hotel room to pick up Gabe's clothing and personal things and to determine whether he had left any notes that might be helpful. I had also planned on Bing's help in finding respectable accommodations for Clara and the kids, but when I mentioned it to the first lady, she said she would find something at the State Game Lodge. I told her they could appropriate my room, if necessary, as I would be spending most of my time in town. It occurred to me that I might just take over Gabe's room at the hotel.

All plans were disrupted when Starling summoned me to one of the secure telephones. When I picked up the receiver, Kate's voice greeted me. I had given her the number yesterday, but she had been warned to speak cautiously because her own party line was not secure.

"Your reservation friend called," she said. "Can you make a visit at one o'clock?"

"If the distance isn't too great." I looked at my pocket watch. It was nine-thirty.

"That will not be a problem. I will be at your place in a half hour. We will need to talk." That meant a maniac would be tearing down the road between the Shamrock and the game lodge. The line went dead before I could respond.

I asked Starling to alert agents at the gate that Kate Connolly would be arriving in the next half hour. I decided I would wait for her on the front veranda. I encountered Grace Coolidge in the hallway and informed her that Kate would be arriving shortly. She asked that Kate visit with her a few minutes if she had time. She said she would be reading in the private lodge room.

I thought about Kate's remarks. I was optimistic that Sage Rainmaker had arranged a meeting with the young brothel escapee. Why else would we be visiting the teacher from the reservation? I reminded myself to remain patient. I trusted Kate, and I assumed she already had the agenda set, whatever it might be.

Chapter 23

KATE

KATE WAS WAVED through the gate when she turned the 1923 Buick into the long, winding driveway. She had purchased the vehicle with the proceeds from sale of some of her calves several years previously, but her father had not permitted her to take it with her to school. He delivered her to the Brookings campus and picked her up personally for vacations and school breaks. A woman had no business wheeling a car about a college campus, he said. Well, in the event she returned to college, she would not be trapped there afoot anymore. She paid for her own education and lodging expenses, and she would be twenty-one years old in the fall. She and Owen Connolly were going to have an understanding before the summer was out, or, if not, she and her cows were moving to other pastures.

When she pulled into the parking lot, she saw Trey waiting on the porch. He was duded-up in jacket and tie today, and, suddenly, she felt rather shabby attired in boots and faded denims. But what did she care about how she was dressed when he saw her?

After she parked and got out of the car, he came down the steps to greet her. As she neared, he reached out as if to embrace her, and then dropped his arms, evidently having second thoughts about it.

"Good morning," he said. "You beat a half hour by two minutes. Impressive. And scary."

"Nothing scary about it if you know the country, and I've hit every curve and twist on the road hundreds of times."

"Nice looking vehicle. Kind of an emerald color and got more curves than the Model T cars assigned to the so-called public servants."

"And my Buick's a hay-burner compared to the Model T. But I don't care if it guzzles some extra gas. I love it."

Trey suggested they sit on the porch, and they sat down in a pair of cushioned, wicker armchairs. From the sober look on his face, she could see he was all business and finished with small talk.

"You said Sage called. But you left me in suspense. Will the girl talk to us?" he asked.

"Yes. At least she told Sage she would. She could back out at the last minute, though, and Sage will not reveal her name until we meet."

"Are we meeting at the school? How long will it take us to get there?"

"We're meeting in Hermosa. At the Congregational church there."

"I've heard that name someplace. Small town, I gather?"

"A village. Less than a hundred people live there. It's a dozen miles from here. We'll take my car. We can be there in twenty minutes."

"A half hour would be fine."

"Sage joined the Congregationalists. Rolf Lium is the student pastor there for the summer, and he will see we have privacy. Incidentally, I'm surprised you haven't been to the church. The president and first lady attended last Sunday according to the Rapid City Journal. They're Congregationalists, and the Hermosa church is going to be their church for the summer."

"I must have had other business Sunday."

"Do you go to church?"

"For funerals and weddings."

"I'm kind of Catholic."

"How can you be kind of Catholic?"

"Well, I was baptized in the church, and we attended mass every Saturday or Sunday faithfully before Mom went off to the war. Then Dad got mad at the priest about something, and we stopped. I might go back to the church or join another when I'm out on my own. I think I need a church. I'm prone to sin."

"Now, why would you say that?"

She was not about to tell him why. "We're all sinners, I guess, but I worry about it some and think I might find peace and strength at a church."

"We were talking about the interview with the young lady before we got sidetracked. Do you think I should change into something less formal for this?"

She studied him thoughtfully and chastened herself for thinking she might enjoy helping him change. Perhaps she should not delay returning to the church. "No," she said. "I think you would seem more authoritative dressed the way you are. She needs to feel she is talking to someone who has the power to protect her."

Trey seemed to be pondering her words. Then he nodded agreement. "I understand that. If I look like a saddle bum, she might wonder if I'm trustworthy. So, that's settled. Now, the first lady would like to visit with you."

"She would? Why?"

"I have no idea. She's in the private lodge room. I'll show you to the room, and then I'll talk to the cook and see if I can beg something for an early lunch. I'll meet you back here when you're finished."

After Trey led her to the private room, Kate tapped on the doorframe before she entered the open doorway. Grace Coolidge looked up from her book. "Come in, dear. Thank you for joining me." She waved her hand in the direction of a chair on the other side of the lamp table.

"My pleasure, ma'am."

The first lady held up her book. "Edna Ferber. Show Boat. It's a very uplifting novel. I hope to see the musical and the film that's going to be made."

"I love her work. I read So Big and it really touched me."

"Yes, it won the Pulitzer Prize. She's one of the few popular novelists to join that elite circle of writers. I will give you my copy of Show Boat when I have finished it."

"Thank you. That's very kind of you." Surely, she was not summoned to discuss literature with Mrs. Coolidge.

"I would like to ask a favor of you."

"Certainly."

"The president has been in something of a funk for a day now. We ordinarily talk about anything that's troubling either of us, but, occasionally he turns even more quiet than usual. He's on the back patio enjoying the morning sun . . . he didn't even go fishing this morning. I would like to you to speak with him."

"Me? Speak with the President of the United States about a funk?" The mere thought horrified her.

The first lady laughed and reached across the table and patted her arm. "Good heavens, no. He just enjoys your company. We both do. Maybe you're the daughter we never had. I think it might brighten his mood if you accidentally wandered onto the patio. Pretend to be surprised to find him there. Then strike up a conversation. Just talk. You don't have to pry."

"This sounds rather devious."

Grace Coolidge laughed again. "Yes, it is devious. Sometimes a woman's happiness requires us to resort to such tactics. We must be certain, of course, the cause is worthy."

"Well, certainly, I would like to help." Kate smiled. "And it sounds like fun."

Chapter 24

KATE

KATE STEPPED OUT onto the stone pavers that formed the patio. President Coolidge was sitting in a rickety rocking chair that looked like it had more than served its time. Coolidge was rocking slowly, staring off into the dark hills, his face pensive. He turned his head at her approach, and then smiled and stood up.

"Kate. This is a nice surprise."

"I'm sorry, Mr. President. I didn't mean to interrupt," she lied.

"Please sit down. And I'm Uncle Cal. Remember?"

He moved a chair closer to his rocker and, only after she was seated in the chair he offered did he return to his rocker. Imagine, she thought, being seated by the President of the United States.

"You are Uncle Cal in my mind," she said. "But you are also the president, and I would not feel right not recognizing that."

Coolidge sighed. "Can I tell you something confidentially?"

"Of course."

"I am tired of being president."

"But the newspapers say you are planning next year's campaign. And no one in your party will challenge you for the nomination."

"You are reading political things?"

"Only since I met you. I'm trying to make up for lost time. I never paid attention to politics before. It seems like a nasty business."

"It is that. Always has been, and always will be, I fear."

"How do you handle all the criticism and outright vicious attacks that come your way?"

"One just cannot take it personally. I rarely respond, and the fuss burns itself out for lack of oxygen most times. But, as I say, I no longer enjoy what I am doing."

"Are you saying you are going to quit?"

"Oh, no. I have a contract with the people for another year and a half. I have a duty to complete my term. I will do that, and I will do my very best. I speak often of persistence as a high virtue. I will persist. But I must decide soon whether I will seek another term."

"You would be reelected."

"Perhaps. But the voters are very fickle and can change their minds with tomorrow's headlines. I never aspired to the presidency, you know. I was governor of Massachusetts and was surprised when Harding selected me to join him on the ticket as the vice-presidential candidate. Then, of course, his death put me in the White House. After completing my own term, I will have served six years. Another term would extend to ten years. I question whether it is good for the country to have a president for that long. Kings and emperors were not the vision of the founding fathers. And as Lord Acton said, 'power corrupts.' I believe that. The best of men . . . or women . . . succumb to that aphrodisiac, if exposed for too long. They come to believe they are indispensable where, in fact, at any point in history there are thousands of people in the country capable of assuming the responsibility and serving very well."

"You have already made up your mind, haven't you?"

He was silent for several moments, rocking silently in his chair, gazing at the distant mountains again. "Yes, I suppose I have. But I didn't realize it until just this minute. Thank you, Kate."

Kate got up and placed a soft kiss on the president's forehead. He gave her a startled look. "You will always be my Uncle Cal," she said. "And whatever you do, I will be honored to have known you. Your secret is safe with me, Mr. President, until you decide to release it to the world."

Chapter 25

TREY

KATE DROVE HER Buick to the rendezvous with Sage Rainmaker and the Sioux girl. We did reach the little clapboard church in twenty minutes, and it was a harrowing experience. I have never cared much for speed, either on horseback or in a motor vehicle, and I vowed I would not return to the lodge with this woman unless she surrendered the steering wheel.

When we pulled into the graveled parking area, I saw a lanky, blond man leaning against a railing in front of the newly whitewashed church. "That's Rolf Lium," Kate said. "He's the student pastor who is serving the church this summer. I met him at an ice cream social the church ladies held a few weeks back. He's very nice, but he's rather shy. Don't be obnoxious with him."

Before we stepped out of the Buick, I turned to her and said, "When have I ever been obnoxious with anyone?"

"I found you obnoxious when we first met. Not so much so now." She smiled. "Just teasing. You do need to work on your sense of humor."

I did not reply. I was not in a mood for playful banter. I would have to work on the sense of humor some other time. As we strolled up the brick walk toward the church building, the young pastor walked out to greet us, a nervous smile crossing his sunburned face. He was a blond, blue-eyed Scandinavian, wearing a white-shirt and tie, and I daresay he and I were the best-dressed men in the hamlet that afternoon. He was not packing a gun, however.

"Good afternoon, Rolf," Kate said, cheerily.

"Kate, it's good to see you again."

Kate? Rolf? This guy's eyes looked damn lustful to me. And I supposed a woman would not find him unattractive. He would bear watching. Gramps had always been wary of preachers, and I guessed the wariness had rubbed off on me.

"Rolf," Kate said, "this is Trey Ramsey, the BI agent who is supposed to meet with Sage and her friend."

At least she remembered I was with her. Pastor Lium extended his huge hand, and I took it and lost my own in a bone-breaking grip that was well-beyond firm. South Dakota was tough country for my crippled paw.

Rolf said, “My pleasure, Trey, if I may call you Trey?” He spoke with a slight accent. He was probably third generation American. Perhaps, his grandchildren would start to speak normal English.

“Certainly, you may call me Trey. I appreciate your cooperation with setting up the interview here.”

“I don’t know the particulars, but I understand that the lives of young reservation women are at stake. If there is any way we can help, we have a duty to be involved. I have set up a small folding table and chairs on the floor in front of the altar. The two of you may enter the church. You will find Sage and Cleo Yellow Bird seated at the table. I will wait out here to assure you are not interrupted.”

“Just let me know if someone shows up who doesn’t appear to belong here.”

“I will do that.” He nodded toward the church entrance. “I also have my weapons inside the door. Just in case.”

I was going to have to reevaluate this man. He sounded like one who would use a firearm without hesitation, if necessary. "I don't expect to have any problems, but it's comforting to have a lookout who won't just be an usher. Thanks."

"Go on in. I will keep my eye out."

Kate and I continued up the walk and entered the church. When we were inside the vestibule, leaning against the wall, I saw a Winchester, along with a double-barrel shotgun and a rifle I could not identify that appeared big enough to take down an elephant. I had a hunch the student pastor knew how they worked.

When we stepped into the sanctuary, I immediately caught sight of Sage Rainmaker and our witness. As we walked down the center aisle and drew nearer, I was stunned by the apparent youth of the girl. I had imagined a young woman of eighteen or nineteen years. This girl seemed much younger.

Sage stood up as we approached and spoke softly, "Kate and Trey, this is Cleo Yellow Bird, the young lady I was telling you about."

The girl stood up and nodded, her dark eyes wide, like a spooky deer. She was a tiny thing with a boyish figure, perhaps reaching five feet on her tiptoes, and she was strikingly pretty, even in the tattered, faded jeans and cotton shirt she wore. I noticed that she wore her moccasins.

They sat down, and Sage continued, "I have told Cleo that she may call our meeting to a halt whenever she chooses. That's one of the ground rules before we start."

"Agreed. You imply there are more rules."

"You must protect her."

"I have thought about this, and I have spoken to the Secret Service. She may return with us to the State Game Lodge, where she will be protected. In a few days she will be escorted by train to Lockwood, Wyoming, where she will stay with my grandparents on their ranch. There are many Brule Sioux in the area. As you know, they are of your Lakota family. An Oglala girl would be welcome there. My grandfather, Ethan Ramsey, and my grandmother, Skye Ramsey, will protect her as their own. She will love my grandmother. She is half-blood Brule. And Gram is thrilled to have her come. I have spoken with them over a secure telephone about this."

Sage looked at Cleo. "Will you do this?"

Again, she nodded her assent.

"Trey, go ahead with your questions," Sage said.

"Cleo. I have been told you were captured by some men and taken to Chicago and somehow escaped and found your way back. I want to hear your story from the beginning. I hope I may learn something that will help me find and arrest these men and stop this from happening to others. I am a Bureau of Investigation agent. Do you understand what that is?"

Cleo spoke so softly, I had to lean forward to hear her reply.

"I have heard of the BI. You are hated and feared by the gangsters in Chicago. I think that is a good thing."

"How old are you, Cleo?"

"Fourteen. In May."

"Are you still in school?"

"I attended Miss Rainmaker's school until I was taken in March. I contacted her when I returned, and she gave me books and helped me when she could. I was afraid to go back to the school. I hoped to go to high school in the fall, but that will not be possible now."

"We'll see about that. The Lame Buffalo Foundation operates a private high school near Lockwood. If you qualify, you might attend there. Otherwise, Lockwood also has a public high school. Do you live with your parents?"

"My parents are dead. The alcohol killed my father, and my mother died from tuberculosis. I live with my grandmother, but she is frightened that I will be found there by the evil men and that we will both be killed . . . or worse."

"Let's start at the beginning. How were you taken by these men?"

"I was a fool. I was told by my friend, Rosa, she is two years older, that a truck full of free clothing was coming to the reservation and that poor girls who had lost their mothers could go to this truck and pick out blouses and skirts, and even undergarments, to take home. I am wearing my best clothes today, so you can see this was very enticing. We were told to go to the truck on the sixth of March at noon. It was to be parked near Lakota Pond."

"Where is that located?"

"Southeast of Rapid City. Just a few miles inside the reservation."

"So, you and Rosa went to meet the truck?"

"Yes. There were five of us there. There were two tables. A pretty, blonde lady was showing the items. She seemed nice, but I found out later she was not. There were two men with her. One was Sioux, but I did not know him. They called the white man 'Bull.' He was strong and very big . . . not fat, just big."

Cleo was speaking noticeably louder now, and her timidity seemed to abate as her anger rose. "Tell me about the truck. What did it look like?"

"It was a Ford. I know that because I saw the name on it, but I do not know much about models. It was covered and painted white. It looked like some of the milk delivery trucks I have seen in Rapid City. There was no sign painted on it, though."

The girl was very well-spoken, I observed. The Lame Buffalo school imposed rigid standards and accepted students without regard to race tuition-free if they could score high enough on admission tests. I hoped Cleo might qualify. "I assume you saw the inside of the truck."

"Yes, but not willingly. When we were sorting through the skirts and blouses, a car drove up and parked near the truck. Two dirty, scroungy-looking men got out. They were friendly with the others, and it made me very nervous. Rosa and I were the youngest. I whispered to Rosa that we should leave, but she refused. She was picking out things she liked. A few minutes later the four men were pointing rifles at us. I started to run, but one of the men fired a rifle in the air and yelled that the next shot would be in my back if I didn't stop. I obeyed, and the woman ran up to me and started slapping my face. She called me a 'red bitch' and worse things."

"After that, you did what they said?"

"Yes, there is no doubt they would have killed us. They herded us like cattle into the back of the truck. It stunk, like it had been used as a toilet. I found out later that had probably been the case. We were ordered to sit down on one of the benches that were bolted to each side wall. After that the doors closed, and we sat in pitch blackness. The other girls started to cry. I did not. I cried later, but at that moment I was just mad. At myself for being so stupid. At those people for taking us away."

"Where did they take you?"

"They took us to a place I later learned they called the chick coop."

"You mean chicken coop?"

"No. They called it a chick coop. I suppose they were trying to be funny. We were cooped up so to speak, and we were all young females."

"Tell me about the coop."

"It was a hole dug out in the rock on the mountainside. Sort of a cave that went thirty or forty feet into the stone and then stopped and branched off two different directions for a short distance. It made kind of a 'T' shape. It could have been natural, but it looked like somebody started digging a mine and just gave up on it. The opening was blocked by a steel gate with bars that had sharp points at the top. The tips of the bars were probably more than ten feet from the ground."

"You said this cave was in the mountainside. How did they get you there? Do you have any sense of where this coop would be located from here?"

"We were locked in the truck most of the way, and we couldn't see out, but could tell when we entered Rapid City from the noise and the stops and the speed. We even pounded on the doors, hoping someone would hear us. After we got through the city, the truck turned left and stayed on what I am certain was a paved road. It seemed like a long time before we turned again, and this time we went onto a rocky road. The ride became rough, and we climbed higher. The road was steep because the climb pushed us toward the rear of the truck. Sometimes, when sharp turns were made, we tumbled over onto each other, and, finally, we just huddled on the truck floor."

"But you cannot estimate the distance?"

"No. It seemed like a long time because we were all afraid. We did not know what they planned to do with us. When the truck stopped and parked, I assumed they were going to rape and kill us. The woman opened the truck doors to let us out in a clearing surrounded by pine. We had only a few minutes before Bull and the two other white men tied black hoods over our heads and made us form a line and each place a hand on the shoulder of the girl in front of us. Bull and the two others led us up a trail. It must have been wide because we did not have to hug the mountainside or be cautioned to watch our step. It was still scary because I couldn't see anything."

"You said there were two other men. Where were the Lakota and the woman?"

"I guess they remained behind and left with the truck. I did not hear another car, so I do not think these were the men who came to help capture us. They must have been waiting for us to arrive."

The girl appeared focused on her story now and spoke in a matter-of-fact tone, as if reciting events that happened to someone else. I noticed that her eyes were fixed toward the back of the church, like the scene was unfolding there. "How long do you think you walked on this trail?" I asked.

"It is hard to say. We moved very slowly. One of the girls stumbled and fell, and the man . . . I think it was this Bull . . . said terrible things to her, called her a whore. It was more than an hour. The climb was very steep because the men were complaining and breathing heavily and were forced to stop and rest. I know Bull wore cowboy boots, and I suspect the others did, also. I would not choose to wear those boots for walking. Anyway, when we arrived at the coop, we were stripped of all our clothing and then our hoods removed. We were shoved in the cave and the gate swung closed and was padlocked."

"Were there other young woman there when you arrived?"

"No, but others were brought there over the next five days until there were ten of us. That seemed to be an important number."

I hesitated to ask the next question. "Were you harmed during this time?"

"I was not. Three of the girls were chosen to be toys for the men. It seemed that the rest of us were to be saved. The three . . . one was my friend, Rosa . . . were taken from the coop daily and raped repeatedly by the men. They gambled, I think, to determine who got first choice. I can still hear my friends' screams from the first day the men ravaged them. I was terrified for them but, also, because I feared my turn would come soon. Rosa would not speak after that first time. She just sobbed. I never heard her speak again, not even on the journey to Chicago."

"Can you think of anything that might help us find this place they call the chick coop?"

"I have only seen it from behind the steel gate. There is a wide ledge in front, at least twenty-five feet, and the ledge on at least one side must taper off to a gentler slope because I could smell smoke from a fire, and the men did not camp on the ledge in front of the coop. One of the girls who was used by the men said the guards slept in grassy area below. I do know the opening was to the east because the rising sun brightened the cave early in the morning and somehow gave me hope. And many miles to the southeast, if I moved to the north end of the gate, I could see Steeple Rock."

Kate spoke for the first time. "That's a rock formation deep in the hills that tourists can't see from any road. Hikers and horseback riders can view it from some of the trails that crisscross the Black Hills. Very tall, but well hidden. It's a spire that looks almost like a giant fang erupting from the earth. It's about four miles due west of our home place on the Shamrock."

"So, the chick coop would be unknown miles northwest of this Steeple Rock. Well, it's a start," I said. I turned back to Cleo Yellow Bird. "Now, I would like to hear about how you escaped."

Chapter 26

TREY

CLEO CONTINUED HER story, telling us in detail about how the ten girls were permitted to retrieve their clothing, which had been stacked in a pile. Then they had been hooded again and herded down the trail like goats and loaded into the same truck that had delivered them to the coop. Three one-gallon jugs of water were placed in the rear of the truck for sharing by the occupants, and they were provided with two empty buckets. Bull had warned they should "shit only in one bucket and save the other just for piss." More than once the buckets tipped at a sudden turn or stop and spilled the contents on the wooden, truck-bed floor, filling the hauling compartment with disgusting stench and covering their sleeping places with slime.

Water jugs were refilled at fueling stops. Waste buckets were dumped from time to time by Bull or the driver. The woman, whom they called Ruby, also somehow squeezed into the truck cab and occasionally tried unsuccessfully to pacify the prisoners and assure the Sioux girls they were on the road to opportunity and that all would be just fine. Twice daily, she rationed out the bread and cold smoked sausage that comprised the menu for the entire three-day trip.

At nights, the girls remained locked in the truck, but the door was kept open and guarded for several hours in the early morning to air out the enclosed back end and to replenish air supply that was all but sucked out between stops. Cleo had quickly figured out that, however mistreated, the girls were valuable cargo at their destination and they were to be kept alive.

I asked, "So, what happened when you arrived in Chicago?"

"That night, we were taken to place that looked like a hotel, but I do not think it was. Then we were escorted to a big room, where we were told to strip off our clothes and bathe in the five tubs scattered about the room. I hurried to claim a tub that was unused, so I would not have to bathe in someone else's dirty water. After that, we were given clean clothing and led to a small dining room, where we received a nice meal, including chicken and small steaks. Later, we were assigned bedrooms, two of us sharing a room. Rosa shared mine, but she still refused to talk. It was very nice. Some of the girls thought this was a wonderful place and were glad to be there. I wanted to go home. But it had been many nights since I slept as well as I did that night."

"In the morning we were summoned to breakfast, and, as soon as that was finished, we were instructed to return to our rooms, where someone would help us get dressed. When Rosa and I got back to our room, an older Chinese woman with a sharp tongue looked us over like a pair of ponies, left for fifteen minutes and returned with an armful of dresses and other things. She decided what we should wear and demanded we surrender our moccasins for painful heeled shoes. We were told to wait in our rooms, and, while we waited, Rosa admired herself in the mirror, and I saw her smile. But she still would not speak."

"But you were being treated well?"

"Of course, but I still wanted to leave. I sensed that no good would come of any of this in the end. If so, why were we forced to come to that place?"

I could see why Cleo escaped. Gramps had always said there are people who thrive in this world despite any hardship that comes their way, seemingly unaffected by the dismal life that surrounds them. Adversity does not break them. It makes them stronger. I suspected Cleo Yellow Bird was such a person. "Go on," I prodded.

"Soon, Ruby came to our rooms and gathered us all up. We followed her like little puppies down a dusky hallway to a big room where five or six men and two women were seated on one side of three tables that were all in a single row. We were instructed to walk in front of the tables very slowly and to gather at the other end of the room. Smile, we were told. I did not. We did this, and then Ruby directed us to walk out one at a time. She sent Mary Hawk Eyes first. She was one of the girls who had been raped by the men at the chick coop. She stood in front of the tables, and a man came and stood beside her and made her turn around. He lifted her dress, so the people at the table could see her legs and rear-end. Then he made her face the spectators, and he pulled down the front of her blouse so they could view her breasts. He announced she was experienced at the art of pleasure and asked for bids. I had attended a horse auction on the reservation and realized, at that moment, what was taking place."

"You were being auctioned?"

"Yes, to operators of bordellos . . . whorehouses. The three girls who had been used were sold first. The rest of us were sold as virgins and brought higher prices. I am ashamed to say I sold for the highest price . . . five thousand dollars. I gather this was because I was both a virgin and the youngest." She lowered her eyes. "My body is more child's than woman's. It was humiliating. Ruby was even asked to probe our sacred areas in the presence of these vermin to confirm our virginity."

I was seething with rage, almost embarrassed to be a male. Slavery still existed in America, and I was determined to strike a blow for abolition. I asked, "So you were sold to one of the bidders. Did they take you away that night?"

"The others. But not me. Autos were waiting outside the building to take us to the bordellos. Anyway, I assumed that. Mary and I were purchased by the same man and were ordered to sit in the back seat of a Model T. The car doors did not seem to be locked, so I unfastened my shoes and took them off and waited. The ugly toad who purchased us was the driver, and he did not seem to be concerned about escape. Where could we go? When he drove the car away, I looked for my chance. It came soon. He stopped at a street corner, and I tumbled out the door and ran. Cars honked, and lights nearly blinded me as

I raced down the street. I made it to the sidewalk and kept on moving. I looked back, and I saw that the man had stopped chasing me after running a short distance. He was probably worried that Mary would get away also. More likely, he was winded. He looked more turtle than rabbit."

I smiled at her humor. Cleo had a way with words and a succinct manner of storytelling that intrigued me. "Somehow you made it from Chicago to the reservation. Please, tell us what happened."

"I turned down a dark, scary alley, but I didn't stop running. When I came out the other end, I almost ran into an elderly Negro lady. I stopped to apologize, and she took my hand and asked if I was running from someone. I said I was. She didn't ask any questions, and she said her apartment was across the street and I should come with her. She promised I would be safe there. Her eyes said I could trust her, and what choice did I have anyway? I had no idea how to get out of the city or how I might find my way back to the reservation. I had no money and only the floozy clothes I was wearing."

"And this lady helped you?"

"Yes, I owe her my life . . . and thirty dollars, as soon as I have it. When we went to her apartment on the second floor of a very tall building, I could see that her furniture was old and worn, but the kitchen and other room . . . I didn't see her bedroom . . . were very clean, and, for some reason, I felt safe. I told her what had happened to me, and she got an atlas book she had. I learned she was a fourth-grade school teacher. We sat down at her kitchen table, and she showed me where I had to go to get to the reservation. I only needed to get to the east border. Once I was on reservation land, I could hitch rides to get home."

"So, this stranger helped you plan your journey back?"

"Her name was Zelda Crocker, and I will never forget her. She made me realize there are good people in this world. Anyway, her son, Reggie, is a truck driver, and he was taking a load of furniture to Minneapolis in two days and would get me that far. Zelda said he would not leave me alone there until he found a reliable trucker to take me to another safe stop. She called it a relay. She said they would try to find good men but that I should not be too trusting and be prepared to run if I had to. She gave me a pocket knife with a long blade, sort of like one the reservation boys called a toad stabber. I stayed with her for the two days. She fed me, and I slept on her couch, and we had talks like I had never had before. When I got ready to leave with Reggie, she gave me the thirty dollars as a loan. She kept it in a jar in her kitchen cabinet, and I could see she was giving me every dollar she had in that jar. I almost cried."

I said, "I have an allowance for information fees. When we take you to the State Game Lodge, I'll give you the money, and you can send it with a letter to Zelda before you leave for Lockwood. Maybe you can write to her from time to time and visit her someday."

Her eyes moistened, and, for the first time, she smiled. "Are you sure? I would love to do that."

"I promise. It's your money, free and clear. Now, tell me the rest. Did you have any trouble getting home from Chicago?"

"Not at all. The relay worked fine. I rode with four different Negro truck drivers. They all were gentlemen and very protective of me . . . except one. He pulled off the road and tried to fondle my breasts and thought he was going to get more until I pulled out my knife and touched it to his throat. He changed his mind. He couldn't get rid of me fast enough after that. One of the drivers told me there might have been trouble if I had not been Indian. My skin is dark enough that it was all right for me to be seen with a colored man. If I had been blonde and white, there might have been problems along the way."

I sighed. "Yes, I suppose that's possible. I would like to talk to you some more and see if we can get more detailed descriptions of the men you encountered. I would also like the names of all the girls who were taken, as well. I'll see if the Chicago office can look in to their whereabouts, but I'm not optimistic. There may be some who don't even want to be found by now. We can go over this at the lodge, if you are willing to go with us."

Cleo looked at Sage. "Will you get word to my grandmother? Tell her I am safe? Nothing else. It is better for her if she can just say I left. When this is over, I will contact her."

"Of course," Sage said. "I think you should do this."

Chapter 27

KATE

KATE SLEPT LATE the morning after the meeting at the church with Cleo Yellow Bird. Late for her was seven o'clock. She was relieved that her father had already eaten breakfast and headed out with Stretch to hay ground with their horse-drawn mowers. After the mowed hay cured for a week, they would be loading it on hay wagons to haul to strategic spots on the ranch to stack for winter feeding. It was hard work, and she felt like a slacker for not helping. Her father had asked her, though, to ride fence lines today and mend fence where she could and make notes of any places that would require replacement. He had employed a fencing contractor who would come in a few weeks to build what new fence they couldn't handle themselves.

Grandma Beth was evidently out collecting eggs from the hen house, but she had left a few biscuits and bacon slices in the oven, which was still warm. The coffee on the stovetop was not hot but warm enough to tolerate. As she spread strawberry jam on her biscuits, she thought back to her return home the previous night. She had arrived home shortly after eight o'clock, but her father reacted like she had been out all night. He wanted to know where she had been all day, whom she had been with and what they were doing. She had fibbed a bit, saying she had been at the State Game Lodge and had dined with President and Mrs. Coolidge, which was true as far as it went. She felt her connection with the BI investigation was confidential business. He asked if she had been with Trey, and when she replied in the affirmative, his face turned beet-red.

Owen Connolly had said, "I don't like that young man. You don't know all there is to know about him. And he's too much of a dandy. He's just after one thing."

Kate had snapped back, "And what's that?"

Her response had flustered her father. "You know what I'm talking about. And if you want a good husband someday, you'll save yourself."

The conversation had taken an uncomfortable turn for her father, and he had done an about-face and stomped out of the room. Later, she wondered about his comment that she didn't know all there was to know about Trey. Was it just a random statement made in anger, or was he aware of some dark secret from Trey's past? As for saving herself? Sorry, Dad. Too late. As for that one thing Trey was supposedly after, she was a little insulted he hadn't made a move for it. Of course, since she was a reformed slut, that didn't mean he would get it.

She smiled as she devoured the last biscuit and recalled yesterday's adventure. That's how she was thinking of her involvement in the BI investigation. An exciting adventure. Trey had insisted he drive Kate's Buick on the return trip to the State Game Lodge, suggesting Cleo Yellow Bird and Kate ride in the back seat and get better acquainted. Kate had no objection and assumed Trey wanted to test the vehicle, but she thought they would have made better time on horseback.

It had been fun to watch Cleo meet the president and first lady. The girl was obviously awestruck and disbelieving that this could be happening to her. Grace Coolidge quickly put Cleo at ease, however, and insisted they join the first couple for dinner. After another interview with the Oglala girl, they had enjoyed a western menu of T-bone steaks, fried potatoes and baked beans, accompanied by a variety of vegetables and fresh-baked sourdough bread topped by cherry pie for dessert. It seemed that his visit to the Black Hills was converting President Coolidge to a new diet, at least for the duration.

Cleo had eaten heartily and didn't leave a crumb on her plate, but Kate had been mildly surprised at her poise and perfect table manners, wondering if Sage Rainmaker included such subjects in her school curriculum. It made sense. She ate quietly, speaking only when a question was directed to her, but her keen intelligence was obvious.

The president had been in good humor, a sharp turnaround from his mood when she had spoken with him that morning. Perhaps, a decision made, whatever it was, had something to do with that, Kate hoped.

Now, she had better get to work. Kate got up from the kitchen table and quickly washed and dried her breakfast dishes and then hurried out to the stable to saddle War Paint. A half hour later she was astride her gelding, saddlebags stuffed with tools, including pliers, a wire cutter, and fence tool, trailed by a pack horse loaded with a roll of wire for fence mending and bridging broken strands of barbed wire, a wire stretcher, and other tools and supplies.

They headed south along the fence line that bordered the crushed-rock road running along much of the east border of the Shamrock. The Labrador, Galahad, ranged in the lush meadow surrounding Kate, sniffing the ground, scaring up an occasional quail or prairie hen that fluttered away, but mostly stalking imaginary prey.

Kate reined in whenever she spotted a gap in the barbed-wire strands that framed the rangelands or a loose wire springing in the breeze. She would quickly repair the damage and move on. Often, she found hair on the barbs near the fence breach, indicating a deer or other critter had hit the wire causing the stress that triggered the wire break. Cattle tended to have more respect for the barrier, unless they sensed a weak spot to exploit when lusher grass was on the other side. This occurred more often in the fall when the pasture had been grazed down.

By midmorning, the rays of a full sun started to warm her back and her shirt was sticking to her skin. Perspiration was forming dark patches under the arms of her pale blue shirt, and, after dismounting to splice two stray wires, she paused and plucked a canteen from her saddlebags. While she drank greedily from the canvas-covered metal container, she heard the chugging of a vehicle motor coming her way from the north. Probably Stretch or Grandma Beth driving the truck out to check on her. The thought annoyed and pleased her at the same time.

She had been fixing fence since she turned twelve, and she was an adult who could look after herself now. On the other hand, folks checked on you because they cared. She had passed through a phase when the watchfulness upset her, and she had responded with outbursts or rebellion. She had now attained resigned acceptance.

As the vehicle approached, Kate had to erase her previous thoughts. The small, battered truck was not from the Shamrock, although it was a Ford model favored by her father. The driver slowed the truck as it passed by, and she observed a front seat passenger looking at her intently. The truck kept moving snaillike down the road, and her eyes followed its movement. She noticed the truck was fitted with side panels extending from the bed, and that several tarps stretched over a few large barrels and boxes pushed against the cab's back. She also saw what might have been a layer of full feed sacks to the rear of the truck's bed. The vehicle's sudden appearance had made Kate uneasy, and she relaxed only when the truck disappeared over the horizon. She supposed the truck's load was headed toward the Lazy K, which had an entry road about five miles south, or a farmstead on one of several small, subsistence farms along the way.

Kate worked her way down the fence line for another hour, pleased to discover only a few minor breaks. She reined in her gelding when she came upon the cluster of cottonwood trees she had been looking for near a stream that cascaded out of the Black Hills to the west and sliced through the Shamrock ranch valley. She looked beyond the stream and caught sight of one of the ranch's angus herds grazing against the shadowy backdrop of the saw-toothed granite mountains. She nudged War Paint away from the fence line and down the gentle slope toward her oasis. Then, she dismounted, removed the lunch she had packed from her saddlebags and released the horse to graze, trusting, as usual, that her friend would not wander. She staked the packhorse within easy reach of the stream.

Galahad knew the lunchtime routine, and he stopped his roaming and raced eagerly toward Kate, as she sat down beneath a mammoth cottonwood and opened her lunch bag. Before she bit into her sandwich, she tossed the dog a thick slice of roast beef, knowing he would be begging for more and holding a few more slices in reserve for when he started his begging. Sharing lunch was a tradition, and she always packed extra for Galahad.

After eating her sandwich, and several shortbread cookies, Kate leaned back against the tree's base and dozed off. She was awakened a few minutes later by Galahad's low, rolling growl. She lifted the brim of her hat and looked around. At first, she saw nothing, but when she got up and surveyed the landscape a second time, she caught sight of movement on the creekbank downstream. As she focused on the object, she saw it was a man, and he was walking with some speed and deliberation in her direction. She could not imagine why any man would be walking in their pasture, and she was not about to meet him without horse and rifle. She cast her eyes for War Paint, and spotted him some fifty yards distant, further than the gelding usually wandered. Then she caught sight of another man walking down the slope from the road. He was carrying a rifle. She whistled for the horse, and he raised his head and started trotting her way. She took off running to meet War Paint, and Galahad followed on her heels.

A rifle cracked, and the horse shrieked in pain, stumbling forward to his knees, and she saw rivulets of blood running down the gelding's neck, just in front of the shoulder. She began to tremble, and her stomach threatened to heave at her fear for her old companion. She kept on running toward the injured horse until a man yelled, "Stop, or I put another bullet in the critter."

She obeyed and turned. It was the Indian who had stalked the president, absent his braided long hair. She shot a glance toward the shady spot where she had staked the packhorse and saw that the mare had pulled loose and disappeared, likely frightened by the gunshot.

She wheeled to run west across the stream, but she was intercepted by the other man, who caught her by the wrist and twisted harshly, tossing her to the ground. This man was tall, with huge muscular arms and shoulders and fierce, stormy eyes that dared her to resist. She did not. But he suddenly released her when Galahad closed his jaws on the man's ankle, roaring like an enraged lion. The man pulled a pistol that rested on his hip, but the dog latched on to his hand and locked his jaws and began to rip. The big man kicked at the dog and tried to pull his hand away, screaming in pain and panic.

Another gunshot, and Galahad flinched, holding on and dragging the man to his knees. With the second shot, the dog's jaws released the mangled hand, and he slumped to the earth within a few feet from Kate. She crawled to Galahad's side and put her hand under his head, lying down beside the still body and pressing her face to the animal's and sobbing uncontrollably, oblivious to the two intruders.

Finally, the stocky Indian told her. "Get up, young lady. You're coming with us. Now." Only then did she become aware of the moaning from the other man, who had removed his shirt and wrapped it around the injured hand.

Kate got up, trying to put aside her grief for the moment, realizing her own survival was at stake. "Who are you? What do you want?" she asked.

"Shut up, bitch," the big man yelled. "Just do what you're told."

"I'm going to finish off the horse," the Indian called George said.

"No," Kate pled. "Not if he's got a chance."

"What horse?" asked the big man.

Kate turned to where War Paint had gone down. He was gone.

"He must have got up and wandered off," George said. "He won't get far."

Kate prayed the Indian was wrong. Anyway, War Paint's fate was out of her hands—and theirs. And she was grateful for that.

"Now, listen girl," George said in a raspy voice. "You've seen we can kill when we got a need. You're either coming along with no trouble, or I can put a bullet in your brain and leave you to rot with the damned cur. Your choice."

All she could do now was buy some time and hope she had an opportunity to escape or someone caught up to these animals. "No trouble," she said.

George said, "We've got the truck parked on an access drive to the pasture." He pointed south, and she knew the spot, well-sheltered from the north by a thick patch of cedar trees.

George grabbed Kate roughly by the arm and yanked her forward. As they walked up the slope, she looked over her shoulder at the prone form of Galahad and, pulling up her dwindling reserves of determination, fought back the tears that threatened to erupt. When they reached the truck, she was surprised to see Willy Hobson leaning against the front fender. He smiled when he saw her and went over to the gate, released the latch, and swung it open to allow Kate and her captors through. Bull Bullock was still moaning and staggered to the truck cab and opened the door on the passenger side and climbed in.

"What's the matter with him, Uncle George?" Willy asked.

"Dog chewed up his hand. Made a mess of it."

"I heard gun shots. Did you kill the dog?"

"Yep. Shot a horse, too, but the damn thing still got away."

"What are we doing with her?" Willy asked, nodding toward Kate.

"The chick coop."

The place Cleo talked about. Kate reminded herself that this at least gave her a temporary reprieve. They didn't intend to kill her yet. But why did they choose her?

"Willy, help me get this dame in the back of the truck." George jerked Kate's arm and started dragging her to the rear of the vehicle. Willy followed, looking at Kate with puzzlement.

"You know she's cozy with the president and a BI agent, don't you?"

"That's why she's here. Boss wants to get back at her for helping Coolidge get away."

"Do you think that's smart?"

"You ask too many questions. But no, I don't. But Boss is still ramrodding the outfit . . . for now."

"You taking over the outfit?"

"Not yet. Now, shut up and do what you're told."

"Climb up there, girl," George said, when they stood behind the truck.

Kate pulled away. "No." She kicked George sharply on the shin, but his grip was a steel manacle. His fist drove into her eye like a sledge, and her knees buckled, but he still held on. Her head spun, and relentless pain stabbed her cheek and temple.

"Willy, toss her on the truck bed," George said.

He responded literally, and she had a brief sensation of flight before her body slammed on the hardwood bed. "How you going to keep her up here?" Willy asked.

She sensed that the men were now in the truck bed, standing near her.

"Take the lid off the barrel on the right. It's empty."

"You ain't going to put her in the barrel?"

"Damn right, I am."

She flailed, trying to get up and run, but George launched several booted kicks to her ribs, and the agony made her forget about her head. She was only vaguely aware of their arms lifting her and the rough hands stuffing her into the barrel. And then the lid came down, leaving her cramped in blackness in an upright fetal position.

George said, "Pull the sacks of feed to the front and stack them around the barrels to keep them in place. It'll give me a place to sit, too. I'll ride back here. You keep on driving."

"What about Bull?"

"We'll leave him with Boss. He can take care of big brother."

Kate heard the truck start up and groaned as the pain shot through her body when it bounced onto the lip of the road. She was twisted like a pretzel and when she thought she could take the torment no longer, she slipped away into unconsciousness.

Chapter 28

GRANDMA BETH

BETH RIDGEWAY HAD just finished grinding up beef strips and putting a meatloaf in the new electric oven. Stretch had offered to buy the appliance, but to Beth's surprise, Owen had coughed up the money. He made clear, however, that the appliance was ranch property.

Beth peered out the kitchen window. The sun was only a few hours from sinking down behind the hills to the west. The men would be home before dark. She hoped Kate would be home soon. It annoyed her that Owen had laid off the two extra hands after spring calving. He could have kept one on. The work was endless on the place, and she didn't like Kate working without a partner. She started to turn away from the window when she caught a glimpse of movement in the ranch yard. Kate? She focused. It was War Paint, staggering like a drunk.

She whirled and rushed out onto the porch and then nearly sprinted across the yard toward the horse, her heart hammering in her chest. When she reached War Paint, she saw the scarlet trickle of blood dripping down the animal's neck over the brown, crusted blood that had flowed earlier. She grabbed the reins and led the horse to the stable, where she watered and grained him, while she tried to gather her wits. War Paint had obviously taken a bullet. Galahad would never have left Kate, so it was understandable he had not returned. What about Kate? My God, for all Beth knew she could be lying dead out on the range someplace. She didn't even know where Kate had been working. Owen had sent her off someplace to repair fence. But where? She fought off the panic that threatened to consume her and returned to the house.

She cranked up the wall phone and gave the operator the number Trey Ramsey had provided the family. A soft male voice answered, "Secret Service, Quinton."

"Mr. Quinton, this is Beth Ridgeway. I am Kate Connolly's grandmother. I need to speak to Trey Ramsey. It's an emergency."

"I will call him to the phone, ma'am," replied the man in a calm voice.

Shortly, Trey came on the line. "Beth, this is Trey. Quinton said something about an emergency. What is it?"

Beth told him about War Paint and the fact Kate had not returned with him. "Something terrible has happened to her, Trey. I know it has. We've got to find her."

"As soon as I hang up, I'm going to make a call to the sheriff's office. Then I'll claim one of the cars and be at the Shamrock as soon as I can."

Beth then called the veterinarian in Custer to come out to the ranch to examine and treat War Paint. Afterward, she returned to the stable to check on the horse. The gelding seemed steadier on its feet now and had cleaned up the grain, which she took as a positive sign. She walked back to the house, agitated by the feeling she should be doing something, frustrated by the waiting. She checked the meatloaf, which was past due for her perusal and had formed a bit of a charred crust on top. She removed it from the oven, doubting anyone was going to have an appetite this evening. She decided the meatloaf was destined for sandwiches.

She was relieved when she heard the familiar rattle and roar of the truck bouncing up the crushed rock drive and hurried out the door to greet Stretch and Owen, looking forward to the comfort and reassurance she could count on from her cowboy husband. On the other hand, she was on edge about the volatile Owen's response. She knew he loved his daughter, but his reaction to the news could range from calm to rage.

She was halfway along the pathway from the house to the ranch yard when Stretch started rushing toward her. She fell into his arms, savoring the sweat and hay dust smell of the man who had known a life of hard, physical labor long before motorized contraptions became a part of the western landscape. Few knew the keen intelligence and sensitivity that lay beneath the surface of this tall, rawboned cowboy with the windburned leathery face who had reached his sixties without a day of formal education. And he was a mind-reader, invariably knowing her thoughts before they formed in her own mind.

"What's the matter, Babe? It's Kate isn't it?" Stretch asked, his voice soft and gentle.

Beth stepped back and nodded her head, her first tears squeezing out of the corners of her eyes. "War Paint showed up in the yard without her. He'd been shot in the neck but got back here somehow. But I don't know what happened to Kate and Galahad."

Owen came up behind Stretch. "What's this about Kate?"

Beth repeated what she had told Stretch. "I've called the vet and contacted Trey Ramsey. He was going to call the sheriff's office. There should be help here soon."

"We don't need a bunch of damned outsiders in on this," Owen snapped, "least of all, Ramsey. You didn't have any business calling him."

Beth started to strike back, but Stretch, stepped in front of her, speaking very slowly and calmly, "Owen, I've worked for you a long time, but I won't have you talking that way to Beth. You do that one more time, and we're packing up and moving on. And if that's what you want, that's okay, too. Just say so."

Connolly looked at him dumbfounded. "Sorry, Beth. I'm just upset. And you know why I don't like Ramsey sniffing around here like some horny bull after a heifer."

"Under the circumstances, I'll excuse your vulgarity and illogical foolishness. Where was she working today?"

Stretch said, "Owen sent her to work the east fence line. Most of it follows the county and park roads. She took the sorrel mare, too, for a pack animal. If she's not dead, I suppose she's wandering around out in the hills. She'll likely find her way back tomorrow."

"We should have better than an hour of daylight left. I'll run to the house and grab a few kerosene lanterns. Do you have flashlights?" Beth asked.

"In the truck," Owen said.

"You and Stretch head up the road and see what you can find. I'll send Trey Ramsey and the sheriff's people your way when they get here."

Only after Owen and Stretch disappeared into the swirling dust kicked up in the driveway did Beth sit down on the porch step and surrender to the tears she had fought off till now. Her body shook as the torrent soaked the front of her blouse. Less than five minutes later, she willed herself to stop the silliness and stood up. She had lost Coleen to Wilson's damned war. Now the only link to her daughter was missing. Kate was alive out there somewhere. She had to believe that. Her religious faith was fragile, but it occurred to her that Trey Ramsey might be an emissary from heaven sent to redeem his father. Perhaps that explained the bizarre coincidence of Trey and Kate meeting up a world away from the battlefields of France.

Chapter 29

TREY

AFTER I SPOKE to Beth Ridgeway, I called Bing Compton, who, fortunately, was still at the sheriff's office. He grumbled a bit about having to cancel a date with Carrie but promised he would head out to the Shamrock and meet me there. I informed Quinton about my conversation with Beth and told him President Coolidge would want to know as soon as he returned from the ranchers' barbecue he and the first lady were attending at the Tall Tree Ranch a half-dozen miles north of the State Game Lodge.

Dusk was closing in when I pulled the Model T into the Shamrock ranch yard. Beth was waiting outside, and as I got out of the car, I heard tires of another vehicle crunching against the drive rock. I looked over my shoulder and saw it was Bing. He must have pushed pedal to floor board on his run from Rapid City. I turned back to Beth, who embraced me warmly.

"Thank God, you're here, Trey. I'm beside myself with worry. Stretch and Owen left a short while ago to look for Kate, but I have a terrible feeling about this."

Bing came up behind me, and I made hasty introductions. "Where are Stretch and Owen searching?" I asked.

"They took the road south along our east ranch boundary. That's where Kate was fixing fence today. If you drive south on the county road, you should catch up to them. If they stopped someplace, the truck should be parked just off the road. I assume they'll be checking pasture along the fence for signs that Kate was there."

"Let's take my car, Bing. Beth, the Secret Service may be calling for a report. Tell them I'll get word to them as soon as we know anything." And please let it be good news, I thought.

I climbed in the Model T while Bing cranked the starter, and, after a few protests, the car roared, and I steered the machine down the long driveway and onto the main road. We drove in silence until Bing pointed to the Shamrock's truck a football field's length ahead of us, parked on the grassy roadside. As we pulled up behind it, we couldn't see any sign of Connolly or Stretch.

"They must have seen something and climbed over the fence," Bing said. "Let's see if we can find them."

I plucked a flashlight from under the car seat and stepped down from the running board. It was turning dusky, and, although stars would be lighting the sky with sparkle soon enough, they wouldn't provide enough radiance for the search facing us.

Bing and I were both tall men, but the top barbed wire was strung tight and high enough to carve a duet of sopranos if we tried to step over. Therefore, we each took turns spreading the two middle wires with foot and fingers so the other could slip through. Even then, I caught the seat of my trousers on a barb and tore a hole in the fabric large enough to stick a fist in. The price paid by a fool who didn't have the sense to change into outdoor garb before taking off for a search in cow country.

After we squeezed through the fence, we stood silently for several moments, taking in the landscape. I heard voices to the south. "They're down that way," I said and started walking along the fence line toward the voices.

"Watch your step," Bing said. "There are a couple of rolls of wire and materials piled up ahead of us."

I switched on the flashlight, and the beam revealed a pile of fencing tools, wire and other supplies. Then, I started a bit when I saw a large shadowy figure plodding up the slope toward us. By the time the horse whinnied, I had already figured out it wasn't a Black Hills cousin to Sasquatch.

"The packhorse," I said. "They must have found her and unpacked her here and turned her loose again."

We moved on with the horse trailing along behind us. Soon we picked up the glow of two lanterns moving back and forth some distance apart like fireflies in the darkness. As we approached, the lights froze in place, as the cattlemen fixed their eyes on the visitors coming their way.

I waved and yelled, "It's Trey Ramsey coming your way. Deputy Bing Compton's with me."

"Howdy, Trey," Stretch Ridgeway said, extending his big hand and taking mine firmly in a sandpaper paw. "Your help's welcome here."

I noted that Connolly remained silent and sensed he was not so pleased to see me. "I see you found the packhorse. She tagged along with us."

"Yep. She's tame as an old hound dog. We figured we'd leave her out here, and she'll find her way home in a day or two. She'll hang around us till we head back, though."

"Have you found anything else?"

"Not yet. We drove back and forth on the road for a spell until we spotted Mazie grazing down the hill. Then we pulled over, and, after unloading her, we started walking the fence line. We found some fresh splices and patches on the wires, so we know Kate was working here, but there are more than three miles of fence so that doesn't narrow it down a lot. I'm thinking Mazie might have stayed around where she last saw Kate, but who knows?"

I had not realized Bing wandered off, when he called from the bottom of the hill. "Hey, I found something. Better get down here."

I could barely make out Bing's shadowy image, but his flashlight beam swept over the earth about him and provided an ample target. We scrambled down the slope as fast as the tricky footing over the loose rock would allow. As we neared Bing, I heard the murmur of water rushing over stone from the stream behind him. My heart stopped for an instant when I saw him kneeling in the grass above a still form.

"It's the dog," Bing said. "He's been dead awhile. Shot twice. But look." Bing fixed the beam of light on the animal's face and muzzle, which were covered with a dark crust. "Blood. And it's nowhere near his wounds."

Then something seemed to catch the deputy's interest, and he wedged his fingers into the Labrador's mouth and pried the jaw open, picking at the creature's teeth.

He plucked an object out and held it up, shining the flashlight on it.

"What the hell is that?" Connolly asked.

"Looks like part of somebody's pinky finger," Bing replied. "I'm guessing this guy chewed up somebody pretty good trying to protect his mistress."

"Galahad didn't have a mean bone," Stretch said, "unless somebody threatened Kate."

Bing pulled a handkerchief from the back pocket of his faded denims and wrapped his trophy in it before stuffing it in his shirt pocket.

I said, "It's obvious Kate was stalked and trapped here. It seems likely somebody took her, but we need to walk this area, I'd say twenty feet apart, and see what we turn up in a sweep." I turned to Bing. "You've done some tracking?"

"I've been a hunter since I was a tadpole. Pop spent most of his time hunting and trapping. Couldn't quite make a living at it so did some seasonal cow-punching for neighbors."

"You take the end nearest the road and see if you can find sign of where they left the pasture. They had to have transportation to get here and take her away." I hoped this was a snatch as I suspected and we didn't find her here.

"Hold your horses, young man," Connolly snarled, "who the hell do you think you are to be throwing out orders here? You're on Shamrock property."

I was not up to a pissing contest with Owen Connolly. "This is a federal investigation, Mr. Connolly. I'm a Bureau of Investigation agent, and I represent the President of the United States. You don't have to take orders from me, but you will not be allowed to interfere with our efforts to find your daughter. I can't believe you would even want to do that. You can stand by and watch, or help us. That's up to you. But stay out of our way."

A few minutes later, we had all spread out and were walking in a line following the east bank of the creek. We didn't have to go far before picking up our first sign at the base of a cottonwood tree, where we found the remains of a half-eaten sandwich and crumbled cookies scattered on a paper sack next to a canteen that had tipped over and spilled its contents.

"She stopped here to eat her lunch," Bing said. "Probably where they caught up with her."

Within fifteen minutes Bing found a trail of matted grass sprinkled with dry droplets of blood that led back to a pasture access drive-off, where a vehicle had evidently been parked. I relaxed some when he reported boot prints in softer dirt on the edge of the drive-off that were too small for a man's.

"We dead-end here," Bing said. "The car or truck could have gone anywhere from here." He threw the mess back in my hands. "What now, Trey?"

I tried my best to look authoritative and was silent for some moments, hoping my companions would conclude I was working on a great plan. Of course, I didn't know what in the hell I was doing. "We can't do much in the dark," I said, stating the obvious.

"That's the best the BI can come up with? I guess me and Stretch are going to have to find Kate ourselves," Connolly said.

This guy and I were going to seriously butt heads before our final goodbye, but I didn't have time to debate. I also was certain he was smarter than the palooka he appeared to be during our conversations to date. Who knows? He might even be helpful at some point, I decided. "Bing, could you come out here in the morning and take another look at the scene. Bring somebody to help if you can and gather up anything that might be evidence of what happened. I would appreciate it if the sheriff's office could put out a quiet alert to physicians and hospital authorities to inform you if anybody shows up with a chewed-up hand and missing finger."

"I can do that."

"Do you have any snitches in Rapid City who might ask around about local goons with Chicago connections?"

"Oh, yeah, but they're mostly boozehounds. I got a contact named Ollie, though, who works the other side of a bar. Knows a lot and is a stoolie for a price."

I pulled my wallet from my jacket pocket, plucked out a twenty-dollar bill and handed it to Bing. "Here's a double-sawbuck. Tell him there're more of those for information that leads us to a gang with Chicago connections. Soon."

"You sound like you know who you're looking for."

"In a general way. I'll tell you about it later."

"Tell us about it now," Connolly demanded.

"Mr. Connolly, I understand your concern, and I will tell you as much as I can as soon as I am authorized to do so. This involves a secret government investigation, and I must speak with the president before I discuss it with anyone. Now, I am going back down the hill and recover Galahad. I assume you have a suitable place to bury him?"

"I figured we'd leave him here. The coons and coyotes and buzzards will clean him up quick."

"I'll help you," Stretch said, and walked away from Connolly to join me.

We walked in silence until we approached the dog's body. I peeled off my suitcoat and said, "Maybe we can lay Galahad on this and use it as a sling to carry him."

"That should work. We have an area marked off as a pet cemetery back at the home place. Owen's buried some of his own dogs there. He wouldn't have left Galahad here. He was just trying to get your goat."

"Well, he succeeded. He doesn't like me for some reason."

"It's complicated. He just never got over losing Coleen. It turned him bitter."

"But that's not my fault."

"No, but like I say, it's complicated."

Stretch wasn't telling me all he knew, but I wasn't going to press him. All that mattered now was finding Kate and bringing her home alive.

Chapter 30

TREY

AFTER HELPING STRETCH bury Galahad, I returned to the game lodge. I was surprised to find the president sitting in a leather-covered, stuffed chair reading Scott Fitzgerald's, The Great Gatsby. It was several hours past the president's customary bedtime, and, although he was an avid reader of nonfiction, I had never seen a novel in his hands before. He looked up, and his tortured expression revealed the depth of his concern.

"Sit down, Trey." He pointed to a chair on the opposite side of the thick, oak coffee table that separated us. "Tell me about Kate. Is she okay?"

"She's not okay, Mister President, but I think she is alive. For the moment, anyway." I told him about everything we had discovered that evening and the requests I had made of the sheriff's office.

"What can I do? Should I call in troops to help with a search?"

"I don't think that would be wise, sir. I suspect these are the same people who tried to either abduct or assassinate you. And they likely committed the murders of the Sioux girls Gabe Riley and I were sent here to investigate. Not necessarily the same men, but the same organization."

"Are you suggesting the mafia is involved?"

"No. We wouldn't be sitting here together if the mafia were behind this. And Kate would have died the day she came upon a stranger fishing for trout. These men may have Chicago mafia customers, but they appear to be a clumsy imitation as near as I can tell."

"Chicago customers? I don't understand."

"I didn't have the opportunity to explain about Cleo Yellow Bird."

"The Indian girl who was sent to your grandparents? I was told she was an important witness, that's all. I assumed she had information about the case you are investigating, and I had no reason to inquire further."

"She escaped from a Chicago bordello."

The president's eyebrows lifted, and, for an instant, his stoic face betrayed rare surprise. "I see." He rubbed his chin thoughtfully. "No, I do not see."

I gave him a quick synopsis of Cleo's capture, her experience at the chick coop, and delivery to Chicago. His eyes widened as the tale unfolded.

"Are you suggesting these men plan to sell Kate into white slavery?"

"That seems far-fetched. Too many risks with somebody of her sophistication. But I fear she will not live to see Chicago."

"If they were going to kill her, wouldn't they have done so when they found her at her father's ranch?"

"It does seem strange. These clowns might even be thinking ransom. Regardless, I'm guessing somebody doesn't want her death to be that simple."

"Not torture?"

"Of a sort. Via rape and beatings, perhaps."

"My heavens. We can't let that happen. We must find her. They are doing this because she interfered with their plans for me, aren't they?"

"It's certainly possible. I can't figure out why they would have picked her out otherwise."

"And you really think there is a connection between Kate's abduction and the Sioux girls?"

"At BI training camp, a speaker talked about modus operandi, the methods of criminal activity that form a pattern and indicate the same person is committing a series of crimes."

"I recall the concept from my lawyering days."

"The leader of this gang, or whatever you want to call it, seems to be fixated on capturing people before he makes disposition of them. I don't know if he planned to kill you or hold you for ransom, but I don't think he had a simple assassination in mind."

"Trey, this young woman is the daughter I never had, and she's in trouble . . . perhaps already dead . . . because she saved my life. Find her. Tell me what you want me to do."

I was initially uneasy about giving instructions to the President of the United States, but this was for Kate. "Call Director Hoover and order him to divert five or six Chicago agents here immediately." I decided I could get used to issuing orders to J. Edgar. "I suppose it will take a few days for BI agents to get here. They should report to a local deputy sheriff, Bing Compton. I will leave instructions with him."

"You're not going to be here?"

"I'm going to be searching for the chick coop."

"Trey, there is something you should know."

"Yes?"

"As soon as I returned from the barbeque and was told about Kate, I had the Secret Service ring up your grandmother. I spoke with her briefly, and she was horrified, of course. She informed me your grandfather wants to talk to you about something important."

"It will have to wait."

"He wants to speak with you personally. He left for Rapid City early this afternoon. If he makes all his connections on time, his train will arrive tomorrow morning." The president plucked his pocket watch from his vest pocket and opened the case. "I should say, this morning. It's half-past two o'clock now."

I did not respond. I could not think of anything I wanted to discuss with Gramps right now. I just wanted to get about the business of finding Kate. Why didn't he just ring me up on the telephone?

"You don't seem very enthused about the news."

"I'm sorry, Mr. President. My focus is on finding Kate, and I don't welcome the distraction by my grandfather."

"Keep an open mind, son. Ethan Ramsey might be a good man to have nearby just now. You go about your business. I will arrange for one of the agents to meet your grandfather at the station and bring him here. If nothing else, I will enjoy his company and counsel."

I sighed and nodded approval, not that Calvin Coolidge required my assent.

Chapter 31

KATE

AFTER REGAINING HER faculties, Kate sensed that the truck was moving up a steep incline, and she felt her barrel-prison start to tip just before the vehicle stopped. Soon, the lid popped open and she was unceremoniously dumped on the truck bed and drug to an automobile before she blacked out again.

Now, Kate was rendered blind by the hood her captors had tugged over her head as soon as the car pulled away from the abandoned truck. Her wrists were bound snuggly behind her back with what felt like rawhide strings that cut painfully into her flesh. One ankle was anchored to an immovable object under the front seat of the vehicle. She guessed it was some metal piece where the seat was bolted to the floor, but it didn't matter. She was no risk for leaping from the car.

There had been a brief stop near Rapid City, where they had dropped off the big man they called Bull. He had moaned and cried during the entire journey, and she was glad to be rid of him. Another man, who the others addressed as "Boss," had come to the car and verbally attacked the abductors for their incompetence. He was particularly angry they had come to his residence. George had asked, "What in the hell did you want us to do with this stupid shit? Dog ate half his hand. We couldn't take him out to the coop with us in that shape."

Boss did not reply, and she had sensed he was examining her. This was confirmed when she felt the pain of fingers sharply pinching her nipples. A hand then inched its way down her abdomen, ending between her thighs, where it lingered a bit, before the man stepped away and said, "This is a choice piece of calico. Tell the boys at the coop nobody takes her till I've had her. I'll be out in a few days before the bus to Chicago arrives."

"You're not fool enough to send her there, are you?" George said. "She's seen Willy and Bull and me."

"No. We're not sending her to Chicago. She's either good for ransom money or buzzard bait," the man called Boss said.

"But if we get ransom money and release her, she'll talk. She knows too much. We'd just as well turn ourselves in."

"I didn't say we were going to release her. I said we were going to collect ransom. After I get my poke. You get the little lady settled in to her accommodations. Then, about this time tomorrow, one of you drive in and pick up Bull. I can't have him hanging around here with a search going on."

Kate took those words as her death sentence, but she had figured out already they couldn't let her live. All she could do was cope and survive until she escaped or was rescued.

The road had turned bumpy, and Kate nearly tumbled over several times as the car crept along, making abrupt turns, and barely straightening out before hitting another twist in the rough trail. Cleo Yellow Bird had provided an excellent description of the trail to the chick coop, but Kate had never expected to travel it. The car stopped, and the rear door opened. A rough hand clasped her bound ankle, and she could feel the bonds loosen, as someone untied the rawhide strips or rope that held her there. Then the hand grabbed her arm and dragged her from the seat and out onto the ground. Her hands remained tied, but she savored the feeling of having her legs free.

If she could only see, she would have taken a chance and run.

To Kate's surprise, she felt a loop of a rope slip over her head and settle around her neck, before it tightened. "Your leash," George said, "in case you get any ideas. Willy here's going to lead you. You try to take off, you could drop a thousand feet. So, pay attention. Willy, you ain't been here before, so you follow me."

Kate estimated it was more than an hour before they stopped. She heard the murmur of male voices ahead of her, almost drowning out the sobbing of a young girl. The pungent smell of a wood fire struck her nostrils, and under other circumstances she would have savored it. She assumed darkness had settled in by now, and, when someone slipped her hood off, she confirmed it.

As her eyes adjusted to regain sight, she searched her surroundings through a fog. But as they cleared, she saw she stood on a wide ledge jutting from a granite cliff that seemed to reach into the clouds. Then the soft moonlight glow revealed the chick coop, a large, dark hole bored into the cliff's face, the mouth blocked by a gate fashioned of steel rods, appearing almost like jail bars. She could see eerie, shadowy movement behind the gate, but that was all.

Three men sat around a fire on the other side, where the ledge sloped off and gradually widened until it disappeared into more level terrain. Kate wondered if that was a back way exit from the ledge, where someone could make her way to the creek valley that snaked between the surrounding mountains. Then one of the men got up from the fire and walked toward them.

"George. You trapped the prize kitten, I see."

There was something about the man that looked familiar, and as he came nearer, she recognized him. The man in Carrie's drawing. Dark—Italian, perhaps. Fine features, pencil-thin moustache. He was dressed like a cowhand, but he looked out of place in dusty, beat-up clothes and boots. And now that he stood in front of her, she was struck by his narrow eyes. Black as coal. Cold as ice.

George said, "We're to hold the girl here, Solly, till Boss decides what he wants to do with her. He's thinking ransom."

"Ransom?" Solly said. "I'm sure she'd bring a price. She'd sell good in Chicago, too."

"That's up to Boss. But I doubt if she's going to Chicago."

"He can't let her loose if she's ransomed. She's seen too much, knows too much."

"He won't turn her loose."

"Want me to get her ready for the coop?"

"Go ahead. But Boss has got first dibs on her. You're a dead man if you hump her before he does."

"Boss is a pig."

"Boss is boss. And you don't want to risk his bad temper. I'm going to see if Spud and Henry can spare a cup of coffee." Many Knives turned to Willy. "You help him, and then come to the fire."

Solly said, "The rabbit's all gone, but they got a pot of beans and maybe a few biscuits left. Eat the beans before Spud gets any more. His farts are already burning my nose and making my eyes water."

"I'll try to sit upwind."

Kate's stomach rolled and rumbled, but it wasn't hunger eating at her right now. It was raw fear.

"Okay, broad, sit down. Willy here's going to pull your boots off," Solly said.

"I can't with my hands behind my back."

"You can't?" He walked around behind her. Suddenly a blow slammed into the tender flesh behind her knee, and her leg gave way and she came down hard on her rear. "See, you didn't need your hands untied. Take her boots off, Willy."

"Yes, sir." Willy knelt in front of her. He was obviously nervous. The implications of his involvement with what she had heard the men refer to as the "gang" were probably just starting to sink in. He reached for a foot with trembling hands and began tugging on a boot.

When both boots were tossed aside, Willy started to get up but was abruptly stopped. "Now her britches," Solly said.

"Her britches? What for?"

"Because she goes in the coop with her feathers plucked, jingle-brain. Now get her britches and underpants off. Then I'll have to untie her to take off her shirt."

Willy obeyed, and in moments her bare butt was resting on the cold granite. Solly untied her hands, and, although she knew there was no path to safety yet, she felt less helpless, as if she were moving to some control over her fate. Solly clutched her arm, digging his fingernails into her flesh, and yanked her off the ground. She stood trying to maintain her balance as jolts of pain ran down her lower left leg. She could bend her knee only a bit because of the blow from what she assumed was his booted foot.

He clutched her shirt front and tore it open, ripping off the buttons. She wore a man's undershirt underneath, and he tore that off next, exposing her breasts.

"I got bigger bubs than you, babe." His fingers pinched her nipple and twisted.

"Nice rosebuds, though." He grinned, displaying wolf-like teeth, until she spit in his face. He slapped her viciously and she staggered and stumbled backward, landing on the rock again.

"Willy, get the broad off her ass and follow me to the coop."

She was still reeling and only half aware as Willy guided her to the cave. She heard the creak of the hinges as the gate opened, and she felt Solly jerk her from Willy's grip before he shoved her through the opening, where once again her body collapsed, and her head crashed against unyielding stone.

Chapter 32

THE RAPID CITY OUTFIT

BOSS BULLOCK LOOKED with disdain at his older brother, who was dripping blood all over the new couch. The big boob had been his cross to bear for as long as he could remember, and although Boss felt nothing for Bull, the pull of blood still counted, and he could not abandon him—not yet, anyway.

Taking Bull to the hospital was unthinkable—too risky. Darkness was not far away, and Kathleen Connolly's disappearance would be discovered soon, if it had not been already. It seemed likely that no one else would be aware that one of the abductors suffered an injury, but that could not be taken for granted. And a mess like Bull's hand would not go unnoticed.

He decided that his only option was to ring up Doc Kerrigan. He had been a competent surgeon when he wasn't smoked. The drunken sot had lost his medical license, but he still earned booze money providing discreet medical services for folks who had reason to avoid the customary sources. He also had a reputation for being the best horse doctor in the county. He ought to be more than good enough for Bull.

Clarence Kerrigan, M.D. arrived in his 1918 Model T less than a half hour after Boss spoke to him. He smelled like stale rotgut, but Boss judged he was close to sober and showed him into the parlor, where Bull still moaned in agony. Kerrigan, a short man on the brink of obesity, had seen fifty-five years but looked seventy-five as he limped into the room. He stood above Bull, who stared up with glazed eyes.

"Hold up your paw," Kerrigan ordered.

Bull weakly lifted his injured hand.

"Good God, man, you stick your hand in a meat grinder? Where's your pinky finger?"

Boss intervened. "Doc, no questions. We called you to patch him up. Get to it."

"He ought to go to the hospital."

"He can't. Now do what you've got to do."

"Take him out to the kitchen table so I can get a better look."

The doctor removed his coat and dropped it on a chair before he carried his scuffed, dirty black bag to the kitchen. Boss helped his brother to his feet, and with his brother's assistance, Bull staggered to the kitchen and sunk down in a chair by the wooden table.

"Do you have a table cloth to put on this?" the doctor asked.

Boss obliged. "Can you knock him out?"

"That's why I said he should go to the hospital. I don't carry chloroform or anesthetics." He stretched Bull's arm out on the table. "Hardly know where to start."

"Listen, you damn quack." Bull stammered between sobs. "Start fixing me, or your brains are going to get splattered on the floor."

The doctor shrugged. "Very well. Claud, do you have any whiskey on the premises, perchance?"

Boss retrieved a whiskey bottle, and when he returned, Kerrigan had several scalpels, curved needles, and suture containers spread out on the table. He handed the physician the bottle. The doctor removed the cork and took a swig of the contents. And then another. And another. Finally, he set the bottle down.

"What in the hell are you doing?" Boss asked. "I thought that was for Bull."

"No. Find him a stick to bite on."

"Are you serious? That sounds like something out of a cowboy movie."

"As a matter of fact, that's where I learned the technique."

Boss looked at Kerrigan incredulously. Was the man joking? He didn't seem to be. He searched the cabinet drawers and found a wooden-handled spatula and gave it to Bull. "Your anesthetic."

"I'm supposed to bite on this?"

"That's what the doctor ordered. Stick it up your ass, if it will help." Boss was getting fed up with the process and was about to tear into the doctor when he saw that Kerrigan was twisting a tourniquet on his brother's arm—the wrong one.

"Doc, what in the hell are you doing. The right arm, not the left."

"Oh, yes. I noticed there wasn't much blood there."

He switched arms, and as near as Boss could tell the blood flow shut down significantly

Kerrigan plucked the whiskey bottle from the table and took another swallow. "One more," he said. "Blood makes me a little woozy."

Boss decided the situation could not get more bizarre. "What do you want me to do, Doc?"

"I want you to hold that arm steady like your life depended on it. I'm going to shoot some stuff near the worst of the wounds, but it's still going to hurt like blazes when I go to work, especially when I trim some bone. Before I start cutting, get me a pan of water and some clean rags."

Once Kerrigan had all his supplies laid out on the table and within reach, Boss pulled up a chair next to Bull and locked his hands on his brother's wrist. "Start chewing wood, big brother," he admonished.

He watched while the physician commenced injecting something into the untorn flesh about the wounds on his brother's hand. Then the doctor took a scalpel and began digging into the stump left by the departed finger. Bull struggled, trying to pull his hand free, and, for a moment, Boss almost surrendered and released his grip. Then the spatula dropped from Bull's mouth and he screamed like a howling wolf before he passed out and his head dropped on the table.

"That should help," the doctor said, and continued working.

The surgery and the stitching took the better part of two hours and an empty whiskey bottle, but Boss was amazed at the deftness of Kerrigan's fingers, as he sliced and stitched and eventually pieced the raw flesh together into something that resembled a hand. Bull regained consciousness intermittently during the surgery, but he drifted away again after a few minutes torture.

When he finished the procedure, Kerrigan rinsed off his instruments in the cold water offered by the kitchen spigot and packed his bag.

"What do you think, Doc?"

"Get him to bed. Get a good batch of aspirin at the apothecary. Get some salve, too. Tell them you want something for healing wounds, maybe something with honey in it . . . or just plain honey. Give him plenty of aspirin and lots of whiskey. He can drink it and rub it on the wounds. He'll likely live, unless he gets infection or hydrophobia from whatever tried to eat him. You owe me a double sawbuck for this."

Boss pulled out his wallet. "Doc, I'm going to give you ten sawbucks for this. That stitches your lips."

"A hundred bucks seals them for eternity."

"They'll be sealed for eternity, if word gets out about this. Understand?"

"I understand perfectly, sir."

After Kerrigan departed, Boss helped his brother back to the couch, where he collapsed and faded away again. Boss did not know if he was sleeping or had just passed out. He didn't care. He was pondering now whether he should have killed the good doctor.

Chapter 33

TREY

THE PRESIDENT HAD instructed the Secret Service to give me whatever I requested. Before leaving for Rapid City, I had asked Agent Starling if he could have one of his men find a good saddle horse and a pack animal from the lodge stables. I also asked that they put together provisions for several days. I did not explain why I wanted this done, and I knew it irked Starling not to be told. Fact was, the plan was still foggy in my own mind, but I would have it figured out when I returned early afternoon.

I was in town now to meet with Bing Compton. I intended to put Bing in charge of coordinating the city investigation, while I embarked on my own search for Kate. I had hoped to meet Gramps at the railroad depot, but it appeared I would not finish my Rapid City business in time. Starling had assigned Frank Caputo to the task as my back-up, regardless, and the agent would drive Gramps to the State Game Lodge, where I could meet up briefly with my grandfather before embarking on my search.

When I arrived at the sheriff's office, I found the atmosphere intense and harried in contrast to its usual laid-back tempo. I caught a glimpse of Bing beyond the clustered desks in the open work area. Bing looked up from his desk and waved me back to his office, which consisted of movable partitions fashioned, it appeared to me, from gunnysacks and a few boards that separated Bing's desk from his neighbors. He at least had the privacy afforded by a wall and exterior window to his back.

As I weaved through the narrow trail between the randomly-placed office furnishings, Bing stood and stepped out to greet me with a bone-crushing handshake, which I had decided must be a South Dakota sport. I returned my best grip, conceding I still needed practice before I took on Owen Connolly again.

"Good morning, Bing. I'm a few minutes late. I stopped at the hospital to check on Gabe."

"How's he coming?" He gestured for me to take the straight back chair next to his desk, and we both sat down.

"He's regained consciousness, but the docs keep him pretty doped up. I saw him for a few minutes, but he wasn't talking any sense. Carrie was there, and she says his outlook improves every time she talks to the doctors, so she's confident he's going to make it. His wife and kids should be here sometime tomorrow. Hopefully, that will boost his spirits."

"I hope so. From all you've said, he's a good man."

"The best. And we could use his help now. Have you heard anything that might give us a lead?"

"Not yet. I had another deputy hand-deliver messages to all the physicians in the city about the man with the missing finger. We're calling physicians in surrounding communities like Hot Springs and Custer and Hill City. Seems to me a man in that shape has got to show up at a doctor's office or hospital . . . and soon."

"Unless he's dead."

"Dog bite shouldn't have killed him."

"His friends might have seen him as disposable evidence."

"Hadn't thought of that."

"Have you talked to your bartender friend?"

"Yep. Ollie's on board. I hope you got more of those double sawbucks."

"I do. Uncle Sam provided me with two hundred dollars for 'evidence costs,' the BI calls it. Just be damn sure we get our money's worth for the dollars."

"I'm to check back with him late afternoon. He thought some of this smelled like a local gang he'd heard about."

"Tell me about this gang."

"Nothing to tell right now. He said he had a couple guys in the bar a few weeks back. They were half-sozzled when they got there, Ollie said, assuring me he didn't sell alcoholic spirits. Of course, he's a lying bastard. He doesn't make a living selling soda pop. Anyway, they got to bragging they were a part of the Rapid City Outfit. They sold women they said. That's as far as they went. Ollie said they weren't smooth and slippery enough to be pimps, so he didn't know what the hell they were talking about and didn't care. They weren't regulars. One was a big, rough-spoken guy he'd seen around town, but he didn't know his name. The other fellow didn't look and sound like he came from around here."

"People from the Black Hills look and talk different?"

"I can't explain, but especially in small towns, we can tell a stranger from a local just by the way he looks and talks. Maybe he just sets his hat on his head a certain way or doesn't drop enough 'Gs' or something. Talks through his nose. Hundreds of telltale signs."

"I won't argue the point. I can pick up a deep Southern accent or a Bostonian on occasion, but it takes something obvious for me to identify somebody that doesn't belong someplace."

"Anyhow, Ollie's asking around. He told me to drop by later this afternoon and he'd try to have something for me."

"I'm leaving it to you to follow up in town. I'm going to saddle a horse and see if I can find where they took her."

"That's worse than a needle in the haystack, unless you got an idea."

"I told you about the Oglala girl I interviewed and took into protective custody, so to speak."

"Yeah. You said she was held at a place called the chick coop. You think that's where they got Kate?"

"If she's alive, they're holding her someplace, and that seems a likely spot."

"But you don't know where it's at."

"That's where I need some help from you. Ever heard of Steeple Rock?"

Bing pulled open his top desk drawer and fished out a folded, parchment-like sheet of paper. He laid it on his desk, unfolded the paper, and spread it out. I recognized it as a map of the Black Hills area, probably something printed for hikers and tourists. It appeared to have undergone a few years of heavy usage. "It doesn't have all the tourist traps on it, but you're not on vacation."

"No," I said, "but I hope you've got something interesting to show me."

He picked up a pencil and circled where Rapid City, the State Game Lodge, Custer, Hot Springs, and the Shamrock Ranch were located. "Steeple Rock is about here." He marked an 'X' some distance north of the lodge. "Only locals know about it. My pop and me hunt up that way a lot. It's a big old pointy rock atop a hill, and it goes almost to the clouds. Some say it's a lost child of the Needles, formations made up of a bunch of similar rocks along the highway northeast of the lodge. It's rough country back in there. Tough as hell to make a road to it, so it just sits there by its lonesome. But it's a breathtaking sight. It's also about four to five miles due west from the Shamrock home place, I'd say."

"It looks like the lodge is a natural starting place. I shouldn't have to haul the horses anyplace. I can just saddle up and go."

"That's true enough. But take this map and a compass. You won't have trouble finding Steeple Rock. You'll know it when you see it, I guarantee. But do you know where you're going when you get there?"

"Northwest."

"That covers a lot of territory. You'll be on the back side of the Needles. That country's all owned by the devil. Trails twist all over hell, steep slopes. There's a creek that zigzags downslope from that way. There's some flat along the banks that eases a horseback ride some. I trapped that country one winter. I ought to be going with you."

"I'd like that, but I need somebody I can count on to work this end."

"I'm sure the sheriff would let me cut loose another deputy to go with you."

"No. Thanks, but I'll be fine." As the agent-in-charge, I did not wish to confess I barely knew what I was doing or where I was going. Pretty much the story of my life.

Bing and I theorized for another half hour, and then, at his suggestion, I joined him at the White Castle for an early lunch. I should not have been surprised to find that Carrie was working her shift since she had been wearing her white uniform when I saw her at the hospital. Of course, Bing knew precisely which table placed us in her service area. From the way they looked at each other, it was obvious their relationship had progressed quickly since that night at the hospital. I could not help but cheer for them.

"You and Carrie seem to be getting along well," I said, as we wolfed down our hamburgers.

"Yeah. I'm nuts about her."

"She doesn't seem to find you too offensive."

"I hope not. But I don't think we're going anyplace soon."

"Why is that?"

"She received a call from the Kansas City Art Institute. They're sending an application for a scholarship and want her to put together what they call a portfolio of her work to send with it. This just came from out of the blue. I don't suppose you know anything about this?"

"Me? No. This is the first I've heard about it." I didn't tell him I had talked to the first lady about Carrie's heroism and her artistic talent. I made no requests or suggestions. But the result was typical Grace Coolidge. If the school authorities determined Carrie had talent worthy of development but there were no available scholarship funds, the first lady would call one of her husband's supporters, and the scholarship would appear.

"Well," Bing said. "This would be her dream, and I would never get in the way of it. If we're meant to be, we'll find a way."

I had a feeling I was listening to a wise young man at that instant. Once again, Bing Compton was not the awkward kid I judged him to be at our first encounter. It made sense to me that whatever true love was, part of it had something to do with not stomping on each other's dreams.

Chapter 34

TREY

WHEN I DROVE into the parking area near the State Game Lodge shortly before one o'clock, I was surprised to see two saddled geldings and a packhorse loaded with gear and supplies staked out on the front lawn. I parked and hurried to the lodge, but I stopped on the veranda when Gramps stepped out the front door. I almost did not recognize him because he was dressed for the trail, attired in a well-worn buckskin shirt and faded blue jeans and cowboy boots. A low-crowned hat was pulled down on his forehead, and, of all things, like an old west gunslinger, he carried a holstered pistol hanging from a cartridge belt on his hip.

"Gramps," I said, embracing him briefly and awkwardly. "Where are you headed?"

"Wherever you are going . . . if you will permit me."

"That's why there's an extra saddled horse?"

"Yes. President Coolidge said you were embarking on a search for the young lady. I came up here to spend some time with you, and I asked the president if he had any objection to my joining you. He thought it was an excellent idea and urged me to do so. I selected the horses and helped with packing the gear and supplies. I will stay out of your way and will try not to offer unsolicited advice. I'm a bit rusty, but I have some tracking experience, as you know. You've got veto power. If you say no, I'll spend some time with the president and relax until you return."

I could not envision my grandfather relaxing. He probably could not define the word. Gram Skye had told me once that Gramps's life was always one adventure after another, although many of his quests dwelt in his own head. She understood because she saw life that way, too. She and Gramps were soulmates, she said, and their relationship was an easy one that had never been challenged over the years. They were best friends, she insisted, and each always had the other's back. I was a bit envious when I thought about that. Their bond was something to aspire to, but I doubted few couples attained it.

So, Gramps was here now for another adventure. Who was I to deny him? And he did have experience that might be useful, even though it reached back to his frontier days as a young Army scout. I swallowed my pride. "Gramps, I would be grateful for your help and company." I plucked Bing's map from my jacket pocket and handed it to Gramps. "Look this over while I'm changing. I'll be ready to ride in twenty minutes."

Two hours later, we reined in our horses at the base of Steeple Rock. "Well," I said, "this is our starting place, and I'm relying on a frightened girl's memory. It's a longshot, but this is the best I can come up with."

"From what you told me," Gramps said, "the young lady had a remarkable memory and a bucketful of grit. I'll bet Cleo and Skye are fast friends by now and that when I get home one of the spare rooms is occupied by another orphaned calf again."

I had not thought about it much before, but Gram Skye and Gramps had always had other folks sharing their house: Sioux, whites, Negroes, and mixed bloods of one sort or another, and mostly children. Uncle Jake, a full-blood Brule Sioux, had been the first, Dad told me once, and my grandparents had adopted him. But Dad was their only blood child. I just always took for granted that long-term guests lived in the extra rooms, and I remember dozens of strangers, many calling my grandparents "mom" or "dad," showing up holidays and throughout the year. It struck me then that family is more than blood ties; it's about special connections. Why was I only now becoming aware what unique people Gram Skye and Gramps were? Something else to think about in quieter moments. I forced myself to focus on my mission.

I said, "If Cleo was right, the chick coop is northwest of here, but we're still tossing darts at a bullseye we can't see. Bing said the only way we'd make time in that direction is to follow that creek bottom." I pointed downslope to the winding ribbon of water that raced from the mountains and tumbled over the rocky creek bed on the way to the valley below.

"Makes sense. Lead the way. I'll follow with the packhorse."

The steep trail to the creek bottom forced us to dismount and lead the horses at several places, and I found myself getting impatient over the loss of time. Gramps seemed unperturbed, however, so I kept my complaints to myself. By the time we reached the creek, I figured we had no more than an hour of daylight. We paused to allow the horses to drink, and Gramps reached into his saddlebags and removed a pair of field glasses.

"I talked that grumpy Secret Service chief out of these," Gramps explained.

"Edmund Starling. He knows what he's doing, but I don't think guys or gals would invite him out to make whoopie. He wouldn't know a good time if it hit him between the eyes."

"On occasion your grandmother has accused me of that. But I have been known to surprise her." He smiled and pressed the binoculars to his eyes, obviously roaming the craggy peaks to the north and west.

After some moments, Gramps passed the binoculars to me. "Take a look. I don't know how anybody would access those peaks to the west. On the other hand, as you move more toward the north, there seem to be some stair-step plateaus along the mountainsides, and some of the surface is pockmarked with holes, like there might have been mining efforts some years back."

"Which might have left some hollow spots for carving out a chick coop." I studied the dark mountains which had given the Black Hills its name. I could see what Gramps was talking about, but I would not have recognized what I was seeing if he had not pointed it out. "I guess that narrows the search some."

"Yes, but we're still talking thousands of acres of very rugged terrain."

We mounted our horses and rode upstream until shortly before sundown. Darkness would render any further effort hopeless, so we found a little clearing among clusters of aspen and birch trees to set up camp. A scattering of bur oak nearby offered dead branches for a good fire. Then I had second thoughts. Did we want a fire that might send a signal of our presence to Kate's jailers?

Gramps was stripping the mare packhorse of her load, and I noticed he kept tossing his head toward the mountains as if he saw something there.

"Do you see something up there, Gramps?"

"No. Just looking. We need to keep our eye out for a campfire up there."

"They might have their eyes open for the same thing. I suppose we'd better forget about a fire tonight and settle for cold beans."

"Unless we want them to see us."

"Why would we want them to see us?"

"They would have no reason to suspect anyone would be looking for them up this way. They wouldn't suspect the law had talked to anyone who could lead them to the chick coop. And, if their hideout location were known, why would anybody come in from this direction? But they might be curious enough to send somebody down to take a gander. He'd just see a couple of cowboys out hunting or trapping. Of course, that pea shooter you've got holstered on your belt isn't anything a self-respecting cowboy would carry."

I nodded at the Army Colt Gramps had probably been carrying since the 1870s. "I guarantee my pistol shoots. I'll bet that antique would blow up in your face if you squeezed the trigger."

"I hope I don't have to win that bet, grandson."

We built a shimmering, hot oak fire that was big to enough to accommodate an Army troop. I was delighted to learn I had brought along a personal chef. I grained and staked out the horses in a blanket of grass that appeared untouched by deer, and when I returned Gramps was simmering beans mixed with chopped smoked sausage in the iron skillet. Coffee brewed in a pot on a nest of coals that had been raked off from the fire, and a small Dutch oven, the lid covered with more coals, perched nearby and sent forth a redolence that pushed me to the brink of starvation.

"Is it polite to ask the cook what's baking?" I asked.

"No. But your grandma always struggled with your manners. Since we're not exactly in polite society, I'll answer the question. Apple cobbler. My specialty. I prefer fresh apples, but I had to make do with the canned variety."

"We're eating a little high on the hog for men on a life and death search, aren't we?"

"And how much further along would we be on this search if we were sharing a can of cold beans and stale crackers tonight?"

"Not complaining. I probably would have ridden out with no more than a Butterfinger candy bar in my saddle bags." In fact, I did have a few Butterfingers secreted with my personal belongings, and the verdict was out yet on whether they were subject to sharing. I was addicted to the bar produced by the Curtiss Company that had been put on the market a few years earlier. Second place was the company's Baby Ruth, named for former President Grover Cleveland's daughter, not the New York Yankee slugger, Babe, as most folks thought. I am a trivia aficionado and am always digging up such nuggets of worthless information.

Gramps said, "I've missed some meals in my day but never on purpose. We need fuel to do our job, just like the old Model T. I always travel prepared for my next meal. The Boy Scouts stole their 'be prepared' motto from me."

I had to admit that so far Gramps had seemed to anticipate everything we might need, and I was enjoying his company in a way I had not since Dad was killed. If it had not been for the gravity of our mission, we might have been sharing a fishing or hunting trip together.

Supper tasted as good as it smelled, and I ate the hot apple chunks lying in a lightly browned biscuit bed until I was stuffed. We didn't have any leftovers to carry with us or bury. I handled the clean-up, figuring that was the least I could do, while Gramps fashioned a lean-to shelter from a canvas tarp that he had brought with him. The two wool sleeping bags he tossed under the tarp would be welcome tonight because, despite the warm July day, a chill was settling on the mountains. I hoped Kate was warm wherever she was. Most of all, I hoped she was alive. She had to be.

Gramps built up the fire, and we sat near the dancing flames facing each other. I shifted from time to time, trying to dodge the smoke that seemed uncanny in following my movements. We were silent for some minutes. A chorus of cicadas provided background music, a prelude to the solo that suddenly burst forth from the cliffs upstream. A coyote's mournful howl. A few barks and then another series of howling before the barking and yipping of what sounded like a pack drowned out the soloist.

Gramps spoke softly. "If your Grandma Skye were here, she would say the coyotes are sending a message."

"You don't buy into that?"

"Call me agnostic. I believe in provable facts. But I don't think anything's impossible. That coyote could be telling us that Kate is fine and just keep following the trail, and we'll find her and bring her home safe. Or he could be warning us there is danger ahead and to get the hell out of here. Whether it's a good ending or a bad ending, the coyote gets credit for his clairvoyance either way."

I decided this was a chance to scratch an itch. How did Gramps end up here in the middle of the mountains with me? What was he doing here anyway? "Gramps, President Coolidge told me you were coming to the Black Hills to talk to me about something."

"Well, that's true enough, but I didn't know about Kate when I left home. I don't think this is a good time."

I flared. "Gramps, I don't like being toyed with. If it was important enough to bring you all this way, I think it's time for you to spit it out. Otherwise, tomorrow morning, I'd just as soon you saddled up and headed back to the lodge and caught your train back to Wyoming."

He looked at me, tilted his head to one side and squinted an eye. "Damn, it's good to see you get pissed enough to speak your mind. You've been holding too much in for too many years. You are right. It appears like I'm teasing you with something, but I didn't intend it that way."

He took the coffee pot from the red-hot coals and filled his tin cup. "I never thought I'd need to talk to you about this. There was no point. Then you meet this young woman. Even then, I didn't see any reason. But your Grandma says there's something between the two of you . . . or will be. Damn coyote told her that, I guess, when we came to visit. Anyway, she said you need to know."

"Gramps, get to it. Know what?"

"It has to do with Deuce and the day he died."

Chapter 35

TREY

"SO, THIS IS about Dad?" I asked.

"And a lady by the name of Coleen Connolly."

"Kate's mom? She and Dad died the same day in France."

"Yes, they did. They also died at the same place and likely within minutes of each other."

"This is an unbelievable coincidence. How do you know all this?"

"As you know, I served some months as interim U.S. Senator for Wyoming. This was in the early days of the Harding-Coolidge administration. I had never been satisfied with the reports we received about your father's death. No details about how he died or exactly where. Killed in action. That was the extent of it. I'm certain I'm not the only father . . . or mother . . . who finds himself dissatisfied with the information furnished by the Army. I became obsessed by it, and my appointment to the Senate opened the opportunity for me to get the information I wanted."

"You twisted arms?"

"Yes, with the assistance of then Vice-President Coolidge. That's when our friendship was formed. And several years later when he lost his younger son, also named Calvin, our shared losses seemed to tighten the bonds. But I digress. The War Department released your father's complete file, which included the names of some persons I was able to interview to procure more information. I finally reconstructed the story of your father's last days."

I struggled to contain myself. Gramps was telling his story with a lawyer's deliberation. I would have settled for a two-minute summary, or I thought so at the time anyway.

Gramps continued. "As near as I can determine, your father met Coleen Connolly in a makeshift army hospital in Paris, where she served as a captain in the Army Nurse Corps. He had been admitted there with a shrapnel wound on his forehead. It was not serious, but it earned him a second Purple Heart and a week's medical leave in Paris. I do not know the details and would not care to know, but during this time Deuce and Coleen, according to several friends and comrades of each, fell into a torrid and intimate affair. It was not casual. They were in love."

My stomach churned, threatening to toss up my cobbler. "But Dad was married. He had me. And Kate's mother was, too." I was, of course, stating the obvious.

"This was in mid-June, and Deuce's 1st Division did not see any action for the next month, and the division was encamped near Paris. It appears Deuce and Coleen were together whenever they both had passes at the same time. Coleen had even rented a room where they could rendezvous."

"The bastard. The sick bastard. Did Mom ever learn about this?"

"I think not. Not from me. What purpose would it serve? I guess now you will have to decide if she ever knows."

I felt the weight of a burden I did not want to carry. "I don't know if I want to hear any more of this."

"But you must. Pandora's box has been opened. But there is something I have reminded myself of many times. Yes, there is right, and there is wrong, but there is a good amount of gray in between. We cannot know what private hells any person endures. I loved my son not one iota less for what, on its face, seemed to be a rather tawdry segment of his life in Paris."

"You are excusing him."

"No. Excusing and accepting are very different things. Your father would have been the last man to excuse his actions."

"Gramps, I don't need more philosophy to ponder. Tell me the rest."

"The 1st Division, under French command of all things, joined the 2nd Division and a French Moroccan Division and five French divisions in what was called the Aisne-Marne offensive to halt the Germans on their march to occupy Paris. It was successful, if you do not count ten thousand American casualties. On the third day of August, Major Deuce Ramsey and several hundred soldiers occupied a trench that blocked an unlikely access through rough terrain east of Paris. The Germans massed troops to assault that point for that reason, and your father's forces were quickly cut-off from reinforcements."

Gramps paused and poured another cup of coffee. He blew on it and took a sip. "A man my age shouldn't drink this stuff after supper. I'll have to get up to piss five times tonight."

"You were talking about the German attack."

"Yes. Your father was wounded the first day . . . a nasty bullet wound under his ribs, according to the reports. They lost half their troops that day, as they warded off one surge after another. The dead were starting to fill the trenches, and Deuce, as the senior officer, stumbled back and forth through the trench, shoring up the soldiers. A courier evidently got a message back to Paris, and somehow word of Deuce's injury got to Coleen. A friend said Coleen disappeared and went AWOL within minutes. It was learned soon after she had confiscated a wounded medic's uniform. Somehow, late on the afternoon of the fourth, Coleen, attired as an Army medic and lugging packs of medical supplies, showed up in the trench, identifying herself as Corporal Colin Connolly according to the account of a first sergeant who survived. She patched Deuce's wound as best she could and then went to work tending to the other wounded in the trenches."

"She must have been an incredible woman," I said, grudgingly.

"The next day, the Germans seemed to be wearing down, but Deuce's troops were outnumbered five to one by this time. The sergeant reported that the major did not want to die in a trench like some kind of a rat. As the German army mustered for another attack, Deuce rallied his remaining troops out of the trenches and, leading the charge, raced toward the enemy, his new medic only a step behind. The attack caught the Germans unaware and they took dozens of casualties before they regrouped and swarmed the American attackers. Your father took bullets in the chest and head that day, either of which could have killed him. His body was found beneath that of Coleen's, who had evidently taken innumerable bayonet stabs trying to shield him. An hour later, reinforcements arrived and routed the Hun. The next day the Aisne-Marne offensive ended."

I suddenly realized tears were streaming down my cheeks. Gramps had stunned me speechless with his tale. This was all too much to sort out in my mind.

Gramps must have sensed my discomfiture and continued. "Your father was awarded the Distinguished Service Cross posthumously for his valor. He was nominated for the Medal of Honor, but it appears that the other circumstances surrounding his death offered potential embarrassment to the military. Coleen's actions, for similar reasons, were swept under the rug, for officially no member of the Women's Nurse Corps ever served in a combat role. Major Ethan James Ramsey II and Captain Coleen Rose Connolly are buried in adjacent graves in the Aisne-Marne American Cemetery in France. I have no idea how that came to be. A silent tribute by a minor military bureaucrat, who somehow knew their story and saw this as a small way to bring justice to the dishonored? A friend with influence? We will never know. I am glad they are together."

"I'm glad you told me, Gramps. I just don't know what to make of it. I wonder what Kate knows?"

"From her conversation with Skye, I suspect she knows no more than you did."

"Her father dislikes me beyond reason. I'm guessing he knows something."

"The records are not public, but I arranged for them to be made available to family members who might request the information. He could have obtained access. I spoke with two of the nurses listed in the report. As I mentioned, one was a friend of Coleen's. The other, a younger woman, had previously been reprimanded by Coleen for repeated tardiness and disliked her superior officer intensely . . . referred to Coleen as a whore for her relationship with your father. If Owen Connolly spoke with her, it would not have enhanced his late wife's standing in his eyes."

"Well, I'm putting this all aside for now, Gramps. I may have more questions. All I want to do is find Kate."

I got up and crawled into my sleeping bag. I was certain after what Gramps had told me, I would not sleep, but I wasn't up to talking anymore. I didn't hear Gramps come to bed, though, and the next thing I knew I was blinded by shards of light from a brilliant sunrise creeping over the hills to the east. I sat up and saw that Gramps had the fire going, and I could smell biscuits baking in his Dutch oven and bacon cooking as it crackled in his skillet. The old man was starting to embarrass me just a bit with his ambition, but not so much so that I would not show up for breakfast.

After I stumbled into the trees and relieved my bladder, to put it delicately, I joined Gramps at the fire, which was more than welcome this brisk mountain morning. It was July for God's sake, and I could see my breath in the frosty air. I sat down, and Gramps handed me a steaming cup of coffee.

"I could get spoiled by this kind of service, Gramps."

"Can't spoil you more than you already are. Breakfast is about ready." Then he spoke in a near whisper. "Just keep staring at the fire, Trey. But be alert. Someone is watching us from the trees upstream, no more than a hundred feet away."

Chapter 36

KATE

KATE WOKE, CONFUSED and dizzy, her head throbbing with pain. She found herself wrapped in a filthy wool blanket. Her nakedness surprised her at first, and then she started to remember. Her eyes had opened to pitch blackness, but, as they adjusted she saw a starlit sky at the mouth of the cave, and she began to make out shadowy figures scattered around her, silent and watching.

She guessed it was up to her to start a conversation with her fellow residents of the chick coop. She lifted herself up on her elbow and slowly scooted into a sitting position, tugging the blanket about her shoulders. Tentatively, she traced her fingers over her face. The left side of her face was tender and puffy, and her eye was nearly swollen shut. There was a knot on the side of her forehead, which she decided must be the result of a collision with the stone floor when she was catapulted through the gate. She could not tell how much time had passed since then, but she could hear the murmur of men's voices beyond the entrance so she concluded she had not been unconscious too long, perhaps only minutes.

"My name is Kate. Thank you for the blanket."

A young woman, her body also shielded by a blanket, stepped forward and lowered herself to her knees in front of Kate. "I am Marta. I feared you might die, but I didn't know what to do. They gave us many blankets. They are dirty and have been used many times by others before us, but they are ample when the night chill arrives. We huddle together in the back of the tunnel to escape the winds, and at least we do not freeze. A blanket was all I could offer."

Kate guessed the young woman to be only a few years younger than herself. Slender and quite pretty. Intelligent, piercing eyes. She did not see surrender or defeat there, and Kate immediately tagged her as a potential ally. "How many are here?"

"Eight of us. I have heard the men talking of moving us soon, perhaps in two or three days. It doesn't seem they plan to kill us, but I feel we have not seen the worst. These are evil men from the place Christians call hell."

"We must escape before they move us. I heard them talking before they brought me here. They plan to capture two more young women and bring them here. I know something about what they do. You will all be taken to Chicago, where you will be sold to become prostitutes in bordellos."

"I will die first," Marta said without hesitation.

The young Sioux spoke with conviction, Kate thought. "And what about the others?"

"Four of the girls are so afraid, they will do whatever they are told by these pigs. They have been beaten and raped so many times, they have become obedient dogs, who follow their masters' commands. I do not understand, but the rest of us have not been raped, only kicked or struck by fists when we do not do as we are told."

"You are being saved to bring higher prices in Chicago. Your virginity will be determined there, and, if you are found chaste, you will be sold to special buyers."

"This is so strange." She shrugged and gave a wistful smile. "I would not qualify for sale to a special buyer, but it would please me to disappoint them."

Kate returned a conspiratorial smile. "I would disappoint them also. But I have reason to believe they will not take me to Chicago. If I do not escape, I will be dead. It is that simple. You said four of the girls will not likely be helpful. What about the others?"

Marta moved nearer and spoke so softly, Kate could barely hear her. "Raven and Olive will help, if I ask. They must be led, but they will be strong followers if they are given clear instructions. But Maybelle cannot be trusted. She will betray us to seek the favor of our jailers. There is a phrase that describes her kind . . . a bird."

"A stool-pigeon?" Kate whispered.

"Yes. A stool pigeon. Be careful what you say when she is near."

They both started at the rattling of the chain and padlock on the steel gate. A man Kate did not recognize spoke in a raspy voice. "Bluebird and Celia, you are going to the dance tonight." He chuckled. "Come with me, we've got company for you to greet."

Two of the girls standing near the wall stepped out and walked toward the gate. Kate could not make out their features, but she could see one was of stocky build, perhaps, a bit on the plump side. The other appeared thin as a walking skeleton. Both walked with their heads bowed.

After the gate was locked and the selectees had disappeared, Marta and Kate got up. While her head ached, the dizziness had abated, and Kate began to orient herself.

"Let me show you the accommodations," Marta said, steering her away from the others and moving deeper into the cave. "The squatty troll was Spud. Watch out for him. He is smarter than he looks. And twice as evil. He will mount both girls before the night is done. The others will get their turns, but Spud and Solly will fuss over who goes first. If I had been chosen, one or more would not live the night, and I would disappear into the mountains."

As they stood together, with their blankets pulled tight around their shoulders, Kate realized Marta was much taller than she, with broad shoulders and sinewy arms—statuesque, an artist might call her. It occurred to Kate that the young woman's apparent strength should be considered in any plan she might come up with. She had already decided she was not going to wait to see what fate had in store for her. She believed people were largely responsible for their own fates.

Kate was surprised to find that the cave narrowed as they went into its depths and that the walls and ceilings were shored-up with timbers. "It must have been the beginning of a mine shaft years ago," she said. "How far does it go?"

"Not far. It turns to our left here, and we sleep just past the turn. It appears they were digging a mine shaft and then one day just stopped. A path to nowhere. After twenty feet or so, it ends at a solid wall of stone. There is also a right turn that hits a dead end after no more than fifteen feet. If you cannot see it, you can smell it."

At that instant the stench struck Kate's nostrils. "The latrine?"

"There are no pots or buckets. You hold back for long as you are able, and then you release your bowels and bladder on the floor. I'm sorry, there is no delicate way to tell you this. Be careful where you step when nature calls."

Kate's urge to pee faded, and they turned back. "Do they feed you?"

"They leave three buckets of water every morning and replace them at night. At the same time, we are given a bag of stale bread or biscuits to divide. When the offering is small, some fight like squealing pigs for more than their shares. While they do that, I drink all the water I can. My father told me that a person can live without food for many days, but water is the first requirement of life."

"There can't be a well up here, so there must be a spring or creek nearby."

"Yes, I assumed that, and when I escape, I will follow that creek, and they will never catch me."

"When you escape? Not if?"

"When."

"I think we are going to be great friends."

As they approached the cave opening, a figure slipped from the shadows and stepped in front of them. "Now, ain't the two of you a pretty pair. Find a friend to share your blanket, Marta? I should warn you, Miss Bluenose, I been told Marta ain't choosy about a person's plumbing when it comes to the lustful side of life."

"Meet Maybelle Red Hawk," Marta said, her voice betraying her hostility.

Kate worried Marta was on the verge of flattening the horse-faced intruder.

Maybelle made little effort to cover her feminine attributes with her blanket, and Kate surmised men would find her body voluptuous, but she was not otherwise an attractive woman. "My pleasure, Maybelle. I've heard so many things about you, I look forward to getting better acquainted."

"Good things, I'm sure," Maybelle said sarcastically, glaring at Marta.

Neither Marta nor Kate replied.

Later, Kate joined the others in what she thought of as the sleeping chamber. There were extra blankets that were welcome in the cave, which tended to be on the cool side even without the chilly mountain night air. After initial awkwardness she wedged her blanket-shrouded form between her cellmates, so each might draw warmth from the others. She was glad to be buffered by Raven on one side and Marta on the other. She had firmed up an alliance with both. The petite Raven, who could not be more than fifteen years old, worshipped Marta and would likely follow her lead, even if it were dangerous to do so. An optimistic, adventurous girl, Kate worried that Raven did not truly appreciate the gravity of their situation, but that fact only solidified Kate's determination to protect her.

Olive was an unknown. She had nodded her assent to the conspiracy to escape, but she rarely spoke. She and Raven were about the same age and could nearly pass for twins. They had apparently been close friends before their capture, and Raven had an annoying tendency to render opinions on behalf of her friend. It was evidently a part of the dynamic of their relationship. Yet, Kate sensed Olive was attentive to every spoken word and harbored a keen intelligence she was not inclined to display.

Olive, not surprisingly, slept on the other side of Raven and had fallen asleep while her friend chattered gossip about their reservation friends. Marta had dropped instantly into sleep, but Kate's mind raced and resisted sleep in this uncomfortable and hostile place. She eventually surrendered to her exhaustion, but it was well after even Raven had ceased her conversation with herself.

Kate jolted awake when she heard stones clattering as someone came down the cave's corridor toward them. An iridescent glow from that area told her that sunrise had arrived. She relaxed when she saw that the disturbance was caused by the return of the two sober-faced Sioux girls who had spent the night with their keepers.

Later, Kate and Marta sat, leaning against the walls, on opposite sides of the cave entry when Willy and the guard named Henry, an older man with a whiskery face dotted with angry pock marks, showed up with water pails and a burlap sack containing stale bread loaves. Henry put down the two buckets he carried while he unlocked the gate. When the gate squeaked open, Willy stepped in and dumped the contents of the sack on the ground. He collected the empty buckets from the previous night. Kate noted that both men were armed with pistols, but during a period of several minutes, access would be slow and awkward.

Apparently, the men were confident that no one would be brave or foolish enough to attempt escape. She supposed part of the strategy of confiscating clothing was to render the captives vulnerable and dependent. She wondered where their clothes had been stashed. The girls who had spent the night with the men might know. She would have Raven make casual inquiry.

After the men left, she took Marta's advice and drank her fill of gritty water from the communal dipper that was deposited in one of the buckets. She plucked a few slices of bread from the crumbling loaf on the cave floor and returned to her spot on the side of cave. As she chewed the dry bread, she studied the gate, the barrier that closed her off from the outside world and freedom. She hadn't even been aware of the lithe form that had slipped in beside her until Olive spoke in a voice that barely rose above a whisper but was smooth as honey. "I can climb the gate and squeeze through the space at the top."

Kate turned her head and looked at the dark, serious eyes that met her own. Then she examined the gate again. At the top of the arched entrance, there appeared to be about a foot of space between the gate and the rock above. The gap would be no more than a foot and a half wide. Yes, the girl could probably squeeze through the space, but the bars were honed into wicked points at the top. One slip, and she could be impaled on the spikes. She looked at Olive again. She was a tiny, pixie-like girl. Probably wouldn't top the scales at a hundred pounds holding a five-pound sack of potatoes.

Kate asked, "What would you do if you got out, Olive?"

"Run. I am faster than the wind. Ask Raven."

"But where would you run to?"

"There seems to be a drop off to a canyon beyond where the guards are camping. There is almost certainly a creek or a stream there. I would follow it southeast until I came to a road, and I would find help."

"You are truly willing to try this?"

"I want to do it. I do not want these men to send me to Chicago."

"You would have to leave after dark. Does that frighten you?"

"Yes. But I will do it anyway."

The definition of bravery, Kate thought. "If you are going to do this, I think it must happen tonight. Let me speak with Marta and then we will talk again."

Chapter 37

BING

BING COMPTON STRODE into the Big Bison Tavern, walking past the saddled, stuffed buffalo bull that greeted customers just inside the front door. He assumed that the saddle was for customer photo opportunities, although the buffalo looked quite docile and bored—not to mention that his hide was patchy and shedding like he had a skin disease. He noted the bull had no testicles and wondered if that was a common taxidermy omission.

Ollie Wicker stood behind the bar, looking as bored as his buffalo friend. When he saw the deputy, he nodded, which Bing took as consent to join him. He ordered a Coca-Cola, which triggered a frown until he dropped a twenty on the bar. As a law enforcement officer, Bing wasn't about to buy an illegal beer. When he considered it, he thought it interesting there were so many taverns still operating openly with prohibition in force. Of course, the alcohol products were not listed on the wall menu, but it was open knowledge that booze could be acquired for a price at these places, and local law folks weren't that interested if things didn't get rowdy. There were only two customers engaged in serious conversation at a corner table, but the bartender still seemed jittery.

"The local guy's name is Bull Bullock," Wicker said, his voice sounding like it was filtered through radio static. "Has a brother called Boss. He's the ramrod of this so-called Rapid City Gang. Worst I've heard about them is they hire whores for the houses in Chicago and do some bootlegging for the speak-easies and other less respectable places. Doesn't seem like serious stuff. Sounds like a low-class bunch. I never done business with them. That's all for a double sawbuck."

"You have enough to make it worth that much?"

"You'll have to pay up front and then decide."

Bing surrendered another of Trey's twenty-dollar bills. "This better be worth it."

"Been doing some heavy thinking. You was asking if I could find somebody that got his hand chewed up by a dog."

"You found somebody?"

"No. But I'll bet your doctors and hospitals ain't turned up nobody."

"No, they haven't."

"Doc Kerrigan's got some booze money. Spreading it around places. Dropped some of it here. Of course, he didn't buy liquor here."

"Of course not. Isn't Kerrigan the guy who lost his medical license because of his drinking?"

"Yep. That doesn't mean he don't have select patients, folks who don't want to go through ordinary medical channels. And he does some vet work on occasion."

"Do you know if he worked on anybody with a mangled hand in the last few days?"

"Somebody paid him serious cash, so it's safe to say he worked on somebody, but I don't know who or what."

Bing shook his head. "I can't believe it sometimes. Booze is against the law, but a drunk can still get drunk easy enough. Practicing medicine without a license is illegal, but a doctor who's lost his license can treat patients. I don't like some laws, but folks can't just thumb their noses at the law."

"Bing, I bet you didn't know I was a college man."

"You graduated from college?"

"I didn't say that. I went two months and took an economics class. I learned a law there that overrules all other laws."

"What are you talking about?"

"The law of supply and demand. Politicians and the voters can pass all the laws they want, but they ain't going to cancel that one."

"You're too deep a thinker for me, Ollie. I'm going to track down Doc Kerrigan and have a chat."

Chapter 38

BING

BING RETURNED TO the sheriff's office and asked one of the clerks to track down an address for Dr. Clarence Kerrigan and to see what she could turn up in the public records on Boss and Bull Bullock. He asked Sheriff Johnson to assign another deputy to the case for backup. The sheriff grumbled a bit about personnel shortages, but when Bing mentioned he would hate to see the Bureau of Investigation get all the credit for solving the case, he gave in with feigned reluctance and put old Sam Piper on the investigation. Bing found Piper something of a curmudgeon, but if anybody started mixing it up with guns, the wiry, seventy-ish man would come in handy. Sam was taking on outlaws many years before the advent of the automobile, and he had not lost his touch with a gun. He still embarrassed all the youngsters at the department's firing range with his weapons proficiency.

Bing stopped at his desk to check messages. Nothing pertaining to the Connolly case, and nothing else mattered right now. The young, blonde clerk handed him several pages of notes and smiled. "I hope this helps," she said, and smiled again before turning away with a noticeable swing of her hips. He was flattered Bonnie apparently had a crush on him. He had planned to ask her out to dinner and a movie. But that was before Carrie.

He shuffled through the notes, which were perfectly organized. An address for Doc Kerrigan. There was also an address taken from property tax records for Claud Bullock. He owned a property just outside of town. No criminal record, so he was either an upstanding citizen or too slick to get caught. One Frederick Bullock aka Bull, on the other hand, had compiled an impressive collection of offenses, most related to drunkenness or assaults of one kind or another. In most instances he got off with fines, but he had served thirty days in county jail a few years back for beating a girlfriend to a pulp. Nice guy. He wondered if Claud was the Boss Bullock Ollie had mentioned. Odds were at least fifty-fifty he figured, since

Bonnie had turned up no other Bullocks in the county records.

First stop, he decided, was Doc Kerrigan's. He stepped over to Sam's desk, where he found the old-timer with his eyes closed and his head slumped forward with chin on chest. Napping, he guessed. Or dead. "Sam, I'm ready to go."

Piper looked up, rubbed his brush moustache with the back of one hand and reached for his ten-gallon hat with the other. He grunted with annoyance and got up and followed Bing out the door.

Kerrigan's house was little more than a run-down box less than six blocks from the courthouse. Bing parked the Model T, and he and Sam Piper walked up to the door, which was warped and badly splintered. Bing knocked. No answer. He tried again with the same result. "I'd guess he's out drinking or tending to one of his illegal patients," Bing said.

"You keep trying," Piper said. "I'll circle the house and see if I can see anything through the windows."

Bing tried the door several more times before he gave up. He turned to step off the porch when Sam sauntered around the corner of the house, his face expressionless.

"Let's go, Sam. Nobody home, or he's not answering. We'll call on Mr. Bullock and swing by here later."

"Might want to take a look inside."

"No warrant."

"Don't need one. There's a man sprawled on the kitchen floor. That's generally an invitation to go in."

Bing wheeled and opened the unlocked door. The kitchen, in what appeared to be a four-room house, was directly off the parlor. Bing entered cautiously and stopped when he saw the prone figure splayed face-up on the floor near a small table. He approached cautiously, not wanting to disturb the scene any more than necessary. He knelt and pressed his fingers to the man's neck, knowing the verdict the instant he touched the cold skin. Cause of death was obvious from the raw, red and purplish ring carved in the flesh around the man's neck.

"Garrote." Sam said. "Only seen that once . . . when I was working in New Orleans twenty-some years back. Mean way to die, I'd think. I'd take a bullet any day."

"Somebody decided to shut him up."

Bing stood up. "We'll go by the office and report to the sheriff. He'll want to claim jurisdiction over the scene and get the coroner here before the city police butt in. Then we'll pay a call on Claud Bullock."

Chapter 39

KATE

KATE WAS SURPRISED and relieved that the men had not summoned any of the girls for their pleasure this evening. It seemed unlikely they would do so now. It must be near midnight, and the camp had quieted. She assumed there was a guard posted someplace, but she doubted if more than one would be out. The captors did not appear unduly concerned about the security of their hideout.

She and Marta knelt not far from the gate, illuminated by moonglow she wished would succumb to cloud cover. Darkness would have been their ally this night. Olive slipped quietly between them.

"Raven will warn us with two owl hoots if anyone is coming this way from the rear," she said softly.

"Anyone" meant Maybelle. She had been called out late afternoon when the Oglala, George, had returned with a pale and sickly-looking Bull, whose hand was heavily bandaged. The big man still whined about his pain, but none of the others appeared to pay any attention to his misery.

Maybelle had returned with a smug look on her face, and Kate did not take that as a positive sign. Something was going on. She assumed Maybelle had been promised privileges or reward for helpful information, perhaps even freedom, which would never happen. Two sharp hoots came from behind. Marta was off her feet and headed toward the back of the cave like a rocket. Kate turned to see Maybelle walking toward them.

"What are you up to?" the woman demanded before she tumbled forward with Raven's arms anchored about her legs. No sooner did Maybelle land on the cave floor than Marta had the spy's head locked between her hands and was pounding it repeatedly like a sledge against the rough granite floor. Kate winced at the crunching sound that came with each strike. Finally, the pounding stopped and Marta returned, with Raven following close behind.

"Is she dead?" Kate asked, shivering at the brutality of the attack.

"I do not know," Marta said, "but she will be no more trouble this night."

They continued their move toward the gate. When they reached it, Kate's eyes followed the steel bars' upward thrust. She shuddered at the thought of Olive impaled upon the sharp spears. She peered through the bars and was relieved to find there appeared to be no sentry on the ledge outside. She hoped he was dozing by the fire at the campsite downslope. It had been quiet for nearly an hour until coyotes had begun howling and barking from somewhere above the coop a short time ago. She welcomed the racket since it might help muffle any noise from Olive's maneuvering on the gate.

"I am ready," came the meek voice of girl beside her.

"You do not have to do this," Kate whispered, "we will understand."

Olive stood, tugged her blanket from her shoulders, and stuffed it between the steel bars. Kate and Marta rose, and Kate linked her fingers into a stirrup for Olive's foot. Marta followed suit. Olive slipped her feet into the supports, and the two women boosted her from the ground. In a moment Kate felt the girl's weight disappear from her hand and looked up to see a naked Olive scaling the gate like a monkey. She held her breath when the girl reached the wicked spikes, but the skinny girl glided through the opening like a bird and easily and silently slid down the other side. She paused just long enough to give them a satisfied smile to acknowledge her victory, and then she picked up her blanket and disappeared into the night.

They stepped back into the depths of the cave, waiting for the guard to sound an alarm, but all they could hear was the coyote jamboree.

"They will never catch her," Raven said. "She can outrun the fastest jackrabbit."

Kate turned around and stepped over to where Marta had left Maybelle. She knelt beside the young Sioux woman and rolled her over. Her head and face were blood-drenched and swollen, her nose nearly flattened against her face. But her chest rose and fell, and her breathing seemed normal except for a wheezing sound that came from her nose. Kate was relieved Maybelle was alive. She did not want to be part of the killing of a fellow captive, even though she was an obvious traitor.

"We cannot leave her here," Kate said to the others. "They will see her. I do not know how we account for her when the guards check in the morning. Of course, we might have to explain Olive's absence as well."

Kate and Marta scooted Maybelle onto her blanket. Then, with Raven's help, they half-carried and half-drug the Sioux stool-pigeon to the shaft in the rear and dropped her with the other four sleeping captives.

Chapter 40

TREY

GRAMPS HAD TOLD me to keep staring at the fire, which is not easy to do casually when some guy might have a rifle trained on your back and a finger pressed tight against the trigger. My stomach won over fear, however, and I finally helped myself to a biscuit and a few slices of bacon. And then a second biscuit and a few more slices of bacon. There was still plenty for Gramps and, likely, another serving for me. Damned if he wasn't a handy old fart to have along, but I wasn't confident I hadn't already slipped into the second-in-command slot. Gram Skye always warned me that Gramps couldn't help himself when it came to taking charge of things, so she'd always found it easier to let him think he was most times.

He had slipped silently into the woods like a cat, and I understood why the Sioux had called him the Puma in his scouting days. It was creepy, sitting there by the fire in the dusky dawn, not knowing who was spying from up the creek and uncertain where Gramps had disappeared to. With my belly full, I was starting to get impatient and thinking of deserting my post when a melee broke out behind me. First, I heard a child's voice cut-off mid scream and Gramps's voice sounding like he was trying to calm somebody. I could not tell for certain, because he was speaking Lakota, a language which, fool that I was, I had spurned in my childhood days, learning only a useless phrase or two that Gram scrambled in with her English and French when it suited her. I got up to go help Gramps because from the racket in the brush and trees, I could not tell who was getting the best of the fracas.

By the time I stumbled my way up the rugged incline that ran along the creek, however, Gramps seemed to have the battle under control. He was on his way down, his hand locked on the forearm of a scrawny, half-naked Indian girl, who had a filthy blanket draped over her front in an unsuccessful effort to conceal her private parts. She was a dirty, gangly thing with a dark, oval face that would likely clean up to be quite pretty. I guessed she could be anywhere from thirteen to fifteen years old.

The girl shot me a look that said she would love to kill me if I came too near. I didn't know how she'd do it, but I respected her wishes and kept my distance. Gramps took her up next to the fire and set her down. She inched closer to the flames, and I realized she had to be half-frozen. I tossed on a few more logs.

"Trey, why don't you see if you can coax her to eat something? I'll find something for her to wear." Gramps headed for the gear stash.

I called after him. "Does she speak English?"

"Of course, she does. She was cussing me out in Lakota, so I gave her a dose of her own medicine."

I picked up Gramps's tin plate, since it was clean, and scooped some biscuits and bacon in it and passed it to the girl, whose anger seemed to have mellowed to mere suspicion. "Eat this while we talk."

She snugged the blanket tighter over her shoulders before accepting the plate. She didn't hesitate once she had the plate in her hands. She tore into the food like a starving hound. I waited and watched since it appeared she would finish her breakfast quickly. When she was down to a few remnants, I asked. "How do you happen to be here like this?"

She opened her mouth as if to speak, and then closed it. She seemed to be pondering her words.

I asked, "Do you know what the Bureau of Investigation is?"

She spoke slowly. "It is police, I think. From Washington."

"Close enough. My name is Trey Ramsey. The other man is my grandfather, Ethan Ramsey. I am a special agent for the Bureau of Investigation. We are looking for a young lady by the name of Kate Connolly, who was abducted by some bad men. We think other young women may be with her . . . probably Sioux women, like yourself. Would you know anything about this?"

"Yes. I know Kate. I am Olive. I saw her last night. She helped me escape."

Kate was alive. The relief that raced through me at that news was like nothing I had ever felt before. "Where is she?"

"A place the evil men call the chick coop."

Gramps returned with a denim shirt that appeared near the end of a long life. "If you will stand up, I'll improve your wardrobe a mite."

She stood, clutching her blanket tightly to her body. Gramps held the shirt up to her. "Stick out your arm." She obeyed, and, after he stretched a shirt sleeve along her arm, he pulled a folding knife out of his pocket, opened it and began slicing off the sleeves well above the shirt cuffs. When he had completed the alterations, he handed her the shirt. "Try this on. You can tie the rawhide around your waist for a belt if you like. We'll turn around and keep our backs to you until you tell us you have your new dress on."

"I can do that. You are a kind man."

Gramps had charmed the young lady quicker than you could blink. He was one smooth old weasel.

"I am dressed," Olive said.

We turned around and found the girl standing there with the hint of a shy smile on her face. She swam in the shirt, and it dropped almost to her knees, the rawhide belt cinching it snuggly to her slim waist. She had a winsome, elfin quality about her that made it difficult to imagine how anyone would wish to bring harm to her.

I turned to Gramps and said, "Her name is Olive, and she escaped from the chick coop last night. Kate is alive."

Olive interjected, her voice soft and calm, "I think they are in terrible danger. There were six men in the camp when I escaped. They are worried about something, and Kate believes they may be changing plans."

"How long did it take you to get this far?" I asked.

"I do not know exactly, but I did not leave until most of the men were sleeping. I would guess it took me five hours. But it was all downhill through this canyon."

"We're not making any time with the horses," Gramps said. "Best to leave them behind."

"Olive," I asked. "Do you know where the State Game Lodge is?"

"When I find a road. Kate told me where I should go when I find Steeple Rock."

"Gramps, what would you think about having Olive continue on to the game lodge? She can ride one of the horses most of the trek and lead the others. We can go ahead on foot. Do you think you can handle a six or seven hour walk up this mountain?" He did not reply, but the look he shot me would have melted iron.

I asked Olive about landmarks on the trail that would help us find where Kate and the young Sioux women were held, and she rattled off information like a travel guide. Her observations were remarkable given she had made her trek down in the dark. Several times on this assignment I had encountered bright, intelligent Indian girls whose spirits had not yet been broken, and I suddenly appreciated the importance of Gram's life work of building educational and financial opportunities outside the reservation world for her Sioux cousins. I vowed to see if Gram could make a place for this shy girl at the Lame Buffalo School.

I asked her, "Can you take the horses and the gear and supplies we don't need with you and continue your journey to the game lodge?"

"Yes, of course. That was my plan before I met you."

"When you arrive, you will be stopped by men who are Secret Service agents protecting the president. Tell them that Trey sent you and that you must speak with Mr. Starling. Tell him about the chick coop and where you met up with us and that he should talk to Bing, the deputy sheriff, about locating the coop. I know you were hooded during the drive to the chick coop but tell them anything you remember that might help locate the place. Also . . . and this is important . . . when we release the young women, we will build a fire that sends up smoke that can be seen for miles. They should head for the smoke."

"I can do this."

"Good. Then let's get you saddled up."

Chapter 41

TREY

TO SAY THAT the climb was rugged was an understatement. The creek twisted like a slithering snake, and the slabs of granite and loose rock footings worsened as we moved upward. The oak, aspen and birch started to give way to towering ponderosa pine and dense undergrowth of smaller progeny and low-lying shrubs. We could see places where Olive had passed or, I should say, Gramps did. He often pointed out places where the Oglala girl had stepped or where she had ridden a loose-rock slide on her butt. I nodded my head in agreement or grunted appropriately, but I rarely saw.

Worse, he made me eat my condescending words with castor oil. He clambered up the rocks like a damned mountain goat, leaving me huffing on the trail behind him. My own ego warred with his stamina, and I only called for rest breaks when I felt I was on the edge of death. We finally took time for lunch, which consisted of water and candy bars. I had carried a leather bag stuffed with assorted bars on my belt, and I snatched the sole Butterfinger before offering the bars to Gramps. He took two Hershey bars, and I had no doubt they had a purpose beyond mere taste.

We sat with our backs leaning against boulders that were scattered in a little clearing off the side of the trail. The sound of the creek's rush nearby made me drowsy, coaxing my focus from our mission. "How far do you think we've come, Gramps?" I asked.

"I think we're less than an hour from the so-called chick coop."

"Really?"

"We've made good time. I'm sorry. I doubted you could move this fast."

I pondered whether his words were compliment or insult. Either way, I guessed he was entitled to a dig.

We each carried our pistols and Winchesters. In addition, Gramps had a nasty-looking sheath knife on his hip and a double-barreled shotgun slung over his back—not much of a long-range weapon, but it would carve out space close-in.

"Is that wicked tool on your belt a Bowie knife?" I asked.

"Yep. I've had it since before I met your Grandma."

"Ever killed anything with it?"

"Three men. Cut up a few others."

I had been joking. I really didn't know this man.

Then he tried to reassure me. "Never killed anybody that didn't deserve it. And it's been a good while. I haven't killed anybody in this century with anything, gun or knife."

"I hope you don't break that record today, but we could have six men to deal with up there."

"I've been thinking about that. It will take a little longer, but I wonder if we should circle around and try to get the high ground on them. If they don't throw their guns down, we could pick off a few of them."

"I'm worried about them holding Kate or some of the others hostage. What if they threaten to kill some of the captives if we don't back off?"

Gramps was silent about that one for a bit. "If I could get in front of the gate with my shotgun, I could separate them from the young women. I could probably blast the lock so they could make a run for it if they needed."

"That's high risk. I'm the BI agent. I claim that job if it comes down to that."

"We've got to see the layout for ourselves before we decide how to approach the attack."

Two gun blasts from upstream echoed through the canyon. "I think our strategies have just been shot to hell," I said. "I just hope they haven't started executions."

Chapter 42

THE RAPID CITY GANG

AFTER SPEAKING WITH George Many Knives that afternoon, Claud Bullock decided he had made a misjudgment. Taking the Connolly girl had been a huge mistake. George said the word from a connection he had in the sheriff's office was that the Bureau of Investigation was taking over the case. The unsuccessful attempt to kill the colored agent should have been taken as a warning the end of his enterprises was near. He had just had a sense of invincibility that made him figure he could weather any storm.

Bull's getting chewed up by that cur had started the landslide. His brother was a walking piece of evidence, and Doc Kerrigan had been a weak link that could tie everything to himself. Boss had resolved that problem as soon as George left to deliver instructions to the chick coop. Boss had gone immediately to Kerrigan's residence. It had been risky because it was still daylight at the time, but he had parked several blocks away and walked to Kerrigan's pitiful excuse for a house. Thankfully, the house had been unlocked—folks in places like South Dakota rarely locked their homes—and he had just walked in.

He was prepared to put a bullet in the old coot's head, but he preferred to avoid the noise. Boss had taken as a positive omen that the outlaw doctor was at his kitchen table, a whiskey bottle within his reach and his head plopped on the surface. Boss had just slipped the garrote out of his jacket pocket, placed the wire gently around the man's neck, and started twisting. Doc woke for just an instant, his eyes bulging and his mouth sucking for air that was cut off. He died quickly without much fuss. Boss was an expert with the instrument, one trick he had brought back from Chicago. He didn't like blood much and usually preferred others do his killing, but this had been fun and a nice opportunity to hone his skills.

Boss had long been prepared for a quick disappearing act, and he was packing his bags now with just that in mind. He maintained bank accounts in Nebraska, Wyoming and Montana under aliases. Banks required no identification to set up accounts. All they were interested in were large deposits. He was not as wealthy as an Arabian king, but he could live without working the rest of his life. He was taking his account information with him so the bank accounts could not be tracked. He planned to take a train to Denver and obtain a hotel room there until he made more definite plans.

He had instructed George to kill the captives, including the Connolly bitch, and leave them where they fell in the coop. He wanted that accomplished by the next afternoon. The Indian tried to convince him to let them live for now and leave them locked up in the coop. They would starve and die eventually, but George didn't think that made him a murderer. It wasn't the same as pulling the trigger.

Boss informed George he was going to personally visit the chick coop early afternoon to verify the job was completed. Of course, Boss expected to be halfway to Denver by then. He also ordered the execution of Solly, Spud and Fred. If Bull were not his brother, he would have been on the death warrant, too. He worried about George's nephew, Willy. The kid seemed soft for the work he had been recruited into, and he might cave. On the other hand, he knew George had been conniving to take over the bootlegging enterprises and, as the contact man, was in a position to step in and work with the low-level flunkies.

If he kept the kid close, George should be able to keep Willy's mouth shut.

He was staying clear of Bull for a long time, maybe forever. His brother knew there was a hefty bank account waiting for him in Cheyenne if the big lout had enough sense to get there.

His bags packed, Boss stepped back and took a last nostalgic look at his office. Remembering he had left his pistol in the desk drawer, he stepped behind the desk and sat down just as the office door opened. A tall, lanky cowboy with a deputy sheriff's badge pinned on his chest stepped in.

The man tipped his hat. "Mr. Bullock, I am Deputy Sheriff Bing Compton. I would like to speak with you."

"How did you get in here? Where's your warrant?"

He reached in the back pocket of his faded blue jeans and pulled out a folded document. "I do have a search warrant."

"You go ahead and search. I have a train to catch."

"I will want to check the contents of your suitcases."

Boss's hand slipped into the desk drawer and emerged with the pistol. He raised the weapon to fire, but thunder roared in his ears, and an invisible force drove into his shoulder and toppled him from his chair before he could squeeze the trigger. His gun dropped from his hand and clattered on the floor. He was sprawled on his back before the pain erupted in his right shoulder. The fingers of his left hand instinctively reached for the hurting and came up wet and bloody.

"Didn't kill the son-of-a-bitch," came a voice from above him. "Didn't try to."

Boss could make out a mustachioed, weathered face standing over him.

"Good shooting, Sam," the deputy said. "Damn glad you followed me in. I'll use his phone to ring up the hospital to get somebody over to cart him off."

The old guy knelt beside him now and started pressing a handkerchief against the wound, trying to stem the blood flow. "Seen a lot worse than this," he said.

"You'll make it to trial and won't see anything but prison walls after that."

"I'm going check out these suitcases," the deputy said.

The Rapid City Gang was dead.

Chapter 43

KATE

SLEEP EVADED KATE, Marta and Raven that night. Olive had evidently escaped into the darkness, but it could be several days before she brought help. Unfortunately, she did not know the location of the road that provided the nearest access. Maybelle was still unconscious but tossed and groaned restlessly throughout the night. Kate had moistened the corner of a blanket with precious drinking water and gently washed the woman's bloody, swollen face. The battered forehead and face were obvious to the touch but barely visible in the pale moonlight that sifted to the cave's rear, but the feel of the misshapen nose reminded her of a scrunched pig's snout. Kate realized Maybelle had to be stopped, but she doubted she could have brought herself to do it with such brutality. Marta seemed annoyed by Kate's ministrations, and Raven simply watched curiously.

Marta said, "In a few hours daylight will arrive and, soon after, the water and the bread. If they do not see us all, they may call for the missing to come out. Then they will know that Olive is absent, and Maybelle is injured."

Kate said. "They cannot catch Olive. By this time, she is free, whatever else happens."

"The 'whatever else' is what concerns me. The men are upset about something. Something has gotten in the way of their plans. They may decide to kill us all."

"I agree. And when they learn Olive is gone, that could end the delay. I think the other girls should be told of the dangers we all face. They must be convinced to help us."

"I will awaken them and tell them what happened and make it clear they will die if they do not help us. But then what do we do?"

"They cannot kill us without coming in here or taking us outside."

"Make them come to us."

By sunrise Marta had recruited more reluctant soldiers, who would likely desert if the battle took an unhappy turn. But at least they would not be belligerent draft resisters.

When they heard the water buckets clanging as their keepers approached, Marta summoned the others to the front, leaving Raven with a big stone clutched in her hand to tend to Maybelle should she awaken. Kate had no doubt the girl would strike without hesitation. She wished Maybelle an uninterrupted slumber.

Kate had suggested they all be armed with rocks heavy enough to inflict damage and light enough to swing with ease. There were ample weapons on the cave floor, and a stone was easily held in one hand concealed beneath the blanket that was clutched about the shoulders with the other.

She was not disappointed to see that Spud and Willy were designated feeders this morning. She suspected Spud's ancestors had shorted him on brains, and Willy clearly was not a natural in the criminal world. He, in fact, appeared to be unarmed, but Spud carried both a Winchester and a sidearm. Willy set down his two buckets and inserted a key in the padlock that fastened the ends of the heavy chain that held the gate to the iron loop imbedded in the rock wall. When the lock opened, he shoved the key in his pocket and left the padlock hanging on one end of the chain. Willy carried two buckets through the partially-opened gate, while Spud remained just outside. Kate could see the man was puzzled and was scrutinizing the cave's interior. Perhaps, she had underestimated him.

Willy had just placed the third bucket inside and dumped the bread on the cave's floor when Spud said, "Hold it."

"What?" Willy said.

"We're short three. Where's the others?"

"They're sick," Kate said. "Puking up their guts and got the runs."

"I want them out here."

"They're too weak. Can't walk."

"Willy," Spud said, "get your ass back there and take a look."

"Me? Why me? Go look for yourself."

Spud stepped just inside the gate and leveled his Winchester at Willy. "This here gun says you do it."

"I'll show you," Kate said and started walking toward the rear of the cave with Willy following cautiously and nervously behind. She looked back just long enough to see Marta pounce like a panther on Spud and drop him to the ground while his victims swarmed the hapless man, hammering him with their rocks. The war had started.

Willy wheeled around when he heard the ruckus behind him.

"Do not yell or you will be dead before help arrives," Kate said. "We do not want to harm you."

Marta was already swinging the gate shut and pressing the padlock closed on the chain.

"Give me the key," Kate told Willy. He reached in his pocket and complied.

"Now we continue our stroll to the back of the cave."

Marta and two other girls were dragging Spud not far behind. The other two were retrieving the bread and water, along with the abandoned Winchester. When they gathered, Kate confirmed Spud was alive, likely in better shape than Maybelle. Esther Quail, a previously beaten-down sixteen-year old, with a new spark in her eyes, handed the Winchester to Kate. "Marta says you should have this."

Kate looked at Marta, who nodded back. She accepted the weapon gratefully.

Kate turned to Willy, who, with a perplexed look on his face, stood amidst the angry females. "Take off your clothes, Willy. To the last stitch."

"Everything?"

"If you want a chance at living through this."

Willy started prying off his boots, and then slowly stripped himself naked, while the Sioux girls began peeling Spud's clothing off his prone form. Marta divided up the garments, tossing Willy's shirt to Kate. "You can't be struggling with your blanket if you have to use the rifle." It was a practical decision, but Kate felt a bit guilty wearing something that covered to mid-thighs. Marta claimed Spud's shirt, which was broad enough to cover her generous bust, but, because of their disparate heights, did not fully cover her buttocks. A few of the girls got socks. Raven was endowed with Willy's hat and britches and seemed delighted with the treasures. The pudgy girl, who had been raped by Spud two nights previous, wore his trousers proudly.

They shredded a blanket and, with the salvaged strips and belts, bound and gagged the men. Spud showed signs of coming around, and Marta said they would take no chances.

When they were finished, Marta approached Kate. "I still am not certain this is the right thing. I think we should have run."

"They would have seen us. Some would have been shot down. Maybe all of us."

"Some would have made it."

They had argued about this during the night. Marta insisted that if the plan worked they should all flee through the open gate. Kate maintained they could hold out in the cave for several days, if necessary, and that the possibility of saving all outweighed the near certainty that some would die. Olive would bring help. They had finally agreed they would run if they could not capture a gun. But the Winchester was in Kate's hands, and she had already decided where the first shot was headed.

Marta held Spud's pistol but had never fired one before. Kate explained the workings and suggested Marta only attempt to fire if they were overrun.

Kate figured it was little more than a half hour later when the Sioux they called George peered through the gate's bars. He was outlined perfectly against the sunlit cave opening, and she was prone on the floor, hidden in the shadows at the cave's rear. She could have taken him down easily, but not yet.

"Willy. Spud. Where are you?" George called.

Marta, from behind the branch-off corner, called back, "They're back here."

"Well, tell them to get their butts out here."

"They have decided to stay here."

"What in the hell are you talking about?"

"We are holding Spud and Willy hostage until you and the others leave this place."

"That ain't going to happen. No way. If you don't turn them loose, we'll come charging in there, guns blazing. There won't be one of you bitches left standing."

"Sorry, George Many Knives, they will not be coming out. And, yes, I know your full name. And so does Olive. She escaped last night and is on her way to bring the law."

"You're lying."

"I will let your nephew reply to that." Marty removed the gag from Willy's mouth. "Tell your uncle, Willy."

"Uncle George?"

"I hear you, boy. How did you fools get in this predicament?"

"They tricked us in here and jumped us."

"Enough." Marta snapped. "Tell him about Olive."

Willy yelled, "They're one short, Uncle George. I don't know her name. But somebody got out. I'm sure of it."

"I want to hear it from Spud. He knows the chicks."

"Spud's out cold. Or dead. Same with your stoolie. These are mean women, Uncle George."

Marta and Raven worked the gag back over Willy's mouth.

Another man stepped up beside George. "What's the trouble?" he asked. Her target.

She took a bead, but the men moved away from the gate and were joined by the others. She could hear them arguing. One sounded particularly excited. "I say we get the hell out."

"No witnesses," George bellowed.

Her target marched over to the gate, aimed his pistol at the padlock and fired. He either missed or didn't crack the lock. He moved nearer and squeezed the trigger. This time the lock snapped, and the chain unwound, and the gates slid open a few feet. He stepped into the entrance, and the others converged behind him.

"No more games," he yelled. "Get out here."

Kate squeezed the trigger twice, confident both struck home. Two blots of blood appeared on the target's chest, and Solly Cleaver looked down in disbelief before his knees buckled and he crumpled to the floor.

Chapter 44

TREY

AS SOON AS we heard gunfire, Gramps and I snatched up our guns and headed up the craggy mountainside. "How far, do you think, Gramps?" I asked.

"Hard to say with the echo in this canyon, but closer than I thought."

In less than a half hour we could hear voices above us, and we stopped to listen. I could not understand what they were saying, but it seemed that a man and a woman were exchanging words. "I think one of us needs to get above them," I said. I pointed to traces of a deer trail that veered easterly from the creek and twisted up the slope. "I'm going to work my way up. You stay with this trail and see if you can move in from below. Maybe we can trap them in a crossfire."

Gramps looked at me with those steely eyes that said he thought he was better suited for my task, but he pinched his lips tight and nodded. I turned away and set out on the path I had chosen, and, out of the corners of my eyes, I saw he was trudging onward. It was Gramps who had taught me about deer trails on the Wyoming ranch. The animals blazed paths that were generally sensible and convenient for all creatures to follow, and I realized now I had given Gramps the tougher of the options. This was the easiest walking I had enjoyed for a spell.

As I worked my way up the incline, I tried to walk quietly, a challenge if you are wearing cowboy boots. I remembered now that I thought it strange that Gramps had abandoned his boots for moccasins before we sent Olive on her way. I had asked him if he wasn't going to bruise his feet on the sharp stones, and, as usual when he thought a question not worthy of reply, he had not responded. No doubt my feet hurt more than his after all these miles, and my quarry could probably hear me coming from a mile away.

I mused that I had not heard gunshots since the first two that pushed us on the move again. My musing ended abruptly when gunfire broke out, more shots than a man could count. And the racket was no longer above me or far away. It came from off to my left someplace. I stepped off the trail and inched northwesterly through the ponderosa.

The gunfire stopped, and a man's raspy voice said, "You'd just as well come out gals. That was a taste of how it's going to be. We got ammunition and food and drink. We can wait you out if we got to. I figure you ain't got more than a dozen cartridges for that Winchester."

A rifle cracked, and I assumed that was the reply. I crept through the trees and undergrowth, and I came upon the scene, something over fifty feet distant, I guessed. And there was the chick coop. A huge hole in a rock wall, closed off by a gate with long steel bars spiked at the top. The entrance was off a wide ledge, where three men, obviously taking care not to step directly in front of the opening, waited with rifles in their hands. Another man lay directly in front of the gate, and I crossed him off as a threat.

I cast my eyes about and caught sight of a trail that wound its way up to the ledge from my side, probably the one that led to the vehicles that delivered the captives. This also suggested there was a car or two parked at the end of the trail, where somebody might run to escape. I decided they would have to go over me first. I wondered where Gramps was. Like a fool, I had not prearranged a signal. My answer came when plumes of thick, black smoke started reaching for the clear, azure sky from below the opposite side of the ledge. The captors saw it, too, and one of the men hurried toward the smoke.

While their attention was focused on the smoke, I broke from my cover, raced for the chick coop path, and moved in on the outlaws. The smoke-chaser had disappeared over the ledge, and the others still had their backs toward me. I could have taken them down right there, but I felt I should try to take them alive.

An explosion roared through the mountains, stinging my ears for a moment. The shotgun. Evidently, Gramps was unconcerned about the etiquette of taking live prisoners.

I yelled at the two survivors. "Bureau of Investigation. Drop your weapons. Now."

A tall man with a bandaged hand dropped his instantly and raised his hands in surrender. The other wheeled and got off a shot before I placed my own between his eyes, and he tumbled backwards. Not to brag, but, from the time I was a ten-year old, I was the best shot in the Ramsey family. Even Gram Skye with only her one hand to work with could outshoot Gramps with a rifle. I suppose that's why he lugged that shotgun up the mountain.

I walked up to the big man, who was whining like a kicked pup, and took his pistol from its holster and picked up the rifles and tossed them some distance away. "Sit down and stay put, if you don't want to end up like your friend."

"Yes, sir. No problems coming from me, sir."

He sat down and clasped his hands behind his head like he had some experience at that sort of thing. I was looking down at the other man, who looked up at me with three eyes. Indian. Presumably Oglala Sioux. I wondered if he was the one who tried to abduct the president. Gramps came up and said, "Damn fine shooting. Still got the touch."

"Thanks, I guess." I had never killed a man before, and it was not a good feeling. I wondered if I would be able to repeat the act if called upon. "Let's get the chicks out of the coop."

I walked closer to the cave opening and yelled, "Kate, whoever's in there, it's Trey. Bureau of Investigation. It's safe to come on out now."

Gramps walked over to the gate and grabbed the dead man's foot and dragged him away from the opening. I swung the gate open and saw a gray mass of ghostly figures moving slowly toward me. The images began to separate as they shuffled into sunlight, and I saw a band of bedraggled Sioux girls, some with blankets tugged about their bodies and others half-dressed in scraps of male garments. But where was Kate? I immediately thought of the earlier barrage directed toward the depths of the cave. Had she been hit? Killed?

"Where's Kate?" I asked a tall woman, who walked several steps ahead of the others. She wore a shirt that barely reached her hips and was otherwise naked.

"She is not injured. She is tending to a witch."

Witch? What was she talking about? I started walking briskly toward the back of what seemed like a huge burrow carved into the mountain. I heard Gramps from outside the cave directing the former captives to the stash of their clothing, which he apparently had come across at the campsite downslope from the ledge.

"Kate," I called.

"Back here," she replied. "Turn left when you reach the end."

A few moments later, I made the turn and found her kneeling by someone wrapped in a blanket. The darkness kept from ascertaining more. Along the opposite wall, I could make out two more figures who appeared bound and possibly gagged given the unintelligible mumbling that was coming from that direction.

"One thing," I said. "Are you okay?"

She stood and stepped into my arms and wrapped her arms about my waist, burying her face in my chest. "I will be," she said. "I will be."

She clung to me tightly for some moments before she lifted her head and said. "I stink. My breath is rancid. But if you can stand it, a kiss would be nice."

What could I do but oblige? And our lips lingered. If this was what it was like to kiss a stinky woman, I would take stinky anytime. But I knew at that instant new struggles lurked on the horizon.

When Kate pulled away, she explained. "This woman is severely injured. She may die. She desperately needs medical attention. We should get her out of here and into the sunlight where we can see what can be done."

"What did these men do to her?"

"They didn't do anything to her. Marta had to shut her up and possibly overdid it a bit."

"I see." But, of course, I did not. "I'll see if I can carry her. My grandfather is with me. He's had some experience with injuries. He might be able to help until we get her to a hospital. What about those two?" I pointed to the two figures on the other side of the shaft. "And who are these others?"

"Prisoners."

This was becoming too complicated. "You can explain later."

I carried the injured woman outside, trying to pretend my back didn't notice but aware that I had just incurred my most serious injury of the adventure. Gramps and several of the Sioux girls were tossing green branches of ponderosa and grass on the fire. Two of the girls seemed to be having fun putting a blanket over the fire and then yanking it away to release dark clouds of smoke.

As I placed the injured woman down in the grass some distance from the fire, I asked, "Smoke signals?"

Gramps chuckled, "Hardly. But it ought to catch somebody's attention." He nodded at the woman. "What have you got there?"

"Thought you might look at her. She's unconscious. Her head and face are really scrambled."

Gramps knelt and examined the woman Kate called Maybelle. "Looks like somebody took a sledge hammer to her face. She'd look better without that pug nose." He cupped his hands over her battered nose and seemed to be manipulating it some way. Then he jerked, and the crunching sound made me shudder.

"Ow, that hurt," came a sleepy voice from the patient.

Chapter 45

KATE

IT HAD TAKEN several hours for the sheriff's department, ambulances, firefighters and other emergency responders to arrive at the chick coop, and, of course, not far behind, the newspaper crowd. The press horde was overpopulated because of the president's presence in the Black Hills, and he had not offered any headlines lately.

At Bing and Trey's insistence, Kate stepped into an ambulance with Marta and Raven and made a trip to the hospital. That evening, as she was being released, Trey stopped by the hospital to confirm she was okay, which she had not required a physician to verify. She felt fine.

"I'm going to be tied up meeting with law enforcement and completing reports the next few days. J. Edgar is obsessive about written reports, and I'm already in trouble. I have a feeling I'll be ordered back to Washington. But we need to talk soon."

She had found that encouraging. She had a bond with Trey she could not quite define yet, but the thought of not seeing him again terrified her. "My father and Stretch are on their way in to pick me up. You will call me when you're free then?"

"Of course. But there is something you must do immediately. Gramps told me about the reason your mother and my father died on the same date. It was not coincidence. It's not for me to explain. Ask your grandmother about it. I believe she knows the story. I'm certain your father does. Tell her you're entitled to the truth."

"You are not making any sense, Trey," she had said.

He had taken her hand and kissed her softly on the lips and said, "I love you, Kate. No matter what." Before she could reply, he had turned and walked out of the room, leaving her head spinning with confusion.

Now she was seated in the kitchen with Grandma Beth. Kate had pondered overnight Trey's insistence on her confronting her grandmother, and possibly her father, about the coincidental dates of death of Deuce Ramsey and Coleen Connolly. This morning she had made a decision and had approached her grandmother, who had been noticeably unnerved and sent Stretch to find her father, who was tending to a lame horse in the stable, "Tell him to get his butt to the house. You can take care of the horse. Owen's not a horseman anyway." Stretch had tossed Kate a look that said there was something brewing, and she suspected he was more than glad to retreat to the stable.

Beth placed two steaming cups of coffee on the table and sat down beside Kate. "Your father needs to be a part of this. We can talk more later, if you wish. Understand that your father views this differently than I do, and with some cause. But carrying anger too long can eat you up inside and force you to close your eyes to possibilities that might bring joy and fulfillment to your life. It is sad when that happens, but it is the choice of the one who bears the anger."

"Anger? Choices? Grandma, I'm getting tired of all this mystery and dancing around whatever happened ten years ago."

The front door slammed, and Connolly stomped into the kitchen. "It doesn't look like there's an emergency here. Stretch said you wanted to talk to me immediately."

"Would you care for some coffee, Owen?"

"No, just tell me what your trouble is, so I can get on my way."

"Sit down," Beth commanded. "Kate wants to know about Coleen's death, and it's time."

His face turned scarlet and he hesitated. "I don't know why," he said, but obeying Beth's order.

Beth said, "Kate says Trey has been told the story. They seem to care for each other. Until they met, this was unnecessary and pointless. I still don't think it's relevant to their relationship, but I know you think differently, and it's time to lay out all the cards."

Kate said, "What is this all about? You are both driving me crazy."

Connolly said, "Your mother was an adulteress, Kate. That's it. A slut. A whore. She spread her legs for Trey Ramsey's father. And, fittingly, she died with him on a battlefield in France."

Kate felt her breath had been sucked away.

"Owen," Beth snapped. "You speak that way about my daughter once more and Stretch and I are finished here. I'm damn tired of your anger and bitterness tainting all of our lives, especially Kate's."

Connolly's eyes shot sparks. "Don't threaten me, Beth. Stay or go. Nobody's irreplaceable."

Beth ignored him and turned to Kate. "I didn't want to tell you this behind your father's back, but he couldn't resist sharing all the information he dug up about your mother's death, so I will tell you what we know, my way." She turned to Connolly,

"And you shut-up, Owen, until I'm finished. Then you can have your say."

Beth told the story of Deuce and Coleen as it had been extracted from military records and conversations with several of Coleen's fellow nurses. Kate listened spellbound, silent tears streaming down her cheeks as her grandmother spoke.

"That's what I know," Beth said when she concluded the story. "The military files don't tell us what was in the hearts of these two people. But the manner of their deaths speaks for them, I think. I love my Coleen, and I was always proud to be her mother. I still am."

Owen got up and pushed his chair harshly aside. "Nothing changes that they were sinners. They betrayed those who foolishly trusted them. They're buried together. I hope they're burning in hell together." He glared at Kate. "Stay away from that young Ramsey. If you don't, you'll never see one acre or one cow from the Shamrock Ranch." He turned and walked out of the room.

Kate watched her father leave. She could understand his pain and anger. She had known betrayal by persons she thought were friends. And it stung. But this had been ten years, and the betrayer was long dead. What more punishment could he seek?

"Grandma, I just don't know what to make of this."

"I don't know if it makes any difference, Kate. I have never told your father this . . . no reason to hurt him further . . . but your mother loved this Major Ramsey. She wrote to me several times before she was killed. She struggled with the scandals that would face her, and she was uncertain what would happen after the war ended. She could just not fathom living without him. And you should know she was not happy in her marriage to your father. She said she needed distance to sort things out, and that's why she signed on for active duty in the Army Nurse Corps."

And what did this mean for her and Trey? Her father had made clear that Trey Ramsey in her life shut her father out of it. She had never known Owen Connolly to change his mind on anything. But she loved him, and she loved the ranch. Knowing what she did now, was it possible to disregard her father's feelings?

Chapter 46

TREY

I SAT IN FRONT of Bing's desk in the sheriff's office. Bing had left for a few minutes to check with Sheriff Johnson about something, and my mind had turned to Kate, as it tended to do. Two days had passed since I spoke with her at the hospital. I had tried to ring up Kate twice. The first time her grandmother said Kate was outside doing chores, but she would ask her to call back. I had not heard from her, so I called again this morning before I drove in to Rapid City. This time Beth Ridgeway had apologized profusely and explained that Kate was not up to talking with me now. I told her I had been summoned back to Washington and would be leaving on tomorrow morning's train. I said it was important for me to speak with Kate before I left. She promised to do her best for me.

Bing returned and sat down. "Why so glum?" he asked. "You're a hero. The BI's scored major points with the public. Of course, Hoover has jumped in and is claiming all the credit."

"It doesn't matter who gets credit. We got a lot of bad guys put away one way or another. Hoover has called me back to Washington, but I may turn in my resignation when I get there."

"You're not serious? I'd sell my firstborn to get in with that outfit."

"Really? Then why don't you apply?"

"I've checked in to it, but Hoover's looking for college boys these days. Guys like yourself with accounting backgrounds, or lawyer-types."

"But they waive this for promising recruits with law enforcement backgrounds. You've helped the BI with a major case. If you like, I'll see what I can do."

"I'm not expecting anything, but I'd welcome any help."

"I'll try, but I can't promise anything."

"It would be great if we could work together again."

"That means I'd be staying with the BI."

"I'm betting you will."

"Anyway, I'm leaving the case in the hands of your office and the state of South Dakota. The feds are going to back off and let the state file and prosecute the charges. Willy and Bull Bullock will testify. Bull and Boss will likely go away for life. Bull did some killing and committed rapes, but he doesn't know we can't prove it. It appears George Many Knives and someone unidentified committed the murders Gabe and I came here to investigate. One will get away with it, but George already got the death penalty."

Bing added, "And Spud Fisher will go to prison for a long time for assault and rape among other things. I think Willy will be out in five years. There's no evidence he did actual physical harm to anybody or understood fully what he was involved in."

I said, "I've got to talk to Gabe and Clara at the hospital. It's been good for him to have her here. It won't be long before he's back in Washington at a desk job. Then I've got to hustle out to the game lodge and pack. I'm on the train in the morning, but you know how to contact me."

"What about the gal?"

"What gal?"

"You know. Kate. You two seem a good match."

"The verdict's out."

Chapter 47

KATE

KATE HAD ENJOYED lunch and dinner at the State Game Lodge with the president and first lady on several occasions since she was freed from the chick coop. She loved them dearly. Grace Coolidge always put her at ease, and the president, with his dry wit, made her laugh. She noticed most guests at one formal dinner did not pick up on the president's sense of humor, and she thought that sad.

One day, joining the first lady for afternoon tea, they discussed Kate's plans. "I am returning to college this fall," Kate said. "I have decided to complete my degree. I can easily graduate next spring."

"A wise decision. That pleases me."

"After that, I don't know. Once, I thought I would return to the ranch. Now I have doubts. You do know the story of Trey's father and my mother, don't you?"

"Yes, I do, dear. Not all of it. But enough. Does that have something to do with your separation from Trey?"

"Yes. I didn't tell you I went to the railroad station the morning he left town. I almost called out to him, but I didn't."

"That's too bad."

"What do you mean?"

"I'm married to Silent Cal, but I don't let him get by with it in private. A husband and wife must talk to each other. People who care about each other must talk."

"You think I should talk to Trey?"

"Why not? Even if it's only to say goodbye. I am meddling, I know, but I fail to see how whatever your parents did, or did not do, should have a bearing on what choices the two of you make."

"You think it's silly, don't you?"

"I do."

As Kate was leaving the game lodge later that afternoon, Agent Starling passed her a note. She read it before she stepped into her Model T. It read: "Kate, I would be honored if you would come to my office at the Rapid City

High School promptly at 10:00 a.m. tomorrow. Thereafter, we will travel to the game lodge for lunch. Uncle Cal."

This was beyond strange. Her dad was going to be irritated she was missing another day's work, although she was caring less by the day.

Chapter 48

August 2, 1927

KATE ARRIVED AT the president's summer office at the high school shortly before ten o'clock. The number of cars in the parking area surprised her. School was not in session, and she knew the parsimonious president had been accompanied to South Dakota by barebones staff. Edmund Starling spotted her in the hallway, and, stone-faced, nodded for her to follow him. He led her through a side door into the president's office.

The president was at his desk and gave her a closed-lips smile and motioned her closer to his desk. Reporters with note pads were filing into the room, pressing latecomers against the wall as it filled up. The president was sitting at his desk with a scissors in one hand cutting up legal-size sheets of paper with something written on it. There seemed to be a short message on each small rectangular piece, some handwritten, others typed. Kate noted that some of the messages were on carbon copies.

The president stood up and handed one of the notes to Kate and then walked around his desk and began passing out the slips to the reporters. "There will be no questions," he said.

As the reporters examined their notes, they made mad rushes to the door, and Kate feared someone would be injured in the melee. Kate looked down at her own message. The president had given her a slip with his original handwriting on it. The note said, "I do not choose to run for president in nineteen twenty eight." It was not dated, and it was not signed.

When the president returned to his desk, he introduced Kate to a distinguished looking gentleman who had been standing a few paces away. The man was Senator Arthur Capper, the Republican U.S. Senator from Kansas and publisher of several farm journals she had read.

Senator Capper rode back to the game lodge with the president, and Kate drove behind the small convoy to join the first couple and Senator Capper for lunch. The thought came to her that she was becoming surprisingly comfortable with her hobnobbing with the government elite. But why not? They were just people, not gods, although she had met a few who did not realize it.

During lunch, the president and Kansas senator were engaged in serious baseball debate. "Babe Ruth will hit sixty home runs for the Yankees this year," President Coolidge predicted.

"Never been done," replied the senator. "The sluggers all burn out before they get there."

"Too bad I'm not a betting man."

"You're a Boston Red Sox fan, aren't you?" Senator Capper asked.

"Yes, and it perturbs me to no end that Boston traded Ruth to the Yankees. They let Herb Pennock get away to New York, too. A twenty-game winner. But not this year, according to his cousin."

"His cousin?"

"Yes, a young man who has been helping me with the budget is a distant cousin. He said his mother was a Pennock from Pennsylvania. His name's Trey Ramsey."

"Related to the former senator?"

"Grandson. He's a genius with numbers. I must confess, he gave me the lowdown on Ruth. He says Pennock will be one game short of twenty."

Senator Capper chuckled. "Well, we'll see about that in a few months."

"Don't bet against Trey."

Kate wondered if the president was sending her a subtle message.

Later, Senator Capper commented to Grace Coolidge, "That was quite a surprise the president gave us this morning."

The first lady had a stunned look on her face, and it was one of the few instances Kate had seen her flustered. My God. The president had not told her. It made for an uncomfortable few minutes until everything was explained. The first lady quickly regained her composure and laughed dutifully about the surprise. Poor Uncle Cal, Kate thought. The first lady's cheerful front was likely to disappear after the guests took their leave.

Kate excused herself mid-afternoon, and, as she was walking toward the door, Grace Coolidge called to her, "Kate, may I speak with you a moment?"

Kate stopped. "Certainly, what is it?"

"I have a letter for you."

Kate took the envelope, which was unsealed.

"I was told to read it," she explained. She waited expectantly while Kate removed the single page.

Kate unfolded the sheet of paper and read it. "Dear Kate, I still remember my last words to you, and they still stand. A stoolie has informed me you have decided to return to school. I have been assigned to an investigation in St. Paul, Minnesota, which will likely take some months. It is within easy driving distance of Brookings. Would you be willing to speak with me if I called on you there? My messenger will see that I receive your reply. Trey."

Kate looked at Mrs. Coolidge. "Isn't it disrespectful to refer to the first lady as a stoolie?"

"As they say, dear, 'if the shoe fits.'"

"Do you have a sheet of paper?"

"I just happen to have one with me." She plucked a small sheet of paper from her dress pocket. "I have a pen, too."

Kate took the writing supplies and sat down at a nearby coffee table. First, she printed at the top of the sheet in large letters, "YES." She signed it, "Kate."

She showed her reply to Mrs. Coolidge, who smiled approvingly.

www.ingramcontent.com/pod-product-compliance
Lightning Source LLC
Chambersburg PA
CBHW030547180626
46816CB00005B/1440
* 9 7 8 1 9 4 3 4 2 1 3 1 2 *